Arc of Doubt

ARC OF DOUBT

A H PILCHER

First published 2020 by Backleg Books, UK
ISBN: 978-1-8382090-0-1
Copyright © 2020 A H Pilcher
All rights reserved.

While some elements of this novel are set around actual events, this is a work of fiction. Characters, incidents and places are largely fictitious.

Backleg Books, UK
ahpbackleg@gmail.com
@ahpilcher

Part One

Arc of Doubt

1

Hampshire, England. 2010

The tide was dead low to the mud, leaving only a tapering gulley of water to the stone quay. The piled ramparts were stained a dirty green by the seaweed to the tideline. On a daytime high tide, this working quay would have dredgers pushing up the creek to unload shingle from the Solent by crane for the belt- driven graders, with their continual slow grinding, echoing over the area.

But now it was still, quiet, the guts of the creek lay exposed, the long-since discarded items partly covered by seaweed stood forgotten. A thin gravel spit pointed to a sign mid channel, the writing worn away by the seasons. The only real sound on this late April evening was traffic from the main road. That too had slackened now, from the relentless, to an intermittent flow under the brick viaduct leading up to the motorway.

The slip road from the roundabout bent back, leading eventually to the quay and marina at the head of the creek. A large sail loft on the edge of the slipway was now smart flats with the boat yard and dingy sailing club beyond.

The Castle pub like most of the houses, was a red brick, late Victorian building, jammed up against an older single storey barn that now served as a boat engine repair workshop for the marina opposite. The pub's customers varied considerably, depending on the time of year and strength of the sun. For a mid- week evening, it was busy. I had been sat with a friend, tucked away at the table in the bay window talking, when I noticed something move on the edge of my vision, then slipping from view. I tilted my head slightly, enabling me to take in the shambling figure of a man, probably in his early sixties although he looked older. I was to find out later he was known as just Tod, because he was always seen on his own.

It was darker than when we arrived, not quite raining, as he shuffled to the edge of the door. I saw only a hand appear from the doorway offering two cigarettes, an extended arm, the benefactor was out of sight. Tod raised his eyes a little and took the cigarettes slowly, he spoke no words. He seemed to drift past the window, his tired, unshaven face tilted downwards again, lost, his expression blank, heavy and grey with his own thoughts.

It was rumoured he had been ill, a simple drifter, unable to cope with the complexities of modern life. He existed, people said, like a pale shadow, occasionally brushing against other people's fast moving lives. The true story, as I came to find out was quite different. Back inside the pub, the evening slipped, another pint had replaced the first, topics jolted away in spasms, then, without warning, my drinking companion pushed back his chair from the table giving off a short raw scratching sound against the bare floor boards.

He announced that he would be back. Turning and moving slightly too quickly, taking the two steps to the lower bar area badly, he regained his balance, heading through the drinkers towards the toilets.

Looking out of the window again, I turned my attention to the small scene starting to take place on the other side of the road against the long brick wall of the converted offices. A light drizzle was blowing on the wind, a young lad astride a bicycle was bumping the front wheel nervously against the edge of the kerb, being spoken to by two young men with their hoodies up. One thrust out a hand and shook hands with the lad, then dabbed a finger at him with an outstretched arm, as though in warning. It seemed like a relationship of deception. The two older youths moved away, one slapping the other on the shoulder and, with a further handshake, they turned the corner and were gone. Looking back I saw the street was empty. Drugs.

A voice behind me started: 'God, the toilets stink, a real drain problem somewhere ...'

So where did Tod go? What of his life? Judgements, I thought, are often made on the imprint before our eyes. But what of the life that has gone before for this man, I wondered.

The beer was enough by 11. We waved in the street before going our separate ways home.

The following day I took the pick-up, leaving Fareham and driving under the motorway north into the countryside for a few miles. On a clear afternoon, with a coolness still in the air, the May trees were yet to flower among the hedgerows that compressed the road on either side. The scrapyard I was on my way to had been rebuilt recently, a modern industrial building with a rolling curved roof design in silver. With its car park, it fronted a vast, enclosed concreted yard covered and piled high in places with the detritus of the auto empires.

As I stood beside my pick-up, I thought for a moment about how it had been. Historically, simply a breakers' yard in what had once been a farm. Now, with modern technology and a good upfront image, it was a multi-million pound business, devouring our damaged and scrapped vehicles bought and sold from around the county, and firmly embedded in the insurance market.

I passed through the automatic doors among other customers and headed for the bank of service people at the tills. A vast TV screen flicked on the wall above, with endless rolling images of damaged, repairable vehicles for sale. Choosing a vacant corner till, I automatically slid my hand into my jeans pocket, ready to finger my wallet. An older, balding man was before me speaking over his shoulder to a colleague who was disappearing through a doorway, I waited.

He finally turned towards me on the swivel stool and as he did so, his black shirt tightened over a small protruding belly. With a deep Merseyside accent, he said:

'How can I help?'

'I rang about a white wing for a 54 plate Peugeot Partner, it was put by.'

Giving my name, the man touched the keyboard without shifting his weight, and spoke into his mouthpiece. He said: 'It's on its way over now.'

After paying on a card, the printer spat out the receipt.

The wing was good and clean, no dents or marks, and with undamaged corners. Leaving through the same doors, I passed the double tyre bay, noting how they were always busy. The wing was carefully wrapped in an unrolled tarpaulin I had brought especially and it was padded with thick offcuts of foam to stop it moving around. I opened the driver's door and slipped in behind the wheel.

I intended to sort the wing out later in the afternoon. It just took four bolts to fit it, and the van - already cleaned - could then be put up for sale. Pulling out on to the tarmac, I re-joined the country road back. Passing through Wickham village square, the road dipped and narrowed leading to a small stone bridge crossing the Meon River.

Dropping to second gear for the bridge, then queuing to join the main road at the junction, I was looking straight ahead. I say looking, but in reality I was in that vacant space somewhere further in the afternoon, planning the task ahead to repair the wing. While waiting for the traffic queue to jerk forward, my eyes focused on him.

It was Tod. He was standing at the edge of a lay-by on the main road, trying to flag down a lift

I was well back from the junction as I started to look closer at him. He stood more upright than when I last saw him, and was wearing jeans and a predominately red checked shirt partially covered by an open hacking jacket. His hair was tidier, long enough to cover his ears and pushed back in an unruly way. There was something about the way in which he stood, perhaps the slight leaning to one side, that seemed to show indifference as to whether he got someone to stop.

I made the roundabout and flicked into the lay-by, then, reaching over to the passenger door using just my forefinger, released the catch to allow the door to swing open slowly. Before I was upright again he was in the seat snapping the door shut.

He turned and reached for the seat belt and, in a perfectly normal tone of voice, said:

'Good morning, thank you,' leaving me to spike the silence that followed.

We had covered some uphill ground on the long straight road before I spoke.

'I'm going back to Fareham, if it's any good to you?'

'I thought you might be.'

Pausing, he took a slow look out of the side window, then turned back before continuing: 'You were watching me back there…'

I decided to bat this straight back to him.

'I saw you last night, outside the pub. That's why I stopped.'

'Ah,' he said, as though this answered everything.

His pause was longer than the last. I got the distinct feeling that he was completely at ease and gently manipulating the conversation.

'I've seen you working in that workshop in your yard at the far end of the viaduct.'

Again, a pause to draw information from me.

I looked towards him briefly before focusing on the road ahead. He was again looking out of the side window, so I saw nothing of his face.

'I'm on my way back there now, I've just been to pick up a wing for a van.'

The workshop covered three garages and a space beside them to park four vehicles. It was part of a decaying block I rented from a local property dealer, whose maxim appeared to be 'let and forget.' As long as the rent was paid on time, I never saw him. The small area alongside was fronted with rust- streaked security fencing which I had chained together with serious padlocks to block prying eyes.

There was something about this man I could not place, a feeling that most of what made him was below the waterline. I tried direct questions, but the tilting head, the smile and the short silences offset me. Even so, I had an undercurrent of liking for him and felt, perhaps, he had the same for me.

On reaching the yard, I parked with the engine running while I opened the padlock on the makeshift gate ready to draw the van into the yard and out of sight. With my back to him, I heard him start:

'I could give you a hand if you like…. won't take long, then maybe a cup of tea?'

And so it was that Tod and I began our friendship.

Later, he helped get the damaged wing off the van and bolt on the new one. A very straight forward job. It was over a mug of tea that he mentioned, as a throwaway line, that he was born and raised just a few miles further south on the coast. I got the impression he was keen to talk, but not sure whether he was comfortable with me as a listener.

Over the next two weeks, he worked with me on several days. I never saw him when I arrived, although I had the feeling he was around somewhere, watching me. Perhaps even then, he was weighing me up. He learnt the art of removing the plastic signwriting from vans in my yard. It was a hard, laborious job and I offered him money. Although he took it, he didn't seem that interested in it. It was taken without a look or a comment, other than a nod of thanks. I remember how his hand would bunch up over the notes, then they would be stuffed into a pocket - any pocket, with clearly no more thought given.

He helped out in many ways and I soon found out he had more than a working knowledge of diesel engines and, over the spanners, he slowly started to open up about himself.

His name was Philbus Nathaniel Gibson. For reasons he didn't give, he wanted to be called by his middle name, shortened to Nat. He had lived a life, on a spectrum few could imagine, let alone experience. Gradually, it was all laid before me in full colour.

Looking back, I can only assume he wanted to tell someone non-judgmental; someone who would just listen. The questions I asked, he was happy to answer, filling in missing pieces like a jigsaw.

Toward the end of that third week, he underwent a change and began to shave every day. I remember remarking on it, joking that he must have met a woman.

'There was only ever one woman, but she's gone,' he replied, without a smile.

It must have been the Thursday that he didn't show, and I wasn't too concerned. By then, I knew he had a room across the park at the top end of the creek, a sliver of a lane that crept back from the viaduct taking the main line trains. Although there was a quietness about that area, it was tired, with discarded rubbish strewn about and overgrown grass verges. People living there cared, but not enough.

The weather that weekend became unexpectedly warm for the end of April, and a fullness appeared in people. They seemed more active outside, talking and walking, raising their eyes from the ground to look at the sun. The old, discoloured crane on the quay was busy lifting boats into the water after their winter storage. The red-trouser brigade had anti- fouled their boats in readiness and wanted them in the water.

The weather stayed fine through the early part of the following week, and it was the Tuesday morning that the ordinary rhythms of lives around here were jolted.

Arc of Doubt

2

Fareham, England. 2010

On the early flooding tide, the dredger was preparing to unload its cargo, sucked from the sea bed around the Nab channel. It inched its way past the quay and then reversed its engines, after throwing its rudder to starboard. Slowly, on the wide bend, skipper John Peterson added the revs, sending a froth of dirty white water to the surface, as his rusting beauty swung its path beneath him.

Manipulating the vessel fully laden was tricky in such a confined space, but years of experience had taught him. Looking over the port side suction pumping tubes from his cramped position in the wheel room, he allowed the dredger to drift parallel with the concrete piers, where dangling truck tyres lay suspended to cushion its arrival.

At almost the last moment, he applied thrust on the engine to bring it within range of its docking mooring lines. This manoeuvre produced a further sucking flurry in the water and that was the precise moment the skipper spotted something lift and move beneath the piles directly in front of him.

Perhaps it was the change of colour he noticed first. Easing the engine and creating another swell, the dredger slipped back a few feet as a narrow gap hung open. Floating face down was a body.

Then, splintering the air, Peterson shouted through the open wheelhouse door to the stevedores on the

quay: '…don't just fucking stand there, get him in …..
I'll hold off…'

The dredger sat low to the water still, on the flat, windless tide. A dry scraping sound of a starter motor turning was immediately overwhelmed by the coughing burst of a diesel engine coming to life. A long cloud of filthy exhaust pumped from the tube above the crane driver's cab as he cranked the revs and the engine hit rhythm.

With a deft movement, the driver started to lift and swing the large open bucket that was used for unloading the hoppers in the dredgers, up and just off the concrete surface. Holding the bucket's brake lever wedged against his knee, he began beckoning one of the stevedores with short jagged arm movements. To convey his message above the noise, he jabbed a finger at him, indicating he was to get into the bucket.

In the wheelhouse, Peterson, reached with his spare hand across the shelf, over papers and, cigarettes, fumbling for his phone and pressed the number. The call was answered quickly.

'Police.'

With a calm voice that betrayed no emotion, the skipper gave the brief facts.

Keeping his view fixed, he took in the bucket, being guided and lowered the short distance by more arm waving, until it sat just below the surface of the water. Creeping forward, the crane driver allowed the body to almost float over the teeth and into the cavernous mouth of the bucket. Peterson could see they were lifting the obviously dead man from the water.

At that distance, he could see the shape and discolouration of the back of the head, which looked as though it had been stoved in.

The bucket was laid down gently on the quayside and the engine died. The tilt allowed a large pool of water to form quickly on the quay.

The yard manager was watching the dredger pull off from the window on the first floor of the office and his curiosity had been aroused. Then he saw the crane lift and swing its contents, and he only saw a man riding in the bucket. Anger at flouting company rules, and health and safety regulations, made him throw his reading glasses on the desk and head for the single flight of stairs, leading straight to the graders and the material piles. He cursed as he passed under the dripping grading conveyors.

Getting closer he saw the situation for what it was and said, almost to himself:

'Oh God.'

Pausing, he then went on: 'I think it's best to leave him exactly where he is as he's clearly beyond any help from us now.'

It was hard for all of them to turn away, they were both shocked and compelled to stare in equal measure.

From the time that Peterson spotted movement under the quay to the yard manager's arrival had been only a few minutes, and soon sirens from police cars were heard, as they streamed through the split in the traffic across the creek.

The first vehicle pulled into the quay entrance, its front wheels stopping by the weighbridge. The policeman's first act was to close the gates and lock down the site.

Only other police vehicles would be allowed to pass through the quickly positioned blue and white police tape. A temporary closure sign was placed in front of one of the gates to turn away the slow stream of builders calling for sand and ballast.

The nearest Detective Inspector was 16 miles to the east, just pulling out of a Fried Chicken drive through with her sideman. A large open polystyrene tray lay on the dashboard, an all-day breakfast of sorts, and an approaching lay-by on the nearside was an open invitation for a pull in.

Then the radio burst in…'DI Lloyd … .. A body washed in on the tide … Fareham Quay…'

Mentally storing every detail of the message, Lloyd drove on.

With a resigned sigh, she leaned forward and closed the box of food, then turned on the siren.

Col, her sideman, a cocky Scotsman, laughed and said: 'Looks like you've got cold chicken again then.'

The food would have to wait. The thought that some prat with a dash cam might just film her driving a police car with lights and siren going, crashing the red light while chewing on a chicken leg entered her mind. Then the shit would definitely stick to the wall.

The police car sped through the traffic and headed for the motorway.

As she drove, Lloyd thought how this was what she lived for, the rush, the challenge of events, the meticulous order of timed happenings. People, alive or dead, always had their surprises, and hard work would lie ahead now. She was alert, confident and started to go through her arrival check list.

Once on the motorway, she was oblivious to the cars she passed. Although slowing the pace on the slip road, she still slid easily through two more sets of traffic lights, leaving the roundabout and heading under the viaduct to the quay.

The rendered, unlisted Georgian house in front of her, with PVC windows slapped on its face, looked tired. It was now the Aggregate Company's offices. Through the open car window she spoke quickly to the police officer:

'Where's the body?'

'Right under the crane.'

He pointed the way. Her arrival time was 1205 and she saw several police cars and a couple of police vans were already there. No sign yet of a police ambulance, but it would be on its way. In the short time since the body had been found, the efficient progression of police standard procedure was underway. The two further vans near the office were the Crime Scene Investigators. By now, they would have a big scene tent erected over the area surrounding the body.

The CSI investigators, she guessed, were already in anti-contamination suits and further officers had arrived to take statements and make a detailed search of the immediate area.

'Any witnesses?' Lloyd asked.

'No, Ma'am.'

'Get your senior officer over here to brief me please, and no press. I'll give a statement when I'm ready,' and as an afterthought, added: 'Has the coroner's office been informed?'

'Yes they have, Ma'am.'

She manoeuvred the car as far as possible onto the approach roadway and pulled herself out of the car.

The graders were quiet, the bulldozer with its massive bucket outstretched was dwarfed by the house-sized ballast pile. The crane, like all the other machinery, had silently ceased its task and all the employees were corralled in the offices. At that time of day, the yard would normally have been singing at every pitch, now it was relatively quiet, with only the traffic noise as a backdrop.

Reaching the tent, one of the CSI officers came out and, peeling back his gloves and lifting his mask from his face, said as a greeting:

'Lloyd, again, death brings us close to one and other.'

She hadn't seen Joe for a while, different shifts probably. He coughed lightly before carrying on:

'The photographer has nearly finished here. I need another half hour before we're done and you can then come in for a private view of the gallery,' amused at his own joke.

Lloyd had decided long ago that Joe was close to brilliant, meant well and was only very slightly irritating. While they stood talking, she could feel the breeze coming off the water and the dampness in the air. It might soon turn to rain.

'Ok, I'll take a walk'

She would look and fix the area in her mind for a later playback. The first job was to climb down the old, rusted steel ladder that was bolted onto the pontoon wall to check where the body was first seen. But before she could do this, she and Col were joined by the senior officer and given all relevant details.

Lloyd could see the dredger was now moored on the windward side of the pier still with a full cargo. She knew if it wasn't emptied, the falling tide would allow its weight to rest firmly on the mud.

Peterson was, she was told, still in the wheelhouse.

Walking slowly between the bunkers with their variously graded materials, she came level with the mountainous pile of ballast brought in the previous day from the sea bed. It was still leaking the Solent from its base, similar to the body she was soon to see. At the farthest point on the quay, she thought she heard far off that long searching, reaching sound of a fog horn. It held her for just a moment, then turning, she walked back to the quayside ladder.

Leaning forwards, she grabbed the top rail, transferring her other hand to the ladder, swung out and started the short, steep descent. On reaching the lip, she transferred her weight to a concrete beam, conscious of her now wet hands from the coat of seaweed on the lower rungs. The space was limited, but by ducking her head, she could move further under the structure. The cross beam above, where the body had rested before being sucked into the open water, was just beneath the high water mark.

The slap of the tide ran over the edge of her trainers. She swung back to the ladder and returned to the quayside. She could see Col talking to Peterson on the forward deck of the dredger. It would all be recorded. Then she made her way towards the tent. They called it 'the activity centre' – but that depended on how you looked at it.

As she approached, one of the CSI team that she had not seen before was returning from the parked box van. His head was lowered and he was still wearing his anti-contamination suit, and clearly lost in his own thoughts. He had not noticed the detective's arrival until he almost bumped into her. He was younger than Joe by some way.

His opening remark was:

'Well, we're nearly there, photography completed and uploaded to your case site, our collection of sealed samples are all ready to remove for analysis. It's finished here now.'

With these few words at the partially-raised tent flap, he started to remove his suit by taking off his head and boot covers in swift movements.

Next, Joe's head appeared:

'You're next Lloyd, do want a mask or have you still got a strong stomach? The camera is on and only stand on the mat.'

With that she stepped forward while he held the flap. Even before she was inside, the stench reached for her, that foul, putrid fermentation of the smell of the dead, covered her. It was as though a last act of the corpse was to take control of the senses of the living.

Deep in the back of her throat the gag came. Somehow, she controlled this natural and involuntary reaction, and she didn't rush from the tent. Joe was standing a few feet away watching with a broad smile, it was his little game and he worked it every time. The body lay on the concrete in the same spot where it had been landed.

'We're done here now and…'

He broke off as the phone in his hand rang.

'Excuse me just for a moment will you?'

He turned his attention to the phone call. She heard him say: '... yes, we're done,...that's fine, it's all bagged ready to go after you've seen it. I'm just talking to DI Lloyd now, but just shout when you are outside... '

It rang again: 'Good ...just a few minutes.'

Looking up, he continued: 'The coroner's officer has just arrived and this fellow's transport is standing by.'

Lloyd was still looking intently at the body. Joe's voice had faded. Pushing a tissue to cover her mouth and nose, she continued to stare at the corpse, taking in the details. With the flaps of the body bag wide open, she could see a male, probably about 6ft, blue eyes, one gone to animals or fish, dark but heavily flecked wavy, mid-length grey hair, maybe in his 60s, very light facial growth. The body was lying on a paper mat with taped paper gloves on hands and feet. Rigor mortis appeared partial. He was wearing a torn wool suit, smart shirt, no rings. One shoe missing. No watch.

Then, her professionalism slipped for a moment as she saw, emerging from a leaking nostril, sea lice. These wriggling creatures filled her with revulsion, knowing that they were already quietly multiplying inside this man's body. She understood that deterioration starts within minutes of death and decomposition was already well underway. Hence the swollen, blanched, purplish grey hue and pronounced blotching on the face and chest areas she could see. Autolysis was the self-digestion, the continual breaking down of cells. It started in the brain and liver, because of their high water content.

'Joe, what can you tell me?'

'Not a great deal about the cause of death until the pathologist has worked him over, but he definitely didn't die here; obviously a blow to the head. There is a long scar to the inside of the right calf, but I would guess that would be the result of something that happened decades ago.

'One real break for you is that he had two false teeth on a plate; and as a Medicaid private insurance patient, there is a number on the plate. It's all been photographed and uploaded to your crime file.

'His pockets contained a handkerchief, loose change, a note clip with four ten pound notes. No phone.'

As Joe shifted his weight, he stopped talking. Lloyd was looking across the floor of the tent at a small puddle of water that had drained from the outside and pooled at the edge of the bag.

A group of dried blood spots floated towards one and other, and one of the growing number of flying insects was circling them.

Looking at Joe, she pointed to the tent flap and promptly walked outside. He followed. It was then that the rising feeling in her chest made her cough violently. Turning away, she wiped her mouth with the back of her hand, feeling unable to use the tissue that she still held. She thanked him and, moving away a few steps, took out her phone. The coroner's officer passed by with a nod and started a conversation with Joe. She heard his opening line: 'Let's get started then.'

Her phone was answered before she heard the ring tone. 'Col, how's it going your end?'

'Staff interviews and statements finished. Nobody appears to know anything or saw anything, so we've been

26

letting them go. Missing persons being checked, local area being worked over door to door, we're onto the dental plate number - seems it's outside the UK, and it's a private medical company. The fingerprint records are clean. I'm in the temporary incident room when you need me'

'Ok. I'll be over shortly.'

Letting a long breath escape, Lloyd glanced down at her wrist and noted the time.

The afternoon was thinning and the sky was hardening. The first touch of drizzle was on the way. As she reached the incident room, the police ambulance, a black, unmarked, specially fitted out van, went by. Watching it leave the yard, it was promptly sucked into the line of traffic moving westwards.

Lloyd pulled open the ground floor door and stepped across the small entrance hall and climbed the stairs two at a time. Several of the upper rooms were interconnected and four large windows gave a complete view of the quay to the south and the west.

Col immediately pointed to a laptop and said: 'The file is open for you.'

The scene of a disaster is always set on slow, but everything happens so quickly when it's seen on replay over and over in the mind.

Leather-soled shoes and a money clip. No phone, watch or ID, but a smart wool suit. She got the feeling he had been due to meet someone.

Arc of Doubt

Part Two

Arc of Doubt

1

Nat Gibson, Northern Territory, Australia. 1967

So where did it start? You mean all the money, the wealth don't you? Not where Nat Gibson was born. You're curious to find out? Well, it was said that he was never a team player, even in sports when he was younger. This was later interpreted as selfish, but with the single desire to succeed.

No one can be sure about all this, but he couldn't deny that he felt at his best when he wasn't tethered by others. Perhaps it was reading too many adventure stories as a teenager or maybe just being bored brainless by the starter jobs he'd taken since school. Whatever the reasons, he left the UK and took off on what became known as the Hippy Trail.

Somehow an education was played out in months instead of years for him. It was a life most people would never experience: the girls, the drugs, the places. A scarlet life on the road to India and beyond. Eventually, towards the end of 1967, he left the island that used to be called Portuguese Timor, and, having spent most of his remaining cash on a deck passage, he made it to Darwin in Australia's Northern Territory.

He had little more than several packs of cheap cigarettes, a few dollars and a strong desire to find a job. Nat remembered clearly his landfall, being up at dawn to see the faintest smear on the horizon wedged beneath the paleness of the lower sky.

Tiwi and Bathurst Islands grew to a thin outline as the tramp fought its way in the Beagle Channel and finally to the mouth of the small, busy, man-made harbour, backed by a bustling town spread a short distance to the east of it.

Tidying himself up, he pinned his now long hair back with an elastic band, lifted his rucksack to sit upon one shoulder and walked down the gangplank towards the long single storey building that was the arrivals and customs hall. It was hot every day and that day was no exception, but the humidity was high, making any effort laboured. He felt dirty, dressed in shorts, a T- shirt he'd worn for a few days and sandals made from car tyres which had covered the miles from Afghanistan.

His only real asset was the smile of youth. Joining a short queue, he was quickly before a customs officer wearing a clean white short-sleeved shirt, but for some inexplicable reason it was his long socks, neatly folded at the top, and lace-up shoes against the khaki shorts that made the memory imprint.

The customs officer looked carefully at the stamps and visas in his passport then at him for longer. He didn't exactly sneer, but his look was far from one of approval.

'So you've come a fair way.'

Then, pointing at the rucksack:

'Best take a look in there.'

Undoing all the buckles of all the pockets, the customs officer shook it, and the entire contents fell onto the counter - not that there was much. The main item Nat had brought from India was a short wolf skin coat. Using a pencil, the officer turned a corner of it slowly, then let it fall back. With one look in Nat's direction, he swiftly swept it into a large container beneath the counter.

'When will I get....?' Nat's voice trailed away as he knew this was lost.

'Uncured animal product.'

He didn't mind, the officer was already leaning his head in the direction of stamping his passport. Nat repacked his few belongings and stepped forward with hope into a new continent.

Once out of the compound, he stopped, and squatted, picking up a small handful of dirt from the ground. Slowly, and with a smile, he spat into the palm of his hand. The saliva spread over the small stones and dust. Suddenly, clenching his fist, he looked up to the sky then opened his hand to let the dust and stones fall away. The reddish stain was already drying.

Walking out to cross the main car park, he cut between the rows of vehicles as a dirty white utility vehicle, with the row of tall oxyacetylene bottles strapped in the back and a rusting, dented tail gate, started to reverse in front of him. It moved a little before breaking. The driver, a man maybe a couple of years older than him, leaned out of the window grinning.

'Sorry mate, didn't see you.'

Immediately, his chance of a lift into town was apparent and for the asking.

'I've just arrived and I'm all in, any chance of a lift?'

'Yeah, sure.'

He chucked his rucksack in the back among the cutting gear, a selection of torches and the hoses that lay tangled in its base. Rounding the truck, he opened the passenger door and climbed in as the driver finished sweeping his hand over the bench seat, clearing the debris. The inside was like the outside - beaten up, probably without a clean since it had been bought new. The driver pointed:

'The door doesn't shut too good ...'

He went on: 'I think it got buckled a while back. Just slam the bastard to the first catch.'

During the drive, he learnt the town's population of around 30,000 was growing fast. The driver was proud of the 'Top End', as it was known, and he explained, in an accent Nat would soon grow used to, that it was the capital city of the Territory and Australia's link to Asia.

The talk ran away like the miles, easy. The welder briefly questioned him about his travels, letting go a low whistle on hearing his route.

'That's far out man, you may be interested in the house at the top of Quoir Street. It has a reputation in the town as a bit of a hippy commune. If you don't mind roughing it, a lot of travellers go through there. It might do you 'til you find your feet.'

The welder put him down on the opposite side of the road to the post office. His last helpful action was to point in the direction he should walk. With a blast of the deep horn that seemed to bounce in the heat of the day, the truck turned away into a side road and was gone.

Looking around, he couldn't help noticing the amount of traffic. It was very busy and seemed to give off an industrious air of people in a hurry to do business. The town was smaller than he had expected, but he would quickly come to realise that size wasn't that important. Strategically, it really was the road to Asia and beyond, and in due course this town would explode.

It was the only town of any consequence at the Top End of an entire continent. It had both a port and an airport and further unlimited land that would allow both to expand. The only way south out of Darwin was on a single track tarmac surface stretching 1,000 miles to Alice Springs.

The road, locally known as the track, was built by the Americans in the last war. That single tarmac strip with its dirt sides stretched south to the railhead at Alice, and for another 1,000 miles to Adelaide on the coast line, on the other side of this vast continent. His scale was the miles he had covered in Europe. 1,000 miles from London to Vienna, then another thousand onto Istanbul, with people, cultures and customs changing all the time. Here, in this brash, new 'deal with it like it is' world, he felt he would make his mark, one way or another.

He eventually found Quoir Street, and asked someone walking towards him if they knew of the house. The woman, smiled benignly, and turned to point out a house on the other side of the road, further down. Before he could thank her, she was walking away. He passed a few vacant dirt plots before standing in front of a place much the same as the others scattered down the road. This house was built on steel piles with the accommodation built off the ground, open garaging and storage was on the ground floor.

The accommodation was reached from a steel staircase at the side. The house appeared to be clad in some sort of industrial sheeting that was once grey, but was now tired and discoloured. It had been rubbed down by the two seasons, wet and dry. It sat embedded on a double plot with unkempt gardens on all sides. Several banana trees looked trashed. Not far away were two unpruned palm trees with two cars in various stages of dismemberment beneath them on what might once have been a lawn. He saw no movement at all. Dropping his pack to one shoulder, he went to the staircase and climbed it. At the top, just two strides took him to the fly screen door. He listened at first then called out:

'Is anybody in?'

As his last syllable faded, the quiet settled again. Leaning forward, he attempted to see though the glass door behind, but an old net curtain obscured everything.

Brushing a hand across in front of his face to clear the flies that were sticking in numbers, he noticed a small tear in the corner of the screen door. The edge of the mesh had started to roll itself like a spring. Descending the stairs again and walking back down the driveway, he wondered what to do next. The humidity was getting to him.

It was nearing 3pm, and sitting down under a young mimosa tree close to the front boundary, he got some shade. He decided to wait for a while, worn out, hot, dirty and wondering how things might pan out. The sound of galahs bursting from the scrub cover on a neighbouring plot distracted him from his thoughts briefly. They rose, flying in a crowd, then turned on the wing, flashing their pink undersides.

A quarter of an hour had passed when his head turned to the sound of a bicycle bell. A girl dressed in shorts and a tie-dyed T-shirt was riding an old delivery bike and about to turn into the driveway. She slowed, then standing onto the pedals allowed an outstretched foot to bounce lightly before eventually taking the weight of the angled bike.

Pushing her hair away from her face with one hand, she said: 'Hi, can I help? I'm Lucy by the way.'

'Hello Lucy, I'm Nat.'

He shifted his stance a little before continuing:

'I just arrived on a boat today and was told of this house. I need work and help with a place to stay. I was hoping…'

And he let his voice drop away while still looking at her.

'Oh, you'll have to see Mike, but he won't be home until later. There's a house full here, but everyone's out at work. As I'm not working today, I was getting stuff for the evening meal.'

Then she pointed at the bags at the front of the bike.

'OK …ah… should I wait or call back, or can I help you?'

Lifting the two woven bags from the handlebars, she swung them into his outstretched hands, then shoved the bike firmly under the staircase alongside two others. Nat waited for her to close the gap and take the stairs first, but she waved him up:

'You've got the weight.'

Once on the landing, she went round him with the key in her hand, fumbling with the lock.

'It never seems to work very well. You have to jiggle it about. It's well worn, like everything around here.'

The catch popped and the door swung on its hinges.

'… I'm gone from here Friday. Declan and I are moving on, we are going to Alice then on back to

Adelaide where we started out from three months ago. What about you Nat? What are your plans?'

She didn't wait for a reply, but took off through an open door to another room.

Nat placed the two bags in the centre of the long wooden table in the large open room. Looking around, he saw an untidy, cheaply fitted out kitchen, with a banana stalk hanging from the beam near the corner of the sink. It was mainly ripe, with many bananas missing.

At the other end of the room were three put-you- up beds, presumably used as sofas. The two waist-height aluminium framed windows gave a view of the rear yard and the scrub land beyond. The two worn rugs on the wooden floor seemed to be an open wardrobe for some of the house's occupants.

He heard the flush of water somewhere and Lucy appeared again.

'Sorry about that....what about you, what are your plans?'

'I'm... well, right now to eat and sleep. I've been on the move for nearly a year.'

Then he laughed self-consciously. In a slightly lower tone, and much more seriously, he said:

'Get rich and get laid in any order...'

Both of them laughed and then Lucy reached to the wide shelf above the dresser, pressing a tab on a Grundig reel-to-reel tape recorder. The music came instantly, filling their space. He watched her turn the stiff pillar tap to part-fill the deep sink. Then, as she reached for the washing up liquid, the angle of the light caught the fine hair on her forearm. Her movement changed and she plunged both arms into the warm water and started on the dishes. After washing up the breakfast pile, she left it heaped precariously on the drainer.

'There's a large, old marmalade pan in the cupboard over there. We use that for the rice.'

'This one?'

'Yeah, there's a lid for it in there somewhere too.'

Shaking her hands first, she used the towel that had been hanging on the back of one of the chairs to dry them while continuing her instructions.

'The rice is in the top cupboard. Five of those mugs should do it.'

She laid the table while he washed the rice in a yellowing plastic sieve under the same tap, swirling it gently in batches with his fingers until the water was clear, then leaving it drained in the pan for cooking.

He heard her voice behind him:

'There is no shortage of that stuff around here, that's for sure!'

They diced eight onions, and between the laughter and the streaming eyes, she encouraged him to dance to the music that was playing - Itchicoo Park and See Emily Play.

Later, a dog barked outside at the deep throated sound of an approaching car with a busted exhaust. Parking up, the engine was cut, and voices spilt into the space. The sound on the steps was of three people, hustling to get inside the door, laughing and fooling about. They stopped suddenly when someone realised there was a new face in the room.

'Hello mate, who are you?'

Lucy cut in: 'He's new in, waiting for Mike.'

Her explanation seemed to satisfy everyone. Nat just stood still, unsure of their acceptance.

Over the next half hour, the others drifted in, including Mike. He was a short, older man, who said Nat could bed on the ground floor for free if he could stand the ants and the mosquitoes. It would be a couple of dollars a night inside after Friday, when there would be more space.

The evening meal was thick lamb chops, spicy rice and something that passed as a salad, but only just.

As the plates got pushed away, one of the boys took a cigarette from a packet, broke off the filter and split it open in readiness before turning to his next task of fitting his Rizla papers together with a casual, well-practised flick of his tongue. He then part-filled it with the grass he had retrieved from a stash bag somewhere behind one of the makeshift sofa beds.

Carefully, he added the tobacco, and the reel-to-reel played on at increased volume. When he finished the fat joint by twisting its end, he delicately held it between his forefinger and thumb, then started waving it, like a magician producing a rabbit, before lighting it with the stub of his cigarette. The sweet pungent smell, like burnt rope, filled the room.

As it was being passed about, a flagon of red wine was carefully sloshed into glasses and then left dominating the table. The conversation was its own battleground, but it gave Nat threads that would lead him to work.

Later, making excuses, he left with his pack and roll to attempt sleep downstairs. Stopping half-way down the stairs in mid-stride, he saw the cloud seemed low in the sky, compressing the land beneath it. Rain was coming again. Dropping his pack to the concrete floor in the storage, he walked further to the side of one of the dumped cars, taking a brief look over his shoulder. Seeing no one, he started to relieve himself, while glancing down but not particularly observing. Afterwards, he returned to the back of the house, and finding the hose attached to the large corrugated tank, he stretched it to the edge of lawn.

Hanging his small towel in readiness on the tank's pipework, and out of sight from the widows, he stripped quickly to wash with a sliver of soap. Holding the hose above himself, the water ran over his body. It was still warm from the day. Putting a kink in it, he placed the hose under his foot to stem its flow temporarily while he thoroughly soaped himself. It was then he felt the first heavy drops of rain hit him.

Bending quickly, he snatched the hose back to let that same run of water rinse him. Flicking the spanner tap shut, he towelled himself dry as best he could, then wrapped the towel around himself. Stepping lightly into his sandals, he picked up his clothes and skipped back to the safety of the storage, just as the rain got into its stride. He put his underpants back on.

Taking three wooden pallets from a stack, he laid them on the concrete to form the basis of a raised bed. Then he found what he could to cover and soften the boards to avoid contact with the ants. Once in the bedroll, the music above him started to recede and tiredness rushed at him. His last thought before the blackness was that he had made it.

His first job was casual work on a daily basis as a manual loader in the cement sheds in town. The work in the builder's merchant was very hard, with a high turnover of manpower. It only lasted for two weeks until a labourer's job came up at Humpty Doo, the rice experimental station an hour's drive to the southeast. Again, he was on the road.

Mike gave him a lift into town early, dropping him at the Victoria Hotel in Smith St. That street, like many others in the tropics, was visually softened with shade from scattered, planted palm trees.

A smile, a handshake across the bench seat, and he was out of the car with his pack. He saw Mike lean a little towards the passenger side window before his voice reached him:

'Good luck, mate.'

And then putting the car in gear with the column stick, he was gone.

Nat walked slowly with time to spare. He was being met by the Woolworth's store and getting a lift in an old, white Holden pick-up. Arriving, still early, he placed his bag between his feet, straightened and looked south down the wide street. On seeing no white trucks in the steady and growing stream of early workers, he turned his attention to the long, single storey row of shops opposite. Their sun shades reached across to the road gutters, ready to cover the strollers and customers alike. His gaze was halted by the large Catholic Church further down that someone had told him had been built recently.

Standing with two giant arches, the second smaller than the first, the church was a tribute to the new style of architecture and the modern graceful use of concrete. He reflected on how the new municipal buildings were all smart, modern designs. The Commonwealth Bank was probably the most impressive. Some of these were built on former bomb sites, the result of the Japanese raids in February 1942, when they attacked Darwin's crowded harbour.

This town felt good to him. The young welder who had given him a lift was right; expansion here was inevitable. It was just a question of by how much and how soon.

Ten minutes later, a very battered white Holden pulled up near the intersection and a young face appeared at the window. The driver waved and, grabbing his pack, Nat covered the ground to the door of the ute. A tall, thin frame of a man was slouched a little in the dirty cab. Nat was unsure whether to focus on the man's face or the mud- stained message on the slack T-shirt that hung from his shoulders.

'Hi Nat, get in.'

Nat felt an undercurrent in his voice immediately. The tone was unexpected, the interest of meeting a new person was not there. It had not been a welcome, more of an instruction.

For a short time, neither spoke. Then, as they crossed the last junction before the highway, he introduced himself:

'I'm Wayne Waterman by the way.'

To open the conversation, Nat began:

'That's an unusual double W... ?'

'What's wrong with that... '

Came back far too quickly. This was a spiky start.

A pair of wallabies sat in the roadside scrub, dumb faced near a sign announcing The Stuart Highway. He snatched another look at Wayne, this time concentrating on what he saw. The slouched figure was leaning into the corner of the cab; he had a stringy, lean look in his dirty clothes. Nat thought that latent malice was just beneath the surface.

The engine note changed as Wayne slipped up a gear. The beginning of the 'track' was at the city limits and with the speed up and the windows down, the moist heat was driven away temporarily. He settled back for the ride. Occasionally, a vehicle came towards them. If it was big enough to bully them, it would hold its path and the ute would slow to two wheels riding the red dirt in the gully before returning to the tarmac strip.

Wayne loosened up and started to point out stuff as they drove, like the giant ant hills standing sometimes over six feet high, and the magnetic ant that built its mound with thick and thin ends, facing north and south to make less of the heat. He was a native of the Territory, born down the track on a homestead near Pine Creek, a young woodsman hewn of the country, as Nat would learn over the coming months.

The land lay near flat scrub, with a thin covering of stunted trees and the single lane tarmac road stretched like a bootlace to the horizon. Above the sound of the engine, Wayne nodded towards the windscreen

'It's like that almost all the way to Alice … bin there once, barely a bend in the bloody road….'

'Ah, you're a traveller then?'

'Na mate, I haven't got a passport,' and his face creased at his own joke.

'Really, you don't have a passport?'

Wayne replied: 'Why would I need it, we have more than our share of the best beaches in the world, nature provides an extraordinary show of wildlife everywhere. If

I wanted to, I could even ski here on Mount Kosciuszko. We have our own native people, it's got it all here mate. I plan to get out and see the city and do a tour round one day.'

Jabbing a forefinger towards some imagined spot on the windscreen, he carried on:

'We'll take a left up ahead head onto Humpty Doo.'

Leaving the tarmac for a wide dirt road, the car reacted, slewing a little from time to time at the occasional soft spots.

'Got to keep the speed up to ride clear of the corrugation.'

Throughout the journey, the barely undulating, unchanging view of the scrub stretched on with the very occasional tin-roofed single storey building, surrounded by an array of rusting chain link to keep the dogs in and the strangers out.

'What do you know about the station, anything?' asked Wayne.

'Not really, it's a labourer's job. I picked it up at the Labour Exchange. More often than not, it's the experiences they lead to, rather than the job itself.'

'Well....the station covers in all around a few hundred acres, but the farm is built up of around 31 acre fields. Not all are used at the same time. It's experimental strains and stuff, grown and watched over by old John Masters, he's the resident expert, some sort of scientist. Spends most of his time in the poly tunnel or his lab, we don't see that much of him. He gets people come to see him from all over sometimes. It's a good job, not too hard for us lot. We start at 8 and meet at the manager's house. He

doles out the jobs for the day. You'll pick it up soon enough.
By the way can you shoot?'

This caught Nat completely off guard.

'No, why? Have I got to?'

'Yeah, well you don't need to be a good shot, just able to fire the bloody shotgun and stuff really. It's to keep the paddies free of the geese that fly in at this time. They come in huge numbers at dusk. If left, they'd strip the fields. I'll show you, and if you like it OK, we'll go for a pig in the bush one day. Food is all around us here, it's the beer I spend my money on!' 'Ah….'came the open ended reply.

Reaching to the back of his seat with some difficulty, Wayne produced two tins of Pepsi from the unseen cold box.

'Here you go, too early for beer, but it ran out yesterday anyway.'

'Thanks.'

Taking the cold-ish tin, Nat ripped off the tab and drank a deep draught. When they finished, they put the tabs inside the tins and they were ejected without a second thought to join the hundreds of thousands, already rusting, that lined the outback highways.

Humpty Doo lay just a few miles off the Highway on a dirt road stretching to Mount Bundy. It went on to Jabiru, deep in Arnhem Land, where the culture and customs of the Aborigines existed without interruption from white Australians.

'That's the grog shop.'
'What's that…?'

Wayne had pointed to a small building, sideways on to the edge of the road, fronted with only one door and two single benches either side of it. Back through the scrub, sat low and almost blending in to its surroundings, was the small, run down homestead belonging to one Jonas McCoy, the unofficial publican. Cold beer was sold at the weekend, if he felt like it.

'Jonas is a strange old bastard, he drove into the bush after the last war, squatted the land and been there ever since, no one seen him in town ever.' He added in a tone of amazement:

'He also eats the roo, which is only good for dog food and croc fishing…. It's the boongs that go there, very few white fellas. We go into town mostly.'

Half a mile further, he slowed again, swinging left through two wide open metal gates into a vast circular driveway. In front of him were six houses of plain uniformity, very similar to where he stayed in Darwin. But these were properly maintained and tidy. The end house on the right was the manager's, slightly larger than the others.

At the back of the plot was a large, secure, tin barnlike store with its full height doors open. Nat could see heavy machinery, tools and an assortment of equipment stored in an organised fashion. The body and arm of a single fuel pump stood alone close by, with a single brass padlock neatly slotted through the wrist of the fuel arm, firm and immovable like a policeman holds a suspect.

Further away, a long, white poly tunnel abutted a smaller rectangular single storey building clad in dulled industrial sheeting. Wayne stopped the pick-up in front of the houses. Getting out, he said:

'You're in with me... bad luck... we're the singletons, the other houses are for the blokes with families.'

Crossing the gap without looking back, he carried on talking: 'They're a mixed bag, keep themselves to themselves mostly.'

Wayne took the steps two at a time, up the stairs in front of him and opened the screen door. He jammed his work boot against it while he worked the key in the door lock, and the door's light hinges squealed as he lifted his boot momentarily and then flicked it open. Nat was not greeted with chaos as he expected, but order. Neat, clean well kitted out. Waving his arm, Wayne launched into:

'The freezer's got pork, fish, goose fillets... you'll soon be sick of them. And it's well iced up!'

A stork of ripe bananas again hung in the corner of the living area. Several paw paws and a melon were left on the table.

'With the summer gone, the fruits are ending, but if you're into mango the yard is still full of them. Can't be bothered with them myself. Anyway ...' Then waving his hand, he started again:

'That's your room and that's the bathroom. I'll split the cost of the groceries with you. I have a list for when I go into town every week. I'm off to work now. You don't start proper till tomorrow, but you can come out with me now if you want?'

'Thanks...but I'll leave it. I want to look around and settle in.'

Only a shrug was returned before the screen door slammed again. Nat could hear the sound of a mosquito somewhere. The humidity was, as normal, high, and he felt a bead of sweat start from the edge of his hairline and run to the bridge of his nose before he wiped it. In his room, he unpacked his few possessions and carefully put them away in the top two drawers of the matchwood chest beside the bed. Before pressing his canvass backpack to the bottom drawer, he turned it upside down and shook it onto the bed in a final check.

Out of a hidden seam, fell a single, small, perfectly shaped dark pebble, followed by the dust of the road.

Picking up the pebble, he glanced at it just as the fingers of his hand closed over it. Standing straight, he looked out of the window at the heavy afternoon rain shower and the track leading to the paddy fields in the distance. Turning the pebble over several times with his finger and thumb, he placed it gently on top of the chest of drawers.

With a full breath of thought, he felt certain that this house, this space of land would provide the financial and physical recharge that he was seeking. An orderly return to an unusual life.

Hunger was getting to him, that lower abdominal grinding that chews through all conscious thought. Ripping a couple of bananas off the stalk, he ate them quickly, losing the skins to a small bin at the side of the sink.

The taste for something more substantial grew immediately. He saw a large cardboard egg tray concealed by two sheets of The Darwin Sun page three. He was momentarily distracted by the topless girl, before realising there were three editions of an imported mail order hunting magazine under it, but no eggs.

Moving over to the large fridge, he snatched at the long handle. It gave, releasing the suction to the seal with the slightest pop, and he found what he was looking for - a complete tray of two dozen eggs. Taking six, he cracked them open, allowing each to drop unbroken to the bowl. The colour of the yokes showed that rich reddish yellow of birds that had run freely and fed naturally. Two onions were sliced, hands wiped, and the onions were then frying in butter, doused with mixed herbs.

Taking a fork from the drawer, he placed it by the bowl. He then withdrew a small black leather wallet from his trouser pocket. Transferring it to both hands, it fell open revealing a thick bunch of notes of small denominations and various scraps of written notes, names and addresses of travelling semi- strangers whose presence was temporarily lost to him.

His finger and thumb flicked the notes apart, and he withdrew two grubby ten dollar bills. Looking back to the table, he saw the shopping list and placed the notes under it, and as an afterthought, he pinned them down with a box of matches. Picking up the fork again, he thrashed the eggs in the bowl, applied salt with pepper and poured the liquid directly over the caramelised onions. Minutes later, it was folded, cooked and he slid it onto a plate. The next step took no time at all.

Wayne didn't return until it was dark. He didn't say where he had been, but was in an irritated, uncommunicative mood and raised a hand without looking, heading straight to his room. The door shut and that was that for the evening. It wasn't until the next day

Nat found out that he had been playing cards and had lost money again.

An early night was an easy option for him. After a warm shower he returned to his room, stripped naked beside the bed, folded his clothes to a pile on the floor and slid under the single sheet. The heat never seemed to leave. He thought of the briefest moment when he opened the fridge door, and the cold air had lifted to his face. Turning his head sideways on the pillow, he adjusted his body with a shift and then he fell to a deep place of sleep.

The next day started early; whether it was the screaming galahs or Wayne beating the pans, he didn't know. He checked his watch, and the hands lay on five minutes past seven. Throwing off the cotton sheet that had covered him, he stood naked, stretching into the morning. Taking the towel from the bar end at bottom of the bed, he wrapped it in a swift action around himself and headed for a shower.

The water had cooled overnight in the tank to a less that tepid temperature, giving him the rinse that he needed, but not the satisfaction that he had hoped for. Drying himself swiftly, he pulled on his pants, followed by what would quickly become his uniform. Short black shorts, a dark blue singlet, socks and a buff-coloured pair of steel toe capped work boots. Brushing his hair back with a few long strokes, he bunched it at the nape of his neck and roughly banded it. Walking the few steps to the living room he could see Wayne waiting, resting against the back of the sofa, arms folded and straight crossed legs. He was grinning when he spoke:

'Well, you look the business, mate, let's get cracking then, it's nearly 7.30.'

He flicked himself upright in one easy movement, leaning forward and throwing his body into the first steps. Stopping by the door, he took a wide brimmed hard felt hat from a peg. Turning back towards Nat, he asked:

'Do you want one?'

'No, I'm OK, thanks.'

The sky was lighter now with fading clouds, the storm rain with its thunder and lightning during the night had disappeared, leaving the reddish dirt with its slight sheen of mud. The land had sucked away most of the moisture. The bushes and vehicles were speckled with the same dirt, carried in the wind and rain. Outside they started to cross the small wide bladed grass area. Several Rainbow Lorikeet flew off the ground from among the ripe, fallen mangoes. They crowded in a shrill scream, then disappeared as their cries faded. The beads of perspiration appeared light to start with, steadily growing heavier before migrating towards his eyes. Drawing a forearm across his forehead was only a temporary action.

The day was going to be like all the others at that time of year; hot, humid and a good chance of more rain, sooner or later. Nat looked to his right at the sound of raised voices from one of the married quarters. First he saw the dog come down the stairs, then it twisted itself into a scratching position before moving off. From inside the house came the harsh voice of a woman:

'… How the hell do I know...? I've got the baby to feed…'

Wayne turned, grinning, and said:

'That's Barry, the mechanic, she's tongue lashing. He will be pleased to go to work today by the sound of it!'

By the time the manager came out, there were six men and two dogs in attendance. One of the dogs was heavy with pups, dragging her belly low to the ground like an over-fed lizard. The manager nodded towards him while he pinned up the day's work sheet on the office door. Then he launched into a non-stop list of jobs for the day, ending with:

'… and this is Nat joining us. Make him welcome, but don't stop him working! He can pair off with Wayne for a few days. See how they get along.'

Nat didn't hear the comments from two of the others, but he heard the laughter. Wayne tried his best to make light of it, but his shrug covered nothing. Friction in a small community was never far from the surface. They took long- handled shovels, rakes, fence poles and wire tensioners with cutters, as well as hand tools, from the store, and piled the gear into one of the available utes. With two men in the front and two others in the back, the truck began slowly chewing up the dirt road to the paddy fields.

It was just a short drive before they were dropped off at field 14, close to the big sluice, with all their gear as well as Fletch, the younger dog that had jumped onto the tail gate at the last minute with a little encouragement. From beyond the elbow that protruded from the driver's side window of the ute came:

'… Be back at twelve for grub….'

They watched the ute round a bend in the road and head for the far corner of the fields. The sound of the engine twisted at one place, perhaps a gear drop, with the wheel spinning in the soft ground. The noise of the truck receded, sucked into the heavy layer of humidity.

Nat's T-shirt was already soaked in perspiration, even before he started any work. A single ibis in the corner of the field turned its head slowly, peering at them with no more than a glance. Then it lazily lifted its wings a few times and flew away in the opposite direction.

Wayne could read his mind:

'Better make a start… it'll be mid 80s by midday, with 80 per cent humidity as well.'

The sluice for 14 was a small steel winding lid that fitted tightly over the two foot diameter pipe at the paddy end. It was a feeder to the field from the main ditch alongside, which in turn was linked to a network for all the fields leading back to the Adelaide and Mary River system and its tributaries. The water levels in the appropriate sapling fields were checked daily to insure the correct level of water was maintained to keep the weeds at bay. Blockages in any of the pipes or ditches were quickly cleared. They raked and shovelled in ten minute bursts, with Wayne slipping into the ditch in his enthusiasm. He was nearly waist deep in warm, putrid water, cursing at the top of his voice and pulling armfuls of weed from the pipe when he leapt back at a thrashing and churning in the water.

'Christ, that gave me a bloody shock…'

'What was it..?'

'A barramundi. Not that big, but they shoot up their spines and if they get you, it can be bad.'

With a sudden rush, the water powered the remains of the debris through and the water rose to the irrigation level before the lid was closed. The fields were planted in rotation, with various types of seedlings in different parts of the fields. The last harvest in field 21, was a sea of beauty. Rice had ripened yellow to perfection and had been harvested in September, using the small harvester that now sat covered in the store. That field lay dry, ready for the cycle - till, flatten, fertilise, flood, and plant- to start again very soon.

According to the schedules, it would be the following week when they would take the mini tractor from the sheds to drag the plough. The land would be turned and the old roots chopped up. Gathering all the tools into a heap, and making certain not to leave any, they then took a claw hammer and horseshoe nails in their small leather bags, along with the wire with the tensioners. They scrambled to the bank top to walk the field, tightening the boundary wire mesh every so often, pinning back odd lifts on the post where animals had tried to get in. 'You ever get any crocks here?' Nat asked. It had been on his mind since he saw Wayne climb into a ditch.

'Yeah, very occasionally, just small ones. The big fellas, you see them up the mouth of the river near the coast, the salties can grow bigger. They can grow to around half a ton and up to five metres, but they don't come in these shallow ditches, just the odd smaller ones. I shouldn't be in the ditch it against the regs really but...'

And then he tapped the flat of his hand to the eight inch serrated blade, holstered to his side adding:

'I'm not properly dressed without it....'

The look on his face was expressionless. Nat laughed nervously, wondering how much of Wayne's behaviour was bravado and how much was something more sinister.

'Well, I'm staying out of the water...'

'Sometimes I lay a line for the barramundi, well not a line, a thick wire trace and try my luck. They'll bend a rod if you hook one, that's for sure.'

As the day flattened out, Nat was exhausted. Even after the lunch break back at the house, his strength had gone. The afternoon was more of the same, but slower, much slower. Finally, around four, the ute's horn sounded. Two long blasts from the next field.

'That's it. Gather up the gear.'

There was little talk after that. The two of them sagged to the flat bed of the ute when it arrived. The dog had wandered off unnoticed hours before, beaten by the heat. Just as they all arrived back at the store, the sky burst again for its regular unleashing, soaking them before the tools were even stored away. Pulling himself up the staircase, with a slow step and his head down, used up the last of his energy. He heard Wayne call out: 'Shower and grub will see you right, mate.'

Nat didn't reply. He wondered just how long it would take him to adjust to all of this.

The first few weeks flipped away. Some tasks were easier and more fun than others, and he came to enjoy the sunset shoot, as he called it. He used the farm's Land Rover or ute on site whenever he wanted to, and he could take it off- site with permission. The hour before sunset he set off on his own with an old bolt action 22 and a single barrel shotgun, with a full bandolier crossed on his chest.

The shot gun stock was chipped and stained, and it kicked like a fairground fighter. But regardless of the bruising, it was his favourite. As the sun moved further to the horizon, the colour came to the sky in the west, turning it to a blaze and with it came the geese from the north. A smear, widening slowly in the late evening sky, and gradually a formation of dozens of them, thinning to the flankers. They were all seeking the young green shoots of the paddy fields. Once he had worked out the direction of their flight, he could drive, then walk to the edge of the field and stand ready.

The feel of being alone in the quiet, the touch of lightness of the broken gun hanging on his left arm, was good. When the gunsmith carved that stock and worked that inlay years ago, this moment was what it was all for. Using his thumb and forefinger, Nat gently worked out a few shotgun cartridges from the stiff loops of the bandolier strung from his right shoulder and transferred all but one to his trouser pocket for easier access. Tilting the edge of the remaining cartridge into the chamber, it slid almost on its own into position. The action from then on grew quicker, the gun snapped shut, safety catch off, gauge range, swing gun, keep the line, in front, the leader ...BANG... again... reload... repeat... BANG...repeat. The birds would turn and lift, gaining height and speed; driven by fear to another place.

The stragglers might glide, then drop softly with a lowered undercarriage to land further away. The 22 would be used then, but accuracy was more of an issue. In that hour and a half before the sun took its last rays with it, he could lose off a box of 50 cartridges without trying too hard, leaving carcasses spread around the fields like litter in a bus station.

It was late and one afternoon after work, he had picked a mango from the yard tree. Standing still, he cut it in half and removed the stone, allowing it to fall to the ground. Then, concentrating, he gently cut two neat crosses deep into the fruit. Wiping the penknife blade on both sides against his T-shirt, he folded it and slipped it back into his shorts. Holding one half of the mango firmly between his thumbs and pushing the fruit gently from the back, he used his fingers to lift it free of the stringiness near the skin. Even lowering his head for the succulent pleasure didn't stop the sweet juices running down his chin. He bolted first one half, then the other and discarded the skin.

Before he could start wiping his hands on his shorts, he heard Wayne from the small balcony above him: 'Too many of those will give you the runs... ....'

Pausing, he changed direction.

'Barry is going into town Saturday, if you want to go for a drink? Might stop at the Grog Shop for a warm up. I'm stopping over in town, got a mate there, what about it?'

Not wanting to sound disinterested immediately, Nat delayed his response. What he really wanted was breathing space; a chance to see something or someone away from the tight confines of the station, the exploration of one to one. He knew if he went with them, it would be an expensive beer swill, ending with a lasting hangover, just like the last time. But what was the alternative?

There was little socialising on the farm, it was work, play and melt away. So..... '...um ... alright, I'm up for that.'

With those words, he knew that he would be spending cash from his savings, and that moving on at the end of the wet season would be delayed even further. That

Saturday around midday, with Barry driving, they set off for town. Spirits were high, but Nat felt uneasy somehow, it was almost a premonition of something untoward approaching. The Land Rover covered the mile to the grog shop, then skidded slightly and pulled up just short of the small wooden building. Leaning with both elbows on the opened counter was the man they called Jonas.

His grey hair and beard were woven together, seemingly without a natural join. His weathered face showed all of his years. Straightening a little he said:

''Ello what have we got here…?'

Then rising to his full height, shot out an extended arm, pointing at Nat: 'You one of those hippies just blown in from the islands?'

Then his arm dropped and his belligerence melted.

Barry opened: 'Hello Jonas, three martinis in chilled glasses please, and one for yourself.'

'Fuck off.'

Jonas, reaching behind, opened the rust- stained front of an oversized fridge, it was stacked with stubbies of Darwin brewed lager. He extracted four and inserted them with a flourish into their polystyrene coolers, and, with an unexpected speed, slid his hand along the rough string looped to his belt until the bottle opener was in his palm. He took the tops off in one continuous movement, swept the counter free, and let them the tops fall to the dirt at his feet. He extended his hand for payment.

This time, his face had worked to something that could be called a smile. He didn't say how much, that was a given. Barry paid for the first beers and they worked through a round each. Intermittent gossip and banter passed back and forth between them, then, quite suddenly, Wayne stood up. Barry spoke:

'Come on, time to go, before any Abos arrive.'

They were faster drinkers than Nat, his stubby was nearly full.

'Look…..ah….you two crack on. I've changed my mind, I'll walk back later.'

He expected them to cajole him, but they didn't. The response from Wayne was: 'Suit yourself. We'll see you later then.'

The Land Rover opened up and pulled away, eventually leaving just the softer sound of a generator in the homestead behind Jonas' stockade.

'Look after the shop, I'll be back in a minute.'

Leaving the rear door open, Jonas lurched on a failing knee about 20 yards to a tree, stared down to the ground and relieved himself. After the buttoning up, he returned.

'Ah… that's better.'

It was a statement, not an opening of conversation. Nat stretched from the bench and walked to the side of the shed for nothing more than a chance to think of what he might do next. Something far off sounded, first lightly, the noise of an engine growing in intensity by the second. It was still far off, perhaps near Humpty Doo. Three long blasts broke, the hello and goodbye of a truck. The sound grew deafening until the thunderous 'Mac' truck came bearing down the dirt road.

Again a hard blast of the horn and the six trailers snaking the road behind passed in a fine spay of damp red dirt. The noses of the cattle, stuck up against the slats of each trailer, was his primary image. While Nat had been focused on the truck, he didn't notice any other movement, but two men now stood just behind him. He was startled. Their broad features were motionless, their dark skins seemed to catch the passing light. They wore jeans, T-shirts and flip flops, and their postures showed a quiet ease. They grinned, first at him then each other, but didn't speak. The gap seemed to stretch a little before Nat asked them if they were down for a beer. The taller of the two was quick with the simple reply:

'OK, I'd like that.'

The other just nodded. Nat realised he had been outmanoeuvred and went to the front to buy three more beers.

'Those black fellas here are they?' asked Jonas. 'Wara and Koen?'

He moved his head slightly as if to communicate, but said nothing, passing the money to Jonas for the opened stubbies. The change was wet from the slop and to free it from his fingers he quickly transferred it to his belt. He wanted a cigarette, but took the bottles to the side bench and passed them to the two men. They were sitting with their backs against the timber wall, legs outstretched and holding the rolled edge of the worn bench. At the ankle line of their worn jeans he noticed they both had the swellings of bites and their skin was discoloured.

They looked at each other, and a short burst of guttural sounds that he could not understand passed between them. The smaller of the two raised the bottle in his direction and with a genuine wide warm smile just said:

'Good beer.'

The opening conversation stuttered into a run:

'I'm Nat, from over at Humpty Doo.'

He learnt that the taller one was Wara, and other was Koen, his half-brother. They lived several miles further down the road from the farm in a collection of tin sheds and humpies up from the lake. In truth, this was just a marsh where even the water buffalo wouldn't go. He'd seen black fellas wandering the extremities of the station but nothing much went missing. To Nat, they were a thoughtful race that had inhabited this wider area for over 65,000 years, a people to be admired for their deep tribal commitments and their disinterest in material possessions.

Shifting his weight on the bench to one side, he eased out a soft pack of cigarettes from one of the pockets of his shorts. Folding back the edge of the silver paper, then tapping it against the fingers of the other hand, he shook two partly out, and offered them, wondering if they would take them. Their response was immediate, they grinned at each other and both took one. Wara put his straight to his mouth, dabbing the filter with the end of his tongue before clamping his lips around the filter, waiting for the light to follow. But Koen carefully lifted his hair and slid it behind his ear, perhaps to smoke later or maybe to trade.

Striking a tab match brought the sharp flare and acrid smell of sulphur, followed by the stronger, sweet scent of burning Virginia tobacco. The two of them shared that first cigarette in open delight, like young boys at the bottom of the yard.

'Is it true you guys can spear barramundi?'

Wara slapped a hand to his thigh.

'That's easy …you gotta be quiet and fast to get 'em… they clever but not as clever as me…'

'How did you learn?'

'Got taught by the elders, they teach us everything we need. The white fellas teaching not so good. You want to see? You meet us tomorrow up at Coolwak. Late morning.'

Next thing he knew, they were up and moving into the light scrub before the road. Only Koen looked back, his features cracked to a smile and he raised a hand, although not high enough to express a clear message. He guessed they would walk the six odd miles, maybe taking an offered ride in the back of a pick-up if they were lucky. Deciding on a last beer, he found Jonas reading a three day old Sydney Herald, which had somehow found its way to his elbow.

'Those two boongs are OK, not like some of their fellas.'

Again the bottle top was taken off, and the hand outstretched in his direction.

Sitting on the quiet side, Nat took another cigarette from the packet and lit it, first with a short, then a longer drag. Dropping the spent match to the sand bucket, a stream of fumes exited his mouth and nose.

He couldn't help thinking about the Aborigines. Everyone denigrated them because of the life they led, but unlike the white fellas, they took only what they needed, not what they wanted. He had spent almost a year moving slowly, like a tortoise, across the Indian sub-continent and further east, and had been met with only kindness by people of every shade who had less than him to give.

Drawing on the last of the cigarette, he pushed the butt beneath the surface of the sand in the bucket, lifted the polystyrene coolie and drank from the bottle again. Allowing his eyes to rake across the bush, deep, and further away, partially obscured amongst the trees was a single water buffalo. A giant beast with wide, dark horns that matched its skin, it stood completely motionless watching, looking with dark eyes. When the long moment was over, he was gone. Leaning forward, Nat bunched himself up then straightened and walked the few steps along the ribbon-like path back to the counter. He placed the empty bottle alongside the still open newspaper.

'Thanks Jonas.'

'Yep, good luck mate.'

The afternoon was pulling on. He crossed the road on a wide angle and started to walk the mile or so back to the station. The road, even after the intermittent rains, was hard packed and still corrugated in places, the odd soft patch which could work its way to a slip or deep rut would be levelled and rolled when the heavy graders finally made it to this part of the road. They were supposed to be out continuously working in the wet season somewhere, but he rarely saw them. Without thought, he took aim at a recently-thrown lager tin that had not made it to the roadside, and kicked it hard into the edge of the scrub to lie for eternity with all the others.

He walked quicker now, deciding to stop off at the manager's house to clear his using the battered ute for the fishing trip the next day. The door knocker was broken, partly missing. Maybe it had been used to pull the door shut too often, he rapped his knuckles hard against the painted surface, then stood back waiting for a response. A dog barked from inside somewhere, another joined in before dying back. Turning his head, he could see the back garden, neat as a new handkerchief laid out square, with a stone path leading to an empty washing line. The sound of the door catch being drawn made him turn back.

'Hello Joanne, is Pete there?'

When he looked at her, he saw a woman about 40, still attractive but on the turn, her natural beauty had wilted, it had been worn down by life on the station. The smile she gave him wasn't full enough to show real warmth.

'Yeah, I'll get him. He's dozing on the sofa.'

She didn't so much go and get him as shout to him in the next room. It was a long slow call, a tired, resigned sigh of sound.

'Pete. It's Nat, for you.'

A pause and a short space opened up before Pete came to the door, crumpled by his recent sleep. The sudden awakening had done him no good.

'Hello Nat, what are you after then?'

'I just wanted to borrow the station ute tomorrow to go to Coolwak to do some fishing, but thought I should ask first.'

Affirming with a nod, he ended the brief call with 'OK,' and reached somewhere out of sight for the Holden's single key, which he passed over. The door closed.

That evening, the rain held off but the rolling thunder clouds swept the sky to be finally slashed by the setting sun. Then the slow, unfolding darkness blanketed the temperate night. That Sunday it was past 8 when light showed red against his eyelids. There was no hurry. Nat lay still, his senses becoming alert to his surroundings. There was no movement in the house, clearly he was on his own with Wayne still away in Darwin somewhere.

Walking to the shower, he rinsed his body. As the water warmed him, the steam rose to the widening black spread of mould, which needed wiping again from the ceiling, but he would leave it. These thoughts didn't last. In clean clothes, he moved to the kitchen, opened the fridge and pulled out the plate of defrosted duck breast. Taking two eggs, he used his knee to edge the door closed. The intensity of heat from the stove was temporarily covered with the frying pan before it reached upward again. The meat was flattened and cooked in butter, then the eggs, split from their shells, fell in alongside. Later, a single light shake was enough to ease the contents onto his plate for immediate consumption. After fuelling up for the start of the day, Nat passed the side of his hand backwards then forwards across the sides of his lips, clearing the last remnants. He rinsed the plate and cutlery under the hot tap with the slightest tilt, and left them to dry on the drainer.

Twisting lightly, he reached with a still damp hand to turn off the radio, then went in search of his boots.

The Holden was unlocked, windows down and unloaded. The button on the door handle was stiff to the pressure from his thumb, and the strained hinge gave off a creaking sound as it opened and shut, blanking the cacophony of bird sounds with their different pitches. The seat gave as he settled back and worked the key into the ignition. Starting the engine, he revved slightly before settling the heel of his boot amongst the growing pile of dirt and stones that had found its way onto the mat. Jerking at the column steering, he slid it into first gear. Leaving the station entrance, he headed east allowing the ute to rumble over the corrugated road.

As rain had held off the previous night, that familiar light cloud of red dirt rose at the rear of the vehicle. He was in no hurry. A couple of cars passed him, but only one was coming the other way. The casual wave, a hand raised by unknown drivers was personal contact in a detached form. He wasn't driving for long, maybe five or six miles, when he found what he was looking for. Slowing to pull off into a bite in the dirt road, he parked up, easing the ute towards a single low tree in the hope of shade for the vehicle.

It wasn't until he got out that he noticed Koen and Wara sitting in the shade a short away off. Wara stood up and raised his hand palm first at chest height, while Koen reached around the tree for two lightweight aluminium poles about eight feet long. They must have been pulled off a tip somewhere. Rammed into one end of the poles was a small two- pronged piece of metal, fashioned with a wide end to the arrowheads to act like a barb.

'I'm early.'

Wara said: 'Sun's well up.'

Then, scratching his leg through his dirty cotton trousers with abstract force, he continued:

'We been here a while, let's go …'

Nat wiped away the sweat forming on his brow with the palm of his hand, leaving a trace of the red dirt that was covering his skin already. Koen carried the spears. They walked slowly, without deliberate effort, as though to conserve rather than expend the valuable resource of energy. They clearly knew the direction they wanted to go in, heading through the minor stunted tree belt which thinned as the land dropped. The path, if you can call it that, was narrow and marked by occasional wallaby tracks and droppings. The lower limbs of those scrub plants sometimes brushed their shoulders, catching for a moment on their T-shirts, like a fly before it shakes itself free of a spider's web. The sweat was running freely on Nat, but urged on by their looks of encouragement, he kept moving.

After a long 20 minutes, they dropped into a rock gulch. To begin with, they climbed with difficulty over large boulders, passing the spears to one and other so as not to damage them. As they closed on the water's edge, the rock size diminished to allow rough walking. Skirting an outcrop, Wara pointed to the worn out, concrete, wharf-like structure running from the end of the path. Alongside the broadening creek was shallow water, reaching part way up to the concrete before widening to a round lake. They passed the roofless building, its walls beaten down by years of neglect. Then Koen slowly edged to peer over into the water two feet below the pier, while Wara walked away in a loop, signalling with a waving palm that Nat should be still. At different points, they surveyed the water through its shimmering surface, looking for the shadow on the rocky bottom that would betray a fish. Nat saw a stick protruding out of the water casting a bent shadow, which deflected the position of what lay beneath the surface. At nothing more than a creeping pace, they advanced their way along until they neared the end of the wharf.

Wara, not 20 feet away from the other two, turned, raised first a finger to his lips to urge them to be quiet; and then moved his index and forefinger to point at his eyes. With a short stab in a foreword direction, he conveyed the simple message of what he could now see.

Crouching just a little, some of his fingers moved on the spear. It was a subconscious repositioning, almost unnoticed, and placed the spear just above his shoulder. Wara indicated that his prey was unaware of him. With a short single movement, the spear pierced the water to its end and the spell was broken. The dying turn of the fish splashed only once as the spear sank from its upright position. Nat glanced back at both of them just as Koen broke into dance shouting... 'Yeah... ...yeah...'

But Wara took no notice. His attention was on the water. Slipping to the shallows, his head jerked first to one side, then the other, checking the immediate area for any further movement of larger predators. Wara reached the spear and floated the fish before quickly levering it with a heave onto the concrete. It was the slapping noise of the fish hitting the hard surface that stayed with him. The hunt, the prize, food. With one hand on the belly of the large fish, Wara gently prized the prongs from its flank with a twisting motion. Standing now, he accepted the praise of the others with a smile before bending to pick the fish up. He inserted his fingers into its gills and raised it to shoulder height for it to be admired. Its silver scales flicked the sunlight as the water dripped off its tail.

It was Koen that spoke first:

'Must be close on seven pounds.'

Nat had watched the hunt in awe, the simple skill conducted with stealth, a sudden strike of prehistoric precision. Wara wrapped the fish in a piece of cloth that had been tied around his waist, and carried it in his arms like an offering to an unknown god. Koen took up both spears and they took a different path out of the gulch, away from the creek, traversing the valley. Nat followed, wondering vaguely why he was sweating steadily while wearing shorts and they didn't seem to, even with their long cotton trousers. Few words passed between them until they approached a wider section in the path where, on a blind corner, they disturbed a large goanna, maybe a yard long. It was gone as quickly as Nat's brain had registered it.

With its belly just off the dirt, it left just a rustle as it became hidden in its surroundings.

Koen broke out: 'Wooooow…. dat fella could have had fish. He nearly knocked you over.'

'Yeah, if you had been faster with the spear, we would have meat as well!' Wara retorted.

There was still laughter as they made the clearing. It was the sound of voices Nat noticed first, and then he saw the three women. Two were old, how old he couldn't tell, they were chattering together, presumably about the fish and their arrival. Each wore a thin cotton print shift dress with stained patches and odd buttons missing. They seemed incongruous in their surroundings. The youngest woman was still older than him, and she was clearly ill at ease, shifting her weight unevenly while glancing backwards and forwards between Koen and Wara. Then she turned and walked away towards the tin sheds. Those two tin sheds, each just about big enough to put a small car in, were where they lived. At the open door of one of them, stood two small children clothed in similar dirt- streaked clothing. They stood with their feet in the dirt, and one had dropped an arm over the shoulder of the other.

They stood so close to each other they appeared joined. They were watching him too, unsure of the stranger. Nat felt the eyes of all the bush creatures were on him too...judging. Three humpies had been sited further down, near the edge of a dried out stream, reminding him of mushrooms appearing for the first time on a late autumn morning in his previous life. The stream, which looked as though it hadn't seen a tide of water for a long space of time, was marked out by gums on either side. There seemed no sense in marking these so-called rivers on maps.

When he turned back, people had moved. The large bed of hot ash from an earlier fire was being flattened while the fish was being gutted and prepared. The noise level changed as the children broke for space and two skin-stretched underfed dogs, looking as if they were mostly dingo, eased forward from the shady side of one of the sheds.

The older bitch came over last, as though knowing her place, with teats of many litters almost dragging on her low undercarriage. A flurry sent the guts of the fish in their direction. The growl was teeth bared, and the old bitch hung back just long enough to settle for the scrapings. Using all the fingers of one hand, Wara scratched his arm, before squatting down to a sitting position, touching the ground to steady himself.

'Nat, you wanna stay? Eat with us? We bake it wrapped like you never had it, old Elandra and Bindra will show you the old way.'

Nat looked at Koen with the positive confirmation answer all over his face. The younger woman, he found out later, was called Merinda. Her man had gone 'walkabout', perhaps it was tribal or perhaps he was out behind a bar in town. Maybe he'd be back soon, maybe not; she appeared unconcerned either way. She shouted something he didn't understand at the children and then she walked with resigned, slow steps uphill to them. He watched her just longer than curiosity called for. The fish got baked on a flat steel plate, resting on four, rounded riverbed stones and covered with a blackened deep tray making a makeshift oven. As it cooked, the light aromas drifted over them all as they clustered around the fire. He felt a rare calmness on him in their company, it was acceptance without judgment, inclusion without a past.

That afternoon, like so many similar afternoons, bled away. Eventually, he was led back to the place where the pick-up was just as he left it. Koen signalled his parting by raising an arm, smiling. Nat started to thank him but the words never reached him, he was already retreating into the bush. The drive back was uneventful, other than spotting the glistening Slaty Grey snake lying loose like cable flex, stretched out across the dirt road, sleeping. Without hesitation, his foot stamped downwards on the accelerator, then he instantly hit the brakes to skid in the dirt and kill it. He could manage spiders, scorpions, king ants and other things but not… snakes. The Territory had its share.

It must have been about 6 when he got back and dropped off the keys. Tired, he slept early that night. It was noise that woke him, the sound of the door hitting the catch, uneven footsteps. They stopped. The simple, sharp sound of breaking glass was isolated in the stillness before the swearing started.

Nat pulled himself from the bed, ripped on his pants and opened the bedroom door. Lit up on the far side of the room, Wayne stood abjectly staring at the broken glass. His head jerked up:

'Yeah... well....'

It was neither a question nor a challenge, just an opening before he briefly explained his weekend hadn't gone so well. His face on one side was swollen, bringing on colour like a cloud banked sunset, with a grey plaster barely covering the cut above one eye. The Hawaiian shirt was torn at the shoulder and grey slacks hung creaseless and filthy.

'Yeah... well,' he began again... 'At least I'm back.'

The pause was longer than needed. His still drunk state was struggling to organise his line of thought and when it came, it came in a rush.

'Barry's still locked up. He'll be out tomorrow ...hopefully. Barry's damaged the Land Rover, but it's drivable .... Just down one side...'

Slower now and slurring, he went on:

'He hit...'

His hand went to his forehead and using his thumb and forefingers, he massaged his temples briefly, without hope of relief

'God my head ....he hit ...ah... he put it too tight... caught the stone wall out on Harbour Road on the way back with some girls. It will take a lot of explaining.'

With all that said, his head dropped and he stumbled away towards his room. Wayne was right, Barry was let out with a fine. He arrived back at the station homestead in a delivery truck he had flagged down, very late for work on that Monday morning.

The boss, meanwhile, had seen the Land Rover parked up out front, and had already spoken to Wayne. He'd walked the length of it and standing still, used his fingernail to flick away a flake of green bodywork paint on the offside dented wing. He looked a second time at the searing graze that had cut into the passenger door, before addressing the labour gang.

His voice was a low:

'He will... pay…every fucking penny for this, literally and physically. Send him to me when he gets back, the roster is on the wall, now get to it.'

Barry never mentioned it again. He must have made his peace with his wife and paid for the repairs, because the incident just slipped off the map. Life, as they say, just went on. The days leading up to that Christmas were spent with everyday tasks - spraying, sharpening the cutting blades, clearance work.

Two months slid away and the days leading to the Christmas drop began. Work remained steady and uneventful other than when the planter sank to its axels in the partially flooded number eight field. It trapped the new labourer by the ankle, poor sod was screaming wild when he was lifted to the centre path. His bones seemed splintered, although there was little blood, and he lay twisting with nerves exposed.

The shrieking died away to whimpers by the time the morphine went in. It was hard to carry on working that afternoon. Nat kept seeing and thinking of the desolation and fear that filled the boy's eyes. The youngster was taken, after a 'phone discussion, to the hospital by the manager on a mattress in the back of the pick-up. It was the fastest way, so they said.

That Christmas, the station emptied for a week's shut down, leaving Nat and the manager's family the only occupants. Everyone had somewhere to go except him, but he was unconcerned. One day, he decided to visit Peachey's machine store. It was a vast emporium of steel - rods, sheets, both flat and thick, and machinery of all shapes and sizes. There were spares and repairs, wire, rolls of it, razor, round or barbed. If you couldn't find it, order it, or repair it, old Peachey or one of his boys would turn it on one of the lathes from a clock cog to a crank shaft; for a price.

All of this organised chaos was roughly cased and framed with a thick layer of corrugated iron, locked tight as a boar's arse at night, with his part-dingo mastiffs wandering free inside. The sign high on the doors near the black, greased slider said: *the best Peacheys are here.*

It was in that yard, having picked up a gasket set, on an afternoon already thinning that Nat saw Kari, crossing towards him.

'Hello mate, given any more thought to my offer in the Vic then?'

Kari stood, a tall gangling frame showing the wear of his years. Part Aborigine, he had made money catching water buffalo out on the Bamurru plains and taking occasional tourist groups, when he could find them, on edgy bush trips; pushing them beyond their usual boundaries and letting them experience the frontier, probably frightening the shit out of them along the way. Nat had met Kari in The Victoria bar, on a late Saturday afternoon at the time when sweat was being washed away with a few early beers, before the real lifting started. Leaning back with his shoulder against the far wall, and bored by the southern states politics being chucked around by people alongside him, he had jerked himself upright and raised a schooner in his fist.

'Those cute pussies in their polished shoes. You need more than a silver tongue to chase down a living up here…'

Then stepping sideways, rubbing the top of one of ears with a finger and thumb, he began again:

'Hi Roy, who's your young friend then?'

That had been Nat's introduction to Kari. There had been an immediate connection, and, later, Kari had offered to take him hunting.

'Yeah, OK, I'd like that,' said Nat. 'Can you pick me up on your way past the station gate?'

Standing solid with his hands on his hips, Kari nudged the dirt with the edge of his boot, then, as if delaying his thoughts for some reason, he spoke:

'I like you kid, you got what it takes. 6am at the gate on Thursday then?'

With not much more that a nod and a wave, it was done. They both moved away. For two days that Christmas, Nat lived bush, working as a cross between a jackeroo and a rodeo cowboy, loving every minute. He was picked up outside the station 40 minutes late by Kari in a battered Toyota Land Cruiser that had once been blue. The car skidded slightly in the dirt as it pulled up with the passenger door opening early. A black fella, busting with a grin like a split banana, was in the passenger seat. His name, Nat thought, was Durbin, but it was pronounced so gutturally, he couldn't be sure he had heard it right. The truck moved on, and they headed deep for the Bamurru plains, an area he had heard about, but never seen.

Taking off down the main road, and siding north for a narrower dirt track after a dozen miles or so, Kari slipped a gear or two and they slowed on the uneven ground, occasionally with tyres spinning in the soft sand. As the land flattened, the scrub thinned and the sun rose higher. They must have covered another 30 miles when the thought occurred to Nat that he was completely lost.

They had changed direction several times before slowing to a stop by what he took to be a dry, isolated gulch. The engine cut with a cough like an emphysema patient. And there they all were, appearing as if from nowhere, a large family living a life as if they had climbed straight out of another age. Behind them, incongruously and looking like they had just been dumped, were two vehicles, an ageing Bedford truck, maybe a five tonner at a guess.

The second was another Land Cruiser, caked in red dirt, older than the one they were getting out of. It had been adapted with two inch steel tubing, amateurishly welded to form a working   platform on the roof and a double rail at waist height above for enclosure. The front of the vehicle was framed and fitted with the same tubing braced at the sides to the platform. Durbin waved and a young man came forward wearing just torn jeans, and together they took the five gallon drums. Using a red plastic funnel, they started to pour the fuel into both tanks of the vehicles. The bonnet was opened and after some wrestling, the engine fired and started.

A small girl with a frown of concentration revved it as instructed while holding her arms up towards to the steering wheel. With words Nat couldn't understand, Kari swung the small child away from the vehicle. Wriggling and laughing, she was set her down on the ground.

'OK, let's get going. Nat, watch Durbin make the first catch, then you can take over.'

With a slamming and grinding, the vehicle took off, jerking and jolting on the uneven ground. Durbin was on the platform and the back was open, filled with old heavy truck tyres in a neat row with leader rope tucked into them. The banging on the roof started, the race to spot and run the buffalo had begun. Getting close enough, or to tire them out, and then to loop the noose lasso on a guide pole was difficult. Once, he was right over the heaving tonnage, the heat the smell and the animals fear lifted right up to him before the bastard then veered away. The buff could have turned his heavy black horns to the vehicle's thin skin.

Eventually, the catches came. The cruiser jerked sideways, the yelling, finally the veering away, and the jolt of the heavy tyre leaving the cruiser, and the laughter of the hunt as the beast slowed, worn out, dragging its load to a halt. Nat was soaked in sweat with the excitement and the laughter. The buffalo were easy to round up, but had to be delivered alive to the slaughterhouse near town. That's where Kari took over the difficult job of drive and deliver, they would later be slaughtered and minced, right down to the tail, and canned for dog food. It took most of the second day to get the quota delivered. Camping out overnight, they returned later in the day to the same camp to find that several people were about go on a goanna hunt. Nat was drawn over by an old woman, wrinkled like the sands of an outward going tide.

'Watch out, she's got her eye on you mate,' called Kari, laughing.

Half an hour later, a different hunt began in earnest. A fast, throaty, staccato conversation burst backwards and forwards among those nearest the sighting. Bare feet slapped the burnt land that had been low scrub, but had been removed by some previous fire. The goanna bolted to a hole, scratching the earth at speed for its life, but someone had got it by the tail and was heaving against the animal's sharp, strong claws that were out of sight underground.

Gradually, it was pulled back to the opening of the hole, but it had one last trick up its sleeve. It turned with open jaws on its attacker, who let go, leaping clear. As the animal again bolted for the same hole, its tail was grabbed by someone else. This time, when it was partially exposed, it was beaten lifeless by several stick bearers. One of the women took the dead animal, about five foot long, over her shoulder and danced a short jig in the dust, to the musical chatter of tribal voices before they ambled back homewards.

Kari explained to Nat that a fire would be prepared and they would all eat together later. But in the meantime, he was going to take a dip in a shallow pool in a nearby canyon to wash the day from his body.

'You coming?'

Nervously, Nat replied: 'I'm not swimming with crocs.'

'Na... you see the bottom.'

Walking on and skirting wide passed a slit in the rock, Kari shouted over his shoulder: 'Watch out, there could be camels in there. If they rush you, you be down quicker than a cold beer on a hot day.'

The narrow path was no wider than a mattress with irregular steep sides reaching for a plain blue sky. Kari shouted and threw a fist-sized boulder further into the gulch.

'Just in case there is one down there, thinking about coming out this way.'

Further on, the track bent to the left, widening to reveal a broad shelf of rock as smooth as a pebble. It was about 30 yards long and almost full of dull, flat, still water. He followed Kari as he headed around its edge and upwards to gain height. Then, swinging around saying nothing, he waved one arm in a wide open gesture. Nat's gaze followed the sweep. Before him lay a scene of extraordinary, calm beauty. The steep ochre coloured walls of canyon looked as though they had been sculpted to meet the shade of the ghost gums, some full grown, that were scattered around the base of the canyon. The pool now appeared translucent, shafted with the sunlight.

He could see clearly down into its full length, this giant saucer sat low in the canyon base, separated from what, in the wet, might have been a river if it rained that year. Its ridges were marked with trees. He took his time following Kali into the water, lying quietly in the tepid shallows, allowing it to reach his chin and watching occasional insects land or swim their first or last on its surface. The wallabies standing further up the path were watching, but they would have to wait their turn.

A quiet peacefulness reached for him. He drifted feet first, barely breaking the surface of the water, over to Kari, who had stripped and washed and then hung his clothes to dry. Nat did the same. Later they returned to the camp. The fire from brushwood had long since turned to a bed of hot ashes raked over the prepared animal. It was being tended by two men with what seemed a ritualistic approach. As part of the dreamtime story, people were summoned to come together and eat. The goanna's soft white meat tasted to Nat like an oily chicken. He ate all that he was offered, including bush tomatoes, damper - a kind of bread - and lightly-cooked Witchetty grubs. These were like crispy chicken with a yolk centre tasting of almonds. Cool water was the only drink. The rich organs, the heart and kidneys, were given to the elders, nothing was wasted.

Nat slept on the ground that night. A simple slipping to another place, no dreams, just a long tiredness, saturated by sleep. Just after dawn, the awakening of the land came. Noises spread into the air, with animals communicating. As he lay still, he then heard people's voices, movement. Kari touched him gently on the arm, willing him up. It was time to be gone, and with just a drink of water from the offered bottle.

He looked around, smiling, then raising a hand to anyone he could see before following Kari to the truck. Kari turned the key, the Toyota's engine fired with a base grumble before settling and then they were on their way back.

Arc of Doubt

2

Nat, Northern Territory. 1968

After the holiday had passed, the first strains of restlessness crept into him; his thoughts were elsewhere more often than not. The following Saturday, he went with Wayne to hunt for a pig, and that day changed everything. What should have been the start of a fun trip was, in fact, a late start, as Wayne had overslept after a long town night. He was in a dirty mood from the moment he shovelled his breakfast into his mouth, giving Nat instructions with his fork about what was needed while he did so.

When they were loading the Holden pick-up, Wayne was also odd, for reasons Nat didn't understand immediately. He was waiting, sitting in the front passenger seat with one leg in the well and one leg wedged against the door in a vain hope of a cooler air flow. He lazily scratched an armpit, and turning the mirror on the path behind him, he took sight of Wayne approaching. He was walking quickly, carrying across his arms what he took to be a rifle, heavily wrapped in towels that he recognised from the shower room. Piled on top were other items he couldn't make out. The swivelling of his head in both directions, twice, gave it away. Wayne carefully laid everything he was carrying, including the large old woven bag swinging gently from his side, into the back, before climbing into the driver's side. He slammed the door, started the engine and drove away in one easy, progressive movement. They cut through the station entrance, Wayne swung at the wheel and the pick-up slipped a bit, then gained traction with the road.

He then turned, looking a little more relaxed, and just said: 'OK then.'

As though this had some sort of meaning of its own. Nat knew he was supposed to have a licence for the rifle, or have permission to have a gun on the station, or both. They headed east down the road towards Bundy, then dropped south into the scrub on a track that had been used frequently by off-roaders. Several more turnings led them onto what seemed like a bullock track that finally petered out at a dead end. Parked there was a Land Cruiser whose occupant slid from the seat with the greeting:

'What took you so long…?'

Wayne's response was wordless and his face faintly aggressive. He went to the back of the pick-up, ripped back the towels to reveal a bolt action 303 rifle. He slung it up by the strap to his shoulder, took a box of cartridges, put it in one of his side pockets, and pointing, issued instructions to both Nat and the skinny youth.

'You take the bag and water bottles, and you,' pointing at the youngster, 'take the other stuff and the pole, and we'll make for the camp.'

'What's the pole for then?'

'You'll see.'

Nat, trying to brake some ice, spoke up:

'I don't know what's more menacing, the gun or your face.'

But there was no reply, he was already walking away. Without looking back, Wayne tossed back:

'Shouldn't take us too long at this pace.'

It was less than ten minutes before they came to a clearing. At its centre were three poles chained together as a tripod; close by lay a circle of large, piled blackened stones. Charcoal from a long-gone, part-burnt fire was still scattered around, as though kicked to the winds. Lying discarded, not ten feet away on its side, was a big steel-lipped cauldron.

More instructions were issued.

'Fetch the water from the swamp, get the pot over by the fireplace. I'll get the firewood.'

Nat looked at the youngster and shrugged. Picking up two large cans, he went the short distance to the water, followed by Wayne's voice: 'Be careful, only fill where you can see the bottom....'

The cauldron was lifted and set on the large stones, leaving sufficient room to set the fire underneath. The tripod had an anchor loop at its top to attach a rope or pulley. Several armfuls of dead wood were collected and laid ready.

Wayne started again:

'OK, we've got to go downwind. We're going to loop round to a couple of holes I know where we might see a pack or pick up tracks.'

Nat had figured out by now that the youth was from the previous evening in town and Wayne was playing The Big White Hunter part to impress him. But whatever the reason for his mood, he was unpredictable and Nat knew he should stay vigilant.

Wayne played the part, shoving in cartridges with casual ease, dropping to one knee from time to time, twice firing off shots at something or nothing. Nat was beginning to grow bored when, directly in front, not 30 yards away, was a small group of pigs heading in a slow walk, traversing his path. Wayne's gun must have been loaded this time, because the noise of the bolt ramming home a round might have spooked them. Holding a finger to his lips to reinforce the silence, he dropped his arm and curled his forefinger to the trigger position. With the crack of the gun, the full-grown young boar went forwards in one jerk to its knees. It must have been Wayne's movement that caused the rest of them to run, because their heads twitched to sniff the air before they disappeared into the scrub, leaving the injured animal lying on its side.

Closing in on it, Wayne was adrenaline pumped, the youth shouted: 'You got the bastard... You got the bastard,' as though it was in some way personal.

'Shut up… just keep behind me.'

Fingering another cartridge into the rifle, he rammed it home with the bolt. As they closed in on the pig, it gave a massive heave as though in a final defiance of the obvious, attempting to haul itself away before falling back, panting its last hard breaths.

Another shot fired, and an echo came, but it didn't last. Wayne had put a bullet close up through the side of its head. Its bloodied body lay still for its long final sleep. Reaching to his belt, he untied a couple of short lengths of coarse cord.

'Here, tie its feet together, then we'll use the pole to lift it back to camp. Do it quick or the ants will be all over it, and then us, when we lift it.'

Nat tied the back legs first, then the front, feeling the warmness of this dead body run strangely through his hands, a fixed clear stare was its only sight. The walk back was difficult, as the carcass swung on the pole while they moved. The kid suddenly opened up:

'God, this is getting heavy, let's put it down.'

Wayne was clearly irritated, the buzz of the kill was wearing off. He responded with a low grunt as though tiring of his friend's company: 'Keep going.'

Reaching the clearing, Wayne took matches from the bag and headed for a tree stump just back from the fireplace. He slid his rifle from his shoulder and rested it against the stump. His first full cough must have loosened the phlegm deep in his chest, then a rolling clearance brought it to his mouth to expel it.

He blew it out like a shot to the dirt; and muttered:

'Get out and walk.'

Raising his head again to them, he said:

'Bloody hell, it's hot, pass the water skin.'

Afterwards, bending to the side bag and rummaging, he brought out two steel- bladed knives; one longer than the other, and a steel. Testing both for sharpness with his thumb across the blades, he whipped them both a few times with well-practised precision on the steel. He must have been satisfied, as the steel slid from his open fingers back to the bag.

He issued more instructions for the youth to help him steady the filled cauldron at the right angle on the stones before lighting the fire underneath it. The flames took hold quickly, devouring the smaller pieces of dead wood rapidly gaining heat. The fire spread to the larger boughs, burning with an intensity and the water started to warm. Looking at the youth he said:

'It will be a while before the pot boils, bring the pig over here and we'll get him strung up ready.'

The three of them strained, lifting the animal, and tightening the rope until they were able to slide its back legs onto the top hook of the tripod, leaving it with its head just clear of the ground.

'What a stinking beast.'

'Well, it certainly will be if we split his stomach open by mistake when we gut him. You'll be chucking straight up, I can promise that.'

'Well, which one of you two wants to pull out its guts?'

'Yeah ... yeah, I'll do that,' the youth said, holding out a hand for a knife.

'First, I'm going to check it's OK and that it's not got TB.'

Taking the knife with the sharpened side upwards, Wayne inserted it with precision at a low point in the pig's belly between its back legs. Firm slow draws of the blade sliced through the skin tissues, opening up the long dark cavity to the sunlight. Using both hands, he drew open the animal to reveal the beast's organs. Stopping briefly, he turned to look at us for admiration of his handiwork, then he cut out the liver, taking it into his bloody hands. It was dark, clean, and heavy; and blemish free. Next, he checked the stomach to find what its diet consisted of. Finally, with a deft single slice to the neck, he opened to the thyroid gland just above its heart. He seemed to rub its fluids between his fingers, and after a pause, lifted his head and grinning, he gave it the thumbs up.

Passing the knife to the youngster, he said:

'Your turn, cut the tusks for yourself, then cut the guts out of him, you can't do much damage now.'

The blood started to congeal on Wayne's hands. Picking up the oversized ladle from the bag, he scooped water from the cauldron. It was hot, but yet to boil. Splashing some onto his hands, he rubbed them vigorously before shaking them off to dry.

'Nice job mate. Scrape him clean from the arse to the neck, but don't puncture the guts or it really will be a shit job.'

The soft laugh at his own joke faded just as the first bubbles came on the water, and the roll of the boil appeared. A large ladle was tipped many times to scald the skin of the pig before they took turns in scrapping with the flat edge of a knife to part the pig from his skin. Cutting with the speed of a skilled practitioner, Wayne quickly separated the shoulders, belly and loins carefully into large joints, and wrapping them in the towels, placed them in two canvas bags.

'OK, let's clear up. Nat, put what's left of the boiling water in that drum over there for cleaning, then push over the cauldron away from the fire using the pole. That's it, chuck all the guts and the remainder of the pig on the ashes and it will all burn away, it will stop the possible spread of disease.'

Washing and cleaning all the implements didn't take long. Nat was tired and already thinking of the return trip. He didn't actually see what happened next, and when the argument started, he stood back to separate himself from the other two.

'You... are a fuckwit. I wouldn't trust you to buy a bus ticket into town, never mind mess with a sharp knife. It was a mistake asking you out here today.'

When Nat turned around, it was done. The kid had been felled like a tree, knees bent and sagging, he kissed the ground almost without sound. Wayne's twisting of his body and movement with the gun in his hands seemed to happen in slow motion. The butt of it had already swung upwards to the youth's chin.

Hanging his gun on his shoulder, Wayne shifted his weight on his feet, gave a long look at Nat without any explanation and waited for the groggy youth, who was by then on his hands and knees, to stand. Leaning in a little, he spoke in a quiet, menacing tone:

'I said...take two of those joint bags to my fucking truck. If you try another V sign, I'll bury you here.'

Turning his attention to Nat with an indifference that was hard to pin down, he went on:

'You bring the other joint bags, I'll bring the pole and gear.'

By the time they reached the vehicle, a dust cloud was rising behind the youth's truck as he took off fast away from them. The bags lay open, their contents partly spilt across the bench seat of the Holden, as Wayne spat:

'Fuck him.'

Those were the last words he spoke on the journey back to the station. That evening Nat made his decision. Next day, just before 8, he climbed the outside stairs of the manager's house using swift pulls on the hand rail and rapped on the front door firmly. The door was opened by Joanne, Pete's wife, and just as he was about to speak, their mongrel made a rush for the door. Joanne's hand dropped from the door as she bent to catch the collar of the dog. Raising her head and shoulders to look at Nat, all he could see at the top of her print dress was the full, round tops of her breasts. He was caught.

She let go of the dog and it bolted past them for the yard. She was smiling when she used the flat of her hands to straighten her dress. It was the way she flattened that dress, with long slow stokes without taking her eyes from him. When she spoke, it was so full of innuendo as if teasing or inviting him.

'Well.. I know what you were looking at ....'

The pause in her voice stretched deliberately. Then looking directly at him, before carrying on: 'But, what are you after?'

'Ah........'

His words wouldn't rise in his throat. He brushed his hair away from his face, and pushed it behind his ear, giving him a fraction of time to compose himself.

The moment was gone as Pete appeared at her shoulder.

'Hello Nat, what you after..?'

Joanne let him pass in front of her.

'Ah...' he started again, this time addressing Pete.

'I wanted to talk to you, just to say, I'm leaving at the end of the week. It's time for me to move on, head to Alice, then south.'

'Um......OK then.... it was only a question of time with you, I knew that when I took you on. Friday your last day then. Take your money and go it is then?' Nat nodded.

'OK, well good luck to you, but it's to work now.'

He jerked his head at the landing, and they descended the stairs together. Once on level ground, Nat turned. Joanne was still there smiling, looking straight at him. He spent a good part of the next hour thinking about her, then stored those thoughts away for another day. The week dragged through, and on the Friday evening, Wayne took off for his weekly bender, full of optimism, probably to return sometime on Sunday, deflated and angry. Spent in every way.

Nat went to his room, and he lay naked under a sheet, staring at the stained ceiling. Sleep signalled him, and he fell into the deep hole. Broken thoughts and half-reclaimed memories, filled the drifting time when he was almost awake and couldn't return to sleep. Just after dawn, bright sunlight had stolen the night and the day hit his tired eyes.

His brain was turning ideas over, like an engine that wouldn't start. Eventually, his battery flattened and sleep came again. When he woke again, he tried to recall all the ideas that had filled his mind earlier, and how they had fitted together, but he couldn't, they were lost, gone.

Bunching his knuckles slightly, then allowing his fingers to flex and unflex, he scratched an area of his scalp. Lying with his head propped against the wall, one hand rested lightly on his chest, he took in the objects around him. A lamp, a drying towel, the uncurtained window. He knew it was early but not how early. Turning his wrist to look at the face of his watch, a quiet, slow expletive escaped through his almost closed lips. The larger hand had come adrift from its mounting. Unhooking the watch from his wrist, he held it at arm's length away from the bed, then lazily dropped the useless item to the floor.

A few more minutes passed before he peeled back the sheet from his body and stood upright with one swift movement before heading for the shower. Standing still under the water, he blew it away from his mouth and nose, thinking of how this morning was going to pan out. He hadn't expected a leaving party. After work the previous day, people had wished him good luck only if they saw him. The evening had been spent packing his backpack, paring down his possessions, thinking, with the help of a couple of Wayne's tins of lager, how he might hitch a ride back to the Stuart Highway before hopefully picking up rides south.   Pete was leaving for Darwin around nine to see his brother's family. Clean clothes, clean teeth, he was ready.

Just before 9, he heard the Land Rover engine start and looking across the park yard he watched the briefest touch to the brake lights as it passed between the posts, then it disappeared from view. He gave it ten minutes while he topped his pack with tins from the fridge and larder, and filled his large water container. Then he shouldered his pack with a shake to adjust it, and headed for the door. Turning one last time, with the keys in his hand, he looked back, then pulled the door onto the lock. Slowly, he descended the staircase, then hitched the pack again as he crossed the park yard towards the manager's house.

Stopping at the bottom of the stairs, he lowered the rucksack to the underside among the bins and storage barrels and continued up, with the keys in his hand. The door was ajar. He called out: 'Hello?'

Joanne's voice came back:

'Come on in, it's open.'

He went in. She was leaning against the back of the sofa with her arms apart. He held the keys out to her, she ignored the gesture. Lowering his arm, he put them on the sideboard.

'I wondered if you might come this morning, I have a leaving present for you. Shut the door and I'll give it to you.'

He did as he was told and shut the door. Some time later, he descended the stairs again, put the bag on his shoulder. Smiling to himself, this time he didn't look back. Walking just far enough to be out of sight from the station, standing in the shade he waited for traffic. He was lucky, the first car stopped. People have more time for their neighbours off the mainstream. The lift took him to the junction with the track, and with a wave, he turned south to a black bootlace of tarmac that stretched over the horizon, all the way to Alice Springs - almost 900 miles away.

Hot days and nights were spent getting down that road. There was endless waiting, and endless small talk; lapsing into long silences. Several lifts took him past the clapboard fronts of small towns with dusty streets; past junctions leading east. There were isolated fuel stops run by people living isolated lives, but in the end he got there.

The train was then the easy option and he took it.... all the way to the rail head at Port Augusta. It was a slow ride through the opal outposts, the salt flats and the wastelands that make up the large, barren part of South Australia. The whispering of two girls returning to the city didn't worry him. He lay still in the compartment, stretched on the bench seat, asleep like a dog for long periods of time. He played two-up with them for coins. Fun stuff to ease the monotony and finally flipped one of those coins to decide whether to go east to Sydney as planned, or west to Perth on a whim. Flipping the coin from his thumb on the edge of his nail, it spun rapidly making a pinging sound before falling to the centre of his open palm. Staring down, tails beckoned him to the west.

'So, west it is, for what it's worth.'

They thought he was joking, but that's the difference between travelling, and holidays. The decision was celebrated with a long pull of warm water from the gallon plastic drum he'd bought to keep hydrated. As soon it filled his mouth, the taste was like drinking straight from a truck's radiator. Clutching the coin in a closed hand, he offered the water to the girls. One gave him a cigarette in exchange for the water, he cupped her hand as the train jogged, and the lighter jumped, then he let her hand go. The exhaled smoke disappeared through the open windows, leaving them both with a dry, aftertaste.

Having left the train, Nat was now in this God forsaken spot. The café's furnishings were hard and tubular and had lost their shine years ago, when the owner had lost his enthusiasm for the business. A fan beat the space around it, disturbing the air and keeping the flies from settling on the edge of the discarded plate. With each revolution, a light clicking sound could be heard, giving the impression that it might come adrift from its mountings.

One glance at it without moving his head, confirmed that it was ill fitting against the ceiling. Food was an essential, with little enjoyment here. Finishing his water with an open throat, the empty glass was laid alongside the plate. In this borderland of society, he was gently sweating. He had begun to feel like a stranded fish on a beach with the outgoing tide. The road stop was nothing more than a place to get fuel, surrounded by a few trees, a corrugated iron workshop with the rusting remains of evidence of previous years littered within sight and the café. This was Iron Knob, a dust-driven, fly-blown outpost on the edge of the Eyre Highway, west of the train stop at Port Augusta. The first dent in the distance to cross The Nullarbor Plain. In desperation to move forward, Nat accepted a lift with an older man in a Holden saloon retuning to 'the knob', just south of the highway. He was one of the 50 or so people working in the ground there, grinding out a life on high wages for the birth of their tomorrows. The whole area was relatively flat with large, easily accessible quantities of iron ore being ripped from the ground, then freighted back to Port Augusta, destined for China. Loans against minerals was the political game in this country, one day, someday, the payback would come.

That lift did move him on 50 miles, but to the middle of nowhere. It was a desolate spot that had stolen two days of his life so far and it was beginning to look like he was never going to leave. This arterial route carried surprisingly little traffic, most of the goods were rail freighted, leaving the road mainly to cars and Greyhound inter-state coaches, laden and compressed by luggage to rut the graded roads westwards.

Nat spent his time jerking a thumb at passing vehicles, and crossing over to the pumps to ask for a lift with anyone who had the misfortune to have to stop there. The hot, cloudless blue sky touched the westward horizon. It was treeless and flat, like a vast rusting sheet of metal. The lift, when it came, was unexpected and surprising. He heard it first, then, kicking up dust behind it, he saw a motorcycle that was blowing its exhaust coming steadily towards him.

He didn't even hold out his hand to flag it, as it didn't occur to him there was a chance of space. It was being ridden by a man about Nat's age, and there was a plywood platform bolted on to the carrier rack to extend the luggage area. It didn't seem necessary, as all that was strapped on the back was a tent, a smallish kit bag and a few assorted items. The driver, in an open- face helmet with sunglasses, dropped the revs. The noise level lowered to a rumble and, cutting across in front of Nat, he pulled up at the pump and turned off the engine. Strapped to the side were two heavy plastic containers which were filled first, before the cap of the tank was unscrewed for that to be filled as well.

Nat had crossed the road with his pack yet again.

'Nice Triumph, old, but a good one by its looks?'

'Yeah, you ride then?'

'I have a licence, but not today.'

Withdrawing a clip from an inner pocket, the man passed over two notes in payment to the attendant.

'Could you use a cold drink?'

'Yeah… '

'Could you use a lift?'

This, at last, was his get out of jail free card.

Iron Knob receded at a steady 50 miles an hour as they drove deeper into the open space, three times the size of Belgium. Out here, if you wanted to get lost and stay lost as a few do, people wouldn't ask too many questions. They rode steadily and continually, sharing the driving, ripping down the miles with occasional stops to stretch their limbs, re-fuel and pick up information of the next pull-ins. It was hard, dirty riding shoved up on the tank at the front or hanging on, supporting the rucksack as pillion, but they didn't give a damn, they felt above the wind.

For the first night, they camped out under bright starlit skies, they felt the world belonged to them. Simple stuff, lounging round a small fire with a boiling billy can and eating rubbish food, talking and talking of endless plans. Melbourne Mike was going all the way to Perth. The deal was simple... share all expenses. The second day was a long slog with several stops. Tiring rapidly with the vibration of the road up through the bike, their bodies began to feel there was a limit to the cramped riding.

Conversation was difficult and intermittent with wraps around their faces to keep the dust from their throats. Boredom seeped in where enthusiasm had reigned, but still the miles burnt off. They had their laughs. Like the time a car coming east swerved to miss some bolting emus, spilling the luggage from the roof rack across the road. Slowing to a halt, kicking down the side stand, they went across to help pick up stuff. The family put on a brave face, tensions were already running high. A young teenager sat sullenly in the back of the car, arms folded, scowling, while they picked up the dirt-stained clothes to repack at the roadside. The pretence of a smile on the woman's face, suggested that recrimination would start again when they got underway.

On the third day, well into the long morning heading north to Kalgoorlie, disaster came closer than a flat tyre to the road. From the left, movement turned to a heaving mass. The hide of an adult male red kangaroo at full stretch, jumping in a single leap almost across the front mudguard. It was so close, the very smell of its coarse hair was in their nostrils. In the time it takes to clap your hands, it had jumped again, gone.

Mike let go a shout of surprise at what must have, for a millisecond, seemed a wipe out. The throttle sprung back in his hand, fear had released his fingers, his foot came off the peg for the brake, but it was already too late. The shock for the pillion was an involuntary jerking that set the bike sideways. Starting to skid, like a speedway rider drifting a bend, he rode down the speed, bending the handlebars back to the skid. The pillion's weight righted to drift with him before the bike finally touched the ground at low speed.

Nat's leg twisted with a screaming wrench, then both men were pitched off as the engine raced high before cutting out. Stillness descended immediately. All quiet, no traffic at all in any direction to be seen. The smell of fuel leaking somewhere was the danger thought. One of the carriers had split, jettisoning its contents onto the road.

'Fuuuuck …aaah… are… are you all right?'

Nat lay still behind Mike, with his eyes tight shut and teeth gritted, registering pain. It flared like a pizza oven somewhere near the shoulder to the wrist. Opening his eyes to a tear in his jerkin, he carefully removed it to reveal a 'Greek tattoo' running the length of his arm. Getting to his feet and walking, checking himself, he held his injured arm with the other hand tightly, drawing what moisture he could together in his mouth, he spat at the wound several times as he had done since he was small boy. He remembered his dad saying: 'spit on it lad, no blood, you can wear the pain then.'

'Yeah I'm OK. We were damned lucky back there. I don't know how you missed him, and he practically kicked us in passing.'

Mike was already up, dusting himself. Then, limping to the bike, he gave it a handlebar lift, jerking it with considerable force. It came upright easy enough, and he flicked it onto the stand after first moving it away from the fuel spill.

'Jeez... what a mess, but we were so lucky. Born to be hung eh? You'll have to ride, if you can start it. My leg, bloody hell, I twisted it...shit.'

Nat straddled the bike, and leaning forward on the handlebars, dropped his head to make certain the kick-start was turned ready. He pumped the compression once, and lifting himself high he dropped his full weight downward and the Triumph burst back into its noisy roar. Checking and re-roping their load, they gingerly rode on. Slowly at first, but quickly gaining confidence, they eventually made it to Kalgoorlie, the bustling town where tourists got turned over by the hookers for an easy fuck. Streetwalkers and brothels were commonplace.

The boarding house they stayed in overnight, in Flore Street, was back from the striking beauty of the Victorian town centre. It was a cash- only establishment, housing all-comers, including the women who had come to town to turn their tricks to a different type of gold from the vast 'Super Pit' goldmine that operated on the town's eastern fringe.

It was their final push to Perth and the coast the next day. Winding through the suburbs in the slow maze, they stopped eventually at the address that Mike had on the inside cover of a worn paperback. Before them was a small, low, cheap panel bungalow on a narrow plot.

A neat run up with a shaved lawn, trimmed up hedges, all showing the tidiness of ordered fastidiousness. An outer screen door slammed down the side of the building, the sound of hard heavy heel steps reached them before they saw him. He stood upright, strong in his belief, and with an extended arm, pointed:

'Mikey, you can fuck right off where you came from. Don't come sniffing round here. Now, push off or I'll down you.'

'Just give her the book back,' said Mike, and he lobbed it towards the man's feet.

It was retrieved angrily, before the man abruptly turned and went back the way he came. Once out of view, the sound of a metal lid being lifted, then the smack of the screen door reached them again.

'So, it's the beach then…?'

Mike gave no reply, or even an explanation.

Within a week, Nat and Mike were losing touch. Mike sought the security of a job in an office, doing the very thing he swore he would never do, and Nat stayed on the beach out at Cottesloe doing casual jobs. He rented a seven-by-four foot room with a multi- share bathroom down a long hall. It was cheap, but it had to be. After a few weeks, Nat moved to a trailer park well past North Beach, back on the other side of the highway. His trailer was old, even for its years. It had been kicked about by the past occupants, but he grew comfortable there and met a girl. She moved in, tidying up the place, spring cleaning, bringing in flowers, and bunching the curtains.

He thought he might love her and she might love him back, but it never got there. One Saturday morning, he had agreed to meet her after work on city beach at a spot near Bellamy's Beach Bar, have a swim, and maybe lunch if they felt like it. But in the end, he didn't swim, he just sat watching her.

She entered the water, seemingly holding her breath. As the depth rose, he watched her back, her elbows raised a little with each of those slow steps. Her shoulders tightened slightly as the water reached the line of her swimming costume, then she stopped, fluttered her hands with opened fingers in a gesture of belief before walking a few steps more. Turning from the waist revealed her profile against the sun. She smiled at him, then turning back and with a quick swinging motion, she raised her arms and dived under the surface of the water, reappearing quickly on the other side of a small wave. With powerful arm movements, she forced her body through the water using a slow, steady, rhythmical stroke.

He was transfixed by the wake and how the sea seemed to cover her and then recover her as she flexed. A moving shadow passed smartly over the sea as the sun slipped behind a white cloud. It was the only cloud in that morning sky and it didn't last long. When he re-focused, she had stopped moving and was simply bobbing like a fisherman's float. She waved again. 50 yards could feel like a lifetime, but his urge to cross that unseen line on the beach had evaporated.

Earlier that morning, he had filled the kettle for tea and put it on the stove. During the time between the first rattle of power and the slow climb to an even roll, he thought of the conversation they had the previous evening, while setting up the bed in the trailer.

Nat had asked her about her family, enquiring whether they lived nearby. She'd replied: 'I haven't actually spoken to my mother for a couple of years now. She's living further down the Swan River with some guy. He's a rep for the brewery. They've got a neat house with a garden yard.'

Her voice fell away a bit, then she added: 'Who wouldn't want something like that? I've just wasted nearly two years with a bloke who turned out to be a lying snake. I thought I loved him. But what I want is someone I can rely on, someone I can trust.'

Nat realised then that he was at a crossroads in this relationship. He couldn't give her what she so clearly wanted. He would need to be gentle, he didn't want to hurt her when he let her go. The small run-on ad in the jobs section in the Daily News, evening edition, just said: *'Labourers wanted for work in North West. Fit strong men only. Long hours, good pay.'*

He phoned the number and got the job with Ravenstone Minerals. Four days later, Nat flew out of Perth Airport in a 50-seater Fokker, heading for Port Hedland in the north west of the state.

Arc of Doubt

3

Nat, Marble Bar. 1969

He slid off the lower bunk just as the murmurings started near him. The bunkhouse was a converted caravan, stripped of its holiday luxuries and roughly refitted as sleeping quarters for five. Standing at the open door in just his black cotton shorts, he leaned his shoulder against the door frame, scratching his head. Then, looking at his watch, saw it was just past 5 as the sun pushed the starry, pale night sky back. The sun rose, seeping first, before growing to that blaze that could blister most anything not covered.

Small, lump-like hills of similar size and symmetry covered the full width of the line beneath the sky. In turn, they were covered with round, thorny spinifex plants growing on the rocky surface, so close together it was difficult to walk between them. From afar, this palest green togetherness gave the illusion of fertility. Other than very occasional larger rock outcrops, this was all there was to be seen. The stark empty beauty arrested time.

He didn't realise then, that many of those hills were iron ore. Within a few decades, open cast mining would scar that huge area forever. Every few years it would rain in these parts, the graded roads and airstrips would be washed away, dry creeks and rivers littered with ghost gumtrees. Boulders would be awash with a wall of water, which would slide and race across the bleached rocky surface, only to disappear, leaving little trace except isolated rock pools and high and dry flotsam, often wedged amongst the branches of trees. Quickly, the seeds of desert flowers would spring to a short colourful life, but time would erase them just as quickly. This harsh, barren land had given little in return for man's efforts until now.

It was the start of just another day, just like yesterday and, hopefully, tomorrow. The crew for the rig started with breakfast. Joe, the cook, a tall, older man wearing a perpetually stained apron was up before them in the cookhouse, where he also slept. Rudy, his yapping Queensland Blue Heeler and probably closest, if not only friend, slept in a cooler spot somewhere beneath the caravan.

Everyone was converging on the cookhouse for a plateful of the same, every day: T- bone steak and two freshly- baked rolls with a mug of tea. John, the driller, a short, hard man from New Zealand, was striding over wearing shorts with his familiar welder boots shouting: 'Josephine, I'm coming for my breakfast.'

The good humoured response was usually: 'You'll be fucking wearing it to work in a minute'

John had slept where he always did - on a flat space at the back of the rig, vacated by various dirt pipes that were now in use.

The faded yellow mobile rotary drilling rig, with its strange assorted support vehicles had arrived after the advance party in this arid, fly- blown spot, 70 miles from a tiny community known as Marble Bar. It took its name from the nearby bar of Jasper, with its huge, polished red stone slabs that looked like marble. The bed of Coongan River, with its scattered Ghost Gums, ran right across it - on the rare occasion when there was water. That town in the Pilbara region was first to be put on the map in the early 1890s, when gold was found. Some strikes, like the 413-ounce Bobby Dazzler brought the town's population, for a short time, to 5,000. Now there were about two or three hundred. Its fame - such as it was - was its record temperatures; a searing, continual blazing heat, plus The Ironclad Hotel, a sprawling, corrugated iron building with its frontage in Francis Street.

It was a rough and ready place and welcomed all-comers, especially during the horse racing week, when the population swelled to a couple of thousand revellers. Two days later, the crowds would evaporate like low cloud over a salt flat.

The bulldozer driver had arrived earlier in a low loader with the geologist, Daniel, a dark, bearded young man. Fuel tanks, a generator and other equipment, plus the bulldozer, had followed. Now, Daniel was leading the way in a long wheelbase Land Rover wrapped with roo bars, as the drilling rig inched its way over the rough tracks, which had been cut by the bulldozer through the nearest un-graded dirt road, seven miles away.

They had marked out the first four platforms to be linked by the rough tracks, cut as flat and level as possible to take the mobile rig. Daniel had set the platforms in an area that had claims pegged and registered the previous year. His team had, on an earlier trip, found very promising signs of malachite copper deposit rock structures. After analysts' reports, the company had wanted trial holes drilled for further research. Nat understood there were other sites on two other areas nearby known only as Kelly's Copper and Bamboo 500.

The bulldozer was leaving that day for new claim work on the low loader, which had just returned with a fresh supply of fuel, trucked up in 45 gallon drums along the red dirt roads from Port Hedland. The outback was known as The Red Centre for good reason, that red dirt found its way into everything- from a moving car to inside the cases in its boot.

After breakfast, Nat's first job was to refuel the rig and the main generator. Stepping away from the permanent shade of the awning rigged alongside the cookhouse, he walked over to the water line and removed one of the hanging canvas water bags that had cooled in the night air, crossing over the 50-odd yards to the rig on the first platform. By the time he reached the rig, he was sweating freely. Spotting the familiar yellow and black aerosol of Scram on a shelf, jammed in among the spanners at eye level, he took the can in one hand and removed the cap with the other.

Shutting his eyes, he gave his face and ears a blast, then finished the action around the bottom of his shorts. He knew this would keep the blizzard of flies away from the vital areas for a few hours, then lobbed the can back among the spanners. The rig was secured with its legs outstretched and the tower upright, with a full carousel of pipes ready in the parallel rack. Taking turns with each arm, he fitted in the pump, sinking the long nozzle deep into the first drum, and whacked in the fuel to the tanks.

The simple backwards and forwards action was easy to start with, but he soon tired. Swapping hands and settling in an arm-wrestling position, he sweated in the last of it. Gasping at the finish, he turned the empty drum on its side and rolled it clear, using the sole of his work boot. The first half hour of the day had left him sweating hard and breathing heavily. Even wearing buckskin gloves, he always seemed to smell of the diesel. The sun was barely up, but the heat was growing for the 12 to 14 hours of hot, hard work to come. Within ten minutes, the rest of the crew arrived.

John fingered the key on the yellow cord looped around his neck, and in a swift movement had it in his hand, ready to turn on the ignition of 'the beasty.' With the thumb of his other hand hovering over the starter button, he waited until the control panel light flashed up and then went out. Checking that the main drive was in neutral, he hit the red button. First came the coughing sound, then the engine bit, throwing out bursts of black smoke from the exhausts up behind the cab into the blue sky. The acrid smells lingered, and as it fired up, it shook the engine in its mountings for a moment. Then, warmed up, the exhaust stream paled and that low steady thump began. It was the sound that would stay with them all day.

'Chain over some pipes from the truck,' John shouted above the noise, as he faced the panel, deftly manoeuvring several levers together. The result was the release of the chain hoist for the offsider, his number two, known as Cord. He was a strong, heaving man, carrying the unwashed, unshaved smell of several days with casual ease. John waved his arms at Cord to bring the support lorry as close as he could to the rig. Thick buckskin gloves grabbed the chain from its coupling as the weight of it started to loosen and swing. It took the offsider all of his considerable strength to loop it away from the rig to be caught by a fashioned hook being wielded on the support truck.

Once secured around the female end of the drilling pipe, the engine note changed again. The swaying pipe was quickly lifted to the upright position, ready to be slapped in to the open arms of the carousel, loaded like the chambers of a revolver, ready for action.

'Come on Nat, get the shovel, clear the drill position for me.'

Nat, with his shovel bent low beneath the back of drill, moved forward with a staggered step, picking away any larger rocks. He then turned the shovel to its edge and scraped the area where the drill bit would enter the ground, leaving an area the size of a small tablecloth relatively flat and level. Backing out slowly, Nat then cleared a similar space for the geologist to lay out his bagged core samples. The ground rock dust was thrown up on the outer casing of the pipework as it turned. The slamming of the drill box down the side of the rig brought a brief discussion between the driller and the offsider, before the clean multi- headed bit was lifted by Cord. He held it like a baby in his arms as he staggered with it back to the drill plate seat, then lifted it into position. Cord held it upright as the auxiliary engine turned slowly, revolving the first length of pipe that had been held ready in the slipway from the carousel. Its slow spin would see it self- tightening into the multi- headed drilling bit.

John looked to Daniel, and with a nod from him, the first pipe of the day began its rotation from the top of the derrick. The tune from the engine changed again and eyes glanced at the top of the high tower to the hoses, bending and flexing near the power block, then down to the space where the pipe had begun to enter the ground. Just before it hit, John's voice was clear:

'Mind your windscreens.'

At first contact, tiny pieces of rock were spat out in all directions, then came screeching as it turned again, this time to an even whirring sound that wedded itself well to the engine's steady hum. The rock seemed hard on that first of many exploration holes, and slow. But eventually they burst through the water table, and the water came up the casing, hitting the pipe platform like a bucket of water hits a window. Someone usually got the unexpected dirty shower while the others danced out of the way.

The pipe shot down through the water and back into the rock beneath in an instant. John exchanged nods with the geologist, then, jerking at a lever, the engine disengaged and the pipe ceased to turn.

Waving a gloved hand, he shouted: 'Nat, clear the muck.'

Again, Nat bent under the platform with the shovel and with several swift shovelling motions, he moved most of the spoil. Then, with a stiff broom with a shortened handle, he swept the area to reduce contamination of the coming samples. Rock dust samples were taken at both prearranged and on spec depths, as stipulated by Daniel. Slipping and loading more pipework, they gained depth to the lower stratas. Over a few days, or maybe even a week, the drill would create several holes at different angles or depths, under the geologist's instructions. Dust samples were usually bagged and clearly depth- labelled on the yard mark. They sweated the hours till the sun got high and a canopy shade of sorts was eventually poled out, bearing in mind the drillers only drill while labourers do the labouring.

Exhaustion set the pattern of those days. The men were fed and watered from the cookhouse every day and evening, then there was a smoke or two, and sparse conversation. Then all the windows were opened, or they dragged their cots outside for the pretence of a breeze before the sleep that sometimes wouldn't come.

Here, Nat learnt the full understanding of the phrase 'bushed'. He had seen some men lose it completely. Behaviour became irrational, some would use their leave time to recover, but most weren't seen again. The turnover of men was high, but so were the wages. Daniel and Nat were similar ages. Daniel, a serious young man in his late 20s, engaged easily with Nat from the beginning, and their relationship flourished into friendship. One had travelled and was excited by his experiences, the other had a solid education in matters that would prove to be financially liberating and was excited by his prospects. Daniel had done well, buying a plot of land overlooking the Swan River in Perth with his gains.

It was clearly a small club, with geologists coming out of mining school keeping in touch with each other on the bush telegraph. This appealed to Nat, who talked to Daniel at length about investing in shares, even taking the name of his stockbroker in Perth.

Nat skipped his first work break after seven weeks and continued to work on the relief crew. This way, there was no temptation to spend any of his wages, unlike the others who got a free flight to Perth and went on 'the lash.'

He just about made the second term, when fluid started spewing out. A hydraulic hose caused a malfunction on a secondary oil pump. The engine was shut down immediately for fear of severe damage. The site mechanic didn't have the parts or the full tool shop. It took the last four days to fix with replacement parts, while 150 foot of pipe was still jammed in the crust. It didn't bother Nat, his time was up anyway.

The ride in a Land Rover, bush bashing the 70-odd miles back to Marble Bar, was very slow and uncomfortable. It led Nat to easier work, who spent the next few days mending tyre punctures. His time was up in the shed with the compressed air pump and the jack leavers, and when the crossover team came back, the hard work started again. Same team, same place. At the end of a third straight term, Nat was bushed. His temper was thinning, he wasn't sleeping well, and he knew he had to get out.

When the relief crew took over, he flew down from Port Hedland with the others. Sitting next to Daniel, he smoked steadily. He was over-tired, nervously twitching his forefinger and thumb on his left hand without realising he was doing it. The plane lifted away for an uneventful flight. Shifting his knees, Nat adjusted himself in the cramped space, trying to find the comfort spot. The seatbelt sign flashed dully against the brightness of the cabin, just as his fingers flicked at his release buckle. Turning towards Daniel, he started: 'Tell me…'

And so began the hours spent sucking in a stream of information on Daniel's second favourite topic - the stock market, and how to invest in it. By the end of the flight, Daniel had arranged a time to introduce Nat to his broker, two days later. Staying at the YMCA hostel was the cheapest option. He had been totally focused on spending as little money as possible, in order to save for travelling again. Probably the east coast, the Barrier Reef and Sydney - who knew after that. The Pacific islands hung like a chain of pearls in his late night dreams.

Nat met Isaac Buchan, Daniel's stockbroker, at his office, and opened an account with a ten dollar bill and a hand shake.

On the way out, Daniel said: 'So, what are you going to pick as a starter then?'

'I've thought a lot about what you told me, and bearing in mind I want to travel, not work too much longer, and I figure I get nothing from the bank, so why not go for mining shares? If I'm lucky, I might make few hundred dollars for an old motorcycle - at worst I'll lose a bit. My logic is, China is sucking in minerals in exchange for economic support now .The war in Vietnam shows no signs of ending, so demand for minerals is high. Perhaps a big company- Western Mining and something smaller...Ravenstone, maybe. You could be the guy that finds a copper strike up there.'

Daniel stopped walking. He looked straight at Nat, laughed and said: 'Sensible. I'll give you a runner as well. I heard from one of my friends, he's just taken a job with Poseidon in the southern goldfields over at Leonora somewhere, they are doing trials for nickel, he seems optimistic. Now, that *is* interesting.'

Daniel tapped the side of his nose.

'I've got to be off, I'm meeting my mum and I'm late. I'm going back in two weeks, probably on a different set to you for a while, so I'll probably see you at some stage.'

Daniel stepped into the moving crowd on the pavement. Nat turned in the opposite direction, headed straight to the Commonwealth Bank and transferred all his savings to his account with the stockbroker; leaving just over a hundred dollars to cover the time before his return to work.

He arranged for a large percentage of further deposited funds from his wages to be transferred, as and when they were paid in. Then, returning to the stockbroker's office, Nat gave them his instructions. These actions alone lifted his spirits, empowered him in a way that gave him a focus and direction that he'd not had before. Returning to his small room at the hostel, he lay full length on the sagging mattress, interlocking his fingers and clasping his hands behind his head, a slow brief look took in the heavy cream-coloured plain walls, no pictures, no mirror. It had a blankness all of its own, it was as if the world outside was washed away as the door closed.

A couple of days would see him back in the sweat pit though. How much more, he wondered, could he do up there? It was about saving money for later, but the question turning in his head was, quite simply, how much is enough? Most people surrendered to this question with their lives and squandered their money on useless, consumer products; enslaving themselves to a system that would have no mercy on their mistakes. He would be away when the clock struck the hour.

Nat's return saw him transferred to claim pegging duty in an area to the south east of Marble Bar, for four weeks. He was with another geologist and another labourer, both new to him, stuck out in the sticks, camping out of the back of a couple of Land Rovers. They pegged out land on compass bearings, with corner posts built into rock cairns staked with the details of claim deeds attached.

Hot square miles in rolling hillock country, covered only in spinifex and infested in parts with red back spiders, and continually covered in a blizzard of flies. The geologist gave the instructions of where to go, using bearings from his map. He fossicked while they walked endless miles, carrying post and papers. Then the party bumped past the pegged claims with their vehicles, and repeated the process. Nat hated it, his legs were continually sore from the piercing stabs of the needle-sharp grass. Early morning dumps were always 'the red back spider risk', and he was constantly thirsty, regardless of how much he drank.

On top of that, the food was packed rations that even a dog would have questioned. Every four days they were back at 'The Bar' to replenish supplies, and in his case saving his sanity. How easy it would have been on any of those days to go into The Ironclad Hotel with its air conditioning, and let the welcome chatter and beer take him to oblivion. But he didn't.

Then one afternoon, it was over, done. The boredom and loneliness were over, the claim-pegging team came back in. Time burnt its way through the calendar slowly up there, weeks fell to months. September and October had passed with him doing house jobs, the endless ferrying of company visitors, arrivals and leavers – all the crap tasks no one wants to do. The company's office was a four-roomed, square, stone bungalow with a central corridor open at each end to a wide veranda. Its ironwork balustrades, were plain and workman-like. Steps dropped to the overgrown couch grass that marked it on three sides. Three beds were set permanently on the east side, there to catch the night draughts. It was here, while the 'summer of love' was taking place elsewhere, that he passed his free time, sometimes with Jeannie the creamy, picking off blood- fattened ticks with their cigarettes butts from the mooching strays that lived their scavenging lives in the grass. They were just this side of dingoes.

Jeannie fancied him, and was dreaming of a magazine life in the city far away. But the clap was a round of applause he neither wanted nor fancied.

Early November, things changed in a manner that he could never have foreseen. He was put back to work with the same crew on the same contracted rig. His first job was to drive the Land Rover to Port Hedland to pick up some new workers. It was a round trip of 220- odd miles. He never quite got used to the lonesome, empty miles, but out here, station workers would do that distance for a 'drive in' and a beer on a Saturday night at The Ironclad. The road was still good. The rain - if there was to be any that year - was due, but hadn't arrived. Out there hope was a natural commodity. It was déja vu all over again, same dirt, same heat, same grind. He knew he was reaching the end of what he could take out here, a social desert without even a mirage of enjoyment. Then it happened.

The hawser snapped with no notice. It just went, a perfect arc curling across the space between rig and the support truck. Then the noise caught up like the sound of bullet, some of its force was sucked away, lashing at the headlight and wing of the support truck. It all seemed so slow, the damage, the frightened look in the eyes of the offsider's face, that moving wire, then it raced like celluloid frames through a projector.

Nat selflessly dived at John's back, catching him unawares, knocking him down instantly like the death roll of a felled tree. The both fell awkwardly to the ground; the hawser passed very close over them, snaking loose now like a worn out twister, as the drill pipe fell harmlessly away from the lorry. Nat knew he had hurt himself badly almost as soon as he hit the ground. Pain screamed into his ankle, his hand reached for the tender spot, but he couldn't stand.

John was on his feet, dishing blame at the offsider at the top of his voice: 'I told you to change that fucking wire two days ago and you didn't. If it hadn't been for Nat that would have taken our fucking heads off. Serious mistake… sort it now.'

Turning, he went to thank Nat. It was then he realised that Nat had not escaped unscathed.

'Oh man… that looks like you've done your Achilles. This could be very serious. We must get it packed with ice and get you to the doc at Marble Bar quick.'

That ride until they hit the graded roads was the worst Nat had ever experienced. Every bump, bounce, jar shook him down with pain.

The operation at the Port Hedland Hospital was a success, but it left him in the slow lane. His workmates disappeared back into the wilderness, as though they had never been there. It took a week before he was released, with the weight of a plaster cast dangling on his foot.

He was hopping like an injured wallaby. Six long weeks on crutches were his reward. The adventures of the skiving Pom became his by-line. It was mid-December when the crew of the rig changed, and he saw them briefly before they left for another southern week. His last conversation was with Daniel, who asked if he was going to stay on.

'Depends... I checked on those shares back in November, they've moved upwards. Perhaps I should sell them?'

'Which ones did you plug for then?'

'Well, I followed just what you said... put my stake into Poseidon.'

'What... all of it?'

His face had an incredulous mask.

'Christ... you mean you've still got them?'

'Yes...'

'But...'

He didn't seem able to continue, jerking a breath seemed to kick start him again, and he went on

'Well... ah... you don't know, do you? Those shares are the story that dreams are made of. You will make good if you sell, they've gone higher than a sparking rocket and I never bought any, thinking they were too small and risky. Good for you.'

It was two days later, lying on a veranda bed, that he saw a woman approaching down the path between the buildings on Main Street waving an envelope, as she closed down the space between them, she called out:

'Hey, Nat, got a telegram for you.'

Swinging the boot to the floor, he heeled it to the top of the steps reaching out his hand. Turning it over to check it, it was clearly and boldly addressed to Nat Gibson. The content was a single sheet with the words: 'Ring your broker NOW, stock skyrocketing!
Daniel.'

Nat just stared at it for a moment, not knowing what to think or do. It had been weeks since he had given any thought to it. Over two months since he had seen any newspaper at all, let alone a financial paper. He felt strangely dizzy, unsure what to do next.

That one phone call changed his life.

Part Three

Arc of Doubt

1

Jessica, England. 1957

Back then, it was the Eleven Plus that could change the direction of your life. Jessica was eleven in 1957. She was one of those post- war children with middle-class parents, who were not pushy, but, in a quiet way, socially aspirational. Money was tight for everyone, but she was always neatly turned out in printed dresses, polished sandals with white socks, and jumpers or cardigans knitted by aunts. The family lived in a semidetached red-brick house, built just before the war with the rare luxury of a bathroom and a separate WC inside the house. Hard to imagine now, but there were few of the household appliances now taken for granted. Discipline was strict, rules were rules. Fish on Fridays, Church on Sundays and everything else by numbers. Jessica was bathed in religion as a child, but in time she dried off.

Children were left to occupy themselves for a lot of the time. So Jess made her own entrainment, playing in the streets with friends, riding her bike to the nearest park, or dressing up in her mother's clothes and role-playing on wet days. During the school holidays and weekends, she was out for hours with children who lived in the same road, and only came when she was hungry. Her father was a sales rep and was away a lot, and when he was at home, she hardly noticed. As she got older, she and her friends would daydream about their futures, and how they were going to get there. They all wanted to make much more of their lives than their mothers had.

In 1957, Jessica sat and passed the 11- plus exam. This gave her the automatic progression to the local grammar school, an entrée into another life and friendships with girls from wealthier backgrounds than hers. It also came with the new found right to question everything her parents stood for, and she did. Within the first couple of years, dresses had disappeared. Tight jeans and pop music were in. Out went the ponytail and in came messy, back-combed hair and experimenting with make-up.

By 15, she was a regular at the local youth club, dancing with anyone who asked her and staying out as late as she dare. By 16, it was all the way with boys. Then along came Johnny Marshall. They were inseparable for several weeks before he evaporated from her life, not knowing that she was already pregnant.

Jessica was alarmed when she missed her period, then angry. Johnny had disappeared and she had to sort out the consequences. While working out what to do and how to tell her parents, she decided that from now on, she would be the one to write the rules in any relationship. Her fears were confirmed by the local GP, who, because of Jessica's age, asked her to return with her mother for a consultation.

The most obvious route would be to disappear quietly to special accommodation for unmarried mothers, where she could carry on with her schoolwork, have the baby and give it up for adoption. There was a chance she might be able to postpone her exams, and take them the following summer. In front of the doctor, her mother tried to cover up the anger and shame she was feeling and after a few moments' discussion, rose from the polished wood bench and, using the palms of her hands, in a single action, straightened her skirt. She told the doctor they would think through their options, as there was much to be done. The walk to bus stop, the wait, the ride and all the way to the key being inserted into the front door lock of their home, was in silence. But as the door shut to the point that the catch dropped, a dam burst in Jessica's mother. Her face seemed to screw up and spit the words out at her:

'You filthy slut. The shame you've brought on your father and me, after all we've done for you... you've always been an ungrateful child. You had the chance to make something of your life. You had your place at grammar school, you could have done so much better - and now this. I can't believe you've been so stupid. Can you imagine what your father is going to say; your teachers? I don't know how we're going to solve this mess.'

Jess had not waited for the full blast of her mother's temper, but moved to the kitchen in search of a glass, then reaching out, she turned the stiff pillar tap. A rush of water hit the bottom of the butler sink, the noise helped drown her mother's voice momentarily.

Taking a glass from the wooden drainer, Jessica slowly filled it then shut down the flow of water. Turning to brush past her mother with the glass in her hand intending to say nothing, but controlling the surge of her own anger, she spoke quickly:

'I don't care about your shame, your pretence and your small minded lives. I don't need your world. And...'

The words stopped midway with the impact of her mother's hand as it hit the side of her face with force. The pain was instant. It blended in with the shock of it all. Jess stumbled, her own hand reflexed to her face. The glass slipped from her hand and the sound of it as it hit the quarry tiled floor was far away. Regaining her balance with the help of the corner of the dresser and a sideways step it was the sound of the broken glass under her shoe that seemed amplified. The tears rose but never came. In a slow deliberate act of defiance Jess turned until she was squared to her mother, then lowered her hand from her face and said in a flat voice:

'I hate you, and everything you stand for…'

Turning, Jess started walking towards the kitchen door that led to the hall. Then at a safe distance, she turned back. Her mother had not moved. Without saying any more, Jessica slipped into the hall, conscious now of the pulsing heat in her cheek and ear where the slap had landed. The ends of her finger rubbed the area as if to remove a stain, then she ran upstairs into her room, slammed the door and lay face down on the bed. The tears came, but they didn't weaken her resolve, they strengthened it. The expected knock at the door arrived a full ten minutes later, three soft taps, the sound in itself a gentle pleading.

'Go away.'

A quietness opened before she spoke again through the closed door, this time with a hard bitter finality: 'I will never speak to you again.'

Footsteps retreated down the stairs.

That was how it was. Jessica said nothing to any of her school friends. They would know soon enough. Her mother had already written to the head, explaining that Jess would be leaving school immediately. After pleading with her father's parents, telling them everything, and explaining she had to get away from her mother and think things through, they agreed to take her in. She packed what she wanted into two old canvas bags and on a wet Friday afternoon, took the number 22 double decker bus to her grandparent's chalet bungalow. She sat downstairs, counting off the number of bus stops. The ticket collector passed by, glanced at her bags, then her face. When he finally took her fare, she paid him no more attention than a sparrow does a starling.

Her left hand gripped the chromium bar on the seat in front and with her body twisted slightly, she stared out the window. The first heavy drops of rain started to fall, running sideways across the window of the moving bus. With dark skies, there would be more to come. As the bus eased its way up and down the gears, her stomach began to tighten. The future seemed more frightening than the past. Starting to rise when the bell sounded, she heard the conductor call out: 'Harbour Road '

And with a few steps, she was off the platform and onto the street. As the bus pulled away, she walked as fast as she could down the continual row of mixed buildings that had grown prior to post-war planning acts, covering 30 yards to her grandparents' door. The wind-blown rain had defeated her. Her hair was wet, her jeans heavy. The paved pathway at the front of the old bungalow was flanked by large hydrangeas, now faded from the lost summer. Pushing on through the overhanging shrubs, she felt the back spray spatter her knuckles. Walking slower up the side of the building, she reached the main door. Stooping under the canopy and lowering the bags to the ground, with a short breath of relief she pressed the inset electric doorbell lightly. It rang somewhere down the hall. Waiting only briefly, the door opened. Her grandmother just said:

'Hello, love. Come in, come in, oh… we'll soon get you dry.'

Her grandfather came into view, easing his arthritic hip into a stiff walk towards her, and passing over a towel. He took the bags up to the attic bedroom and placed them on the single bed. The kettle hit an increasing pitch and Jessica followed her grandmother into the kitchen. Her grandfather came back, gave her a hug and retreated to the lounge.

'Our house is yours for as long as you need to stay,' said her grandmother, 'But first, I had better tell your parents you are with us and you are safe.'

No questions were asked, and no criticisms were given during those first few days. Jessica's grandmother assumed they would talk the situation through and agree on the best course soon enough. Meanwhile, Jessica made herself useful, but not a burden. She suspected that her mother had been in touch, but she had no wish to talk to either of her parents. As the days passed, she had plenty of time to think. She had heard of girls in her situation having abortions, but these were illegal and dangerous. Giving the baby up for adoption would probably be the only way, but the reality of a living baby seemed a long way off. In the meantime, she felt accepted and loved by her grandparents and gradually her old self confidence started to seep back.

It was during the afternoon, and she had just finished putting the washing through the mangle. She had lowered the airing rail from the kitchen ceiling, fixing it off at a height to make it easy to load the washing, which would dry in the warmth from the coke boiler. Then she felt the first shock of pain, like a belt slicing upwards from her lower abdomen.

Something was wrong. Clutching herself, she stumbled out of the back door, down the path to the outside toilet. Throwing open the door and clearing the mop bucket from the front of the bowl in almost a single movement, she tore down her jeans and pants and sagged to a crouch. Tears of confusion followed as she saw the blood. Her whole body was trembling, what the hell was happening?

The expulsion of blood, mucus and membrane frightened her. With her body already bent, she felt the rising taste of bile and heaving, coughing once, she spat the contents onto the toilet floor. There had been no time to choose the privacy of a closed door, and while staring through the doorway at the flaking paint on the boundary wall, she first heard, then saw her grandmother.

'Oh … goodness Jessie, what's happening? I'll get towels.'

Jessica's tears had subsided, but the terror stayed. It was the sight and smell of her own blood, and the amount of it. Her grandmother passed the towels, then moved quickly away, saying she would telephone the doctor. Instructed to go to the local hospital immediately, a neighbour was called to help and he brought his car to the front of the house. Jess was still in shock when her grandmother wrapped her in a coat and helped her down the path and into the waiting Hillman. Jessica was put in the front seat, while her grandmother levered herself into the back. For some reason, Jess's overriding memory of this clip of her life was the strong smell of leather from the upholstered seats. The drive took about 15 minutes, and after a brief wait in the casualty department and notes being taken, Jessica was admitted into a ward. She was in for two days, while the usual procedures for a case like this were carried out, and then discharged. The hospital staff had been attentive and kind, and assured her that early miscarriages like hers were very common. It wasn't her fault.

During the bus ride home, sitting next to her grandmother, Jessica felt bruised and battered by the experiences she had gone through in the last few weeks. She wanted to forget, blot, and erase it from her life. The time that followed was a period of reflection. She had, a few times, allowed herself to think what it would be like to have a baby, and to keep it with her, but she knew it would be an impossibly tough life. She knew she was not capable – financially or physically – of bringing up a child on her own, but going through the pregnancy and giving the baby away would have been dreadful. She was deeply relieved then that the problem had been dealt with for her, whether by fate or chance. It was all of ten days before she felt she wanted to leave the house and face anyone.

When she did, she chose to visit one of her former school friends, Carla who had been in the same class. It took her about half an hour. She cut through an alley - avoiding the dog crap was an obstacle course in itself - then straight across the park through the wrought iron gates onto St Ann's Road, heading north. This brought her eventually to the red pillar box at the corner of Carla's road, where she stopped.

Looking down the road at the larger, detached houses set well back from the road, many with cars in their drives, she realised she was wasting her time. Her trip was pointless. First, it was Friday and Carla would be in school, and second, they were no longer classmates. Jessica recognised that she and her other former friends were on different paths now, she had left her schooldays behind. It didn't upset her unduly, she just turned away, heading this time in the general direction of town.

Her shoes must have been tight as after a short distance she put out a hand to lean on a lamp post then, using the left leg, eased off the other shoe. Putting the heel on the ground she used the opposite foot to rub the area before slipping her shoe back on and continuing. It was a warm day and she wore a bright, electric blue cotton skirt well above the knee with a white T-shirt, a cardigan clutched in her hand. On a whim, she decided to go to the Labour Exchange in Clarence Square to register for work.

It was a foreign experience, the heavy doors were like the entrance to a bank, opening into a wide hall with a high ceiling and long, metalled widows at measured intervals. Stopping briefly, she assessed what she should do next. Looking around, she was reminded of a betting shop she had once seen in a snatched view through open doors. There were boards on one wall, displaying cards with job descriptions, then the main counter, also a wide shelf at waist height running down most of the length of two walls. The air was stale, and the atmosphere felt somehow masculine with many more men than women filling in forms. There were untidy piles of them scattered on the shelves.

Moving towards a woman who was turning away with a completed form in her hand, Jessica said:

'I'm new, do I need to fill this form out first?'

'Yes, love.'

The woman joined one the queues. Jess looked for a pen, but could not find one. Turning, she avoided a man who was grinding his cigarette butt with his shoe on the grey thermoplastic tiled floor. It was then that she noticed how many people had done the same thing. Holding the uncompleted form, she waited in one of the queues in front of a counter. It seemed a long wait in a short queue before she reached the front, facing a middle aged man with a boyish face, sitting on a high-backed stool so as if to appear the same height as her. There were full, cream, wooden partitions, their colour matching the walls, on either side of him, reaching to the front of the counter, giving the appearance of privacy.

'How can I help?'

His face gave it all away. Committed boredom, resigned to a job that would give him progression through his career so as to rise with the slow, steady consistency of a ball-cock. Her smile didn't quite reach him.

'There were no pens... can you help me?'

Raising his head slightly he said: 'We open at 9.30, they are all pinched by 9.45, best to bring your own next time.'

He took her empty form and so began the questions and answers. She ploughed through her background, offering feigned enthusiasm, while the clerk filled out the form with the necessary information. He then placed it in a basket, together with other sheets, clearly marked

IN. Reaching with his spare hand, he drew across the counter a green metal container, partially filled with alphabetical index cards. Jess watched this, noticing that his nails were bitten to the quick and the cuticles were torn.

As his fingers played among the cards, she looked at the wall behind him. Then, fumbling in her bag, produced a single cigarette from a hidden package.

'Don't mind if I smoke do you?'

She lit up, took a deep drag and leaned back to produce a long exhale of smoke. Looking back at him, she knew her boredom threshold had been reached.

He had arranged three cards neatly in front of him.

'Now, let's see.'

It was almost comic, as though he was going to produce something from a hat like a magician.

'You haven't got any qualifications, or proper work experience, so I can offer you an industrial cleaning job, with some night shift and overtime.'

Silently, she shook her head and took another draw on the cigarette. She was still focused on the calendar on the wall behind him, which, for some reason, was showing what looked to be a decorated Christmas cake even though it was September. She heard a scratching sound, and looked back at the chewed nails that were easing a dented, aluminium ash tray towards her across the counter.

He carried on:

'I have an opening here for work in a branch of Hopkins dry cleaners?'

'Ah, unfortunately, I suffer a bit from asthma,' she lied.

'Right, the last one I can offer you at the moment is a junior office job at Harbone and Thompson Transport, on the ring road, training given, nine to five.'

Jess asked immediately if she could have an interview. He picked up the heavy black receiver, plugged his index finger into several numbered holes on the dial, allowing them to spin, then leaned back slightly raising his eyes as if to a hidden horizon while waiting for the phone to be answered. That afternoon, she got that junior job in the haulage company, working as a 'go- between' in the office, the workshops, and the yard, and with an easy competence that seemed to come naturally to her.

She volunteered for everything, showing enthusiasm wherever possible, hoping to ease her way forward. The harder she worked, the more she liked what she was doing. Her basic typing skills improved rapidly with the steady flow of short memos and dockets, and she quickly settled into the flow of this raw working life. But she saw the glances men gave her that lasted longer than they should. She understood that her looks and height made her a magnet. One morning, her responsibilities changed. When the receptionist didn't show, Jess volunteered to step in, even though she had only taken odd calls until then. She found it was easy, but relatively dull, and towards the end of the day, she amused herself by answering a couple of calls with the firm's name changed from 'Harbone and Thompson Transport' to 'Hardboiled and Thompson Transport.' Nobody noticed.

Jess was pleased to go back to the office the next day when the receptionist returned from what she could clearly see (even if others couldn't) was a day's holiday. Her confidence was exploding almost by the day. On the back end of a warm, dry day, something happened. She walked through the double swing doors that connected the steel landing and staircase to the workshops below. It was just after five and the three mechanics had already cleaned up, changed and bolted for the door on the first strike.

About to turn back, she heard:

'Hey, Jessie something I want to ask you ....'

Coming out of the rest room below at double pace was Tom Hilder, a driver. He took the stairs two at time coming right on to her.

'Come on, Jessie, you know I fancy you ...'

With his wide smile verging on a leer, he hooked his arm around her waist pressing her body against the guard rail. As she twisted, he leaned towards her in the pretence of whispering something, but she felt him edge her skirt and slide his hand up. She spat in his face.

He recoiled: 'You bitch.'

He stood back and wiped the spittle from his face with his shirt sleeve. Jess looked straight at him, and said: 'Just so we understand each other, if you ever try anything like that again, I will bring on tears and be crying rape. You'll be finished here, and your wife will leave you. I will lie to any court... got it?'

She didn't wait for a reply, but pushed open the door that led back to the office. Clearing a few papers, she too left for home. On the top deck of the bus, she took a king- sized cigarette from a gold coloured packet and lit it with a roll of her thumb on the wheel of her smoky zippo lighter, blackening the paper at the end as it lit. The first intake always tasted vaguely of the lighter fuel that was soaked up in its wick. Snapping its lid shut, and glancing at the embossed sword and shield on its side, she dropped it into her bag. Leaning back against the red checked upholstery, she stretched her legs underneath the seat in front. Her anger had died away and she felt good about herself, having taken control of what could have been a very difficult situation.

A few weeks later, after a spell of dullness that blankets the spirits, the sun came out on a dry and bright day. Jessica was offered a lift into town for her lunch hour break by a young trainee mechanic, a good- looking boy, maybe a year older than her, but too shy to make a pass at her. She took the lift and turned it into a return trip as well. The mechanic dropped her at a corner, and waved her away with: 'See you back in an hour then?'

Climbing out of the van, she used both hands to slide the passenger door on the Commer van shut again. The van merged into the traffic heading down the High Street and disappeared. Jess decided to go for a cup of coffee while reflecting on how dull the job was becoming as her initial enthusiasm was wearing away. With a hand on the bar, she pushed the heavy glass door open.

The Wimpy Bar on this Thursday lunchtime was crowded. A stool by the window shelf was vacated and she moved quickly to take it, cursing quietly as she sat, realising that she had shaken some of her coffee into the saucer. Mopping up the spillage took her attention for a moment before she became conscious of two girls, about her age, discussing an interview that one of them was due to go to the following week. An office junior, helping with sales, dealing with the public, answering phones. The wages were a full £3 more than Jess was getting. She continued listening.

'And best of all, Barham and Co are commercial surveyors in the High Street only minutes away from where I live. If I get it, I wouldn't have such an early start in the mornings ...' a thinning burst of laughter followed before the subject changed. They soon moved away, and their space was quickly taken. It was as though Jess had dreamed a scene from a play.

The last of her coffee was nearly cold. Finishing it, she slid from the stool and left. Stopping briefly, wishing she had a cigarette, she wondered what to do for the best. Further down the pavement, a dog offered its leg to a tree at the side of the road. Its owner stood, holding the lead, embedded in a well- folded newspaper for a few moments, immersed in something. The dog moved, the lead tightened and then the owner followed it down the pavement. Jess moved to cross the road, starting to track away from the woman walking towards her. Without thinking, she said: 'Excuse me, can you help me... I'm looking for the surveyors. Barham's?'

'Yes dear... I know that... ah ...top end of here,' and she pointed, stretching an open hand. 'Turn left into Manor Street and it's a glass fronted office tucked in on the left.'

The 'thank you' was to her back, as she was already moving away. Crossing the road and slipping between the parked cars, Jess started to make her way towards Manor Street. Two pigeons lifted from the pavement in front of her only to skip once and settle again near the gutter. Jess didn't see them. She was thinking, and curious, an idea had been worming in her mind. With a limited amount of time, she walked faster, finally reaching The Crown pub.

Taking a wide swing to avoid the small group talking at the doorway, she headed left into Manor Street and passed the smart floor-to-ceiling glass office front. With a slow turn for her reflection in a nearby window, she turned, walked back and took a deep breath, stood straight and pushed the stainless steel bar on the plate glass front door. Turning to close it, she faltered, realising it was self-closing.

There was little in that front office. A large Persian rug, which for some reason was missing the tassels at one corner, with a green leather-buttoned chesterfield fronted by a small, low, brass table. On it lay two magazines, carefully positioned, and a daily newspaper casually folded once after reading. A feeling of spaciousness was immediate. A man, possibly in his early 30s and wearing a charcoal grey, three-piece suit straightened up from the papers he was looking at, took one pace from the desk and said in a warm, open voice:

'Hello, how can I help you?'

'Good afternoon, my name is Jessica Howard. I've come about the receptionist's job and I would like to speak to you or someone else about it please.'

'Um… not really my area …can I take your details?'

'I would rather speak to someone, if it's possible.'

'Ah..well… can't do that. Annie Walters is at lunch…' he plugged on. 'Have you any experience in this field?'

She had the distinct impression that he was humouring her, as he still had not taken any of her details. He just stood, relaxed with one hand in his trouser pocket, just a few paces in front of her. Speaking firmly, trying to sound confident:

'Yes... I work for a haulage company at the moment and manage incoming phone inquiries, type the orders, instructions, liaise with delivery staff and I also deal with customers who come into our offices.'

All of this was true, albeit to a considerably lesser extent than she had suggested.

'Sounds good Jessica... you seem to have the ability to think on your feet.'

She started to smile, relaxing a little, when she heard the glass door behind her start to open. Turning only her head in reflex more than intent, she saw a man about to enter. Turning back, she was caught completely off guard by being asked: 'Could you deal with that chap, please?'

He returned to the desk and started to reach for some letters. Jess turned back to the newcomer, and with barely a shadow of hesitation said: 'Good afternoon sir, how may I help you?'

The tall man pointed vaguely at something in the window, then asked: 'Is Charlie Mayall in?'

'Ah, I think he is at lunch at the moment sir, may I take your name and a telephone number, and I will get him to call you as soon as he returns?'

Jess moved to the desk hoping to find a pen and paper, knowing her confidence was starting to leak, like her armpits. It was then that a woman's voice came from the archway leading to the rear office:

'Very good indeed, but can you type?'

Spontaneous laughter broke out around the room. Annie had come in from the car park at the back, after dropping John at the front to pick up a lease left for him at the solicitors opposite. Charlie was already behind her. She hadn't seen the two men communicate. Her typing test was good enough, and that was how she came to work at Barham and Co.

She didn't return to her former workplace that afternoon but phoned, feigning sickness and said she was going home. She did go home, but an indirect way, first retracing her steps back down the High Street, then angling across to the bus station. Waiting the few minutes for her bus, there was no queue. Standing back from the bus stop, someone passed her shoulder walking quickly while pushing his wallet into his back pocket.

Something small fell alongside her. It drifted downward catching a draught and came to rest very close to her, and casually, as though shifting her weight, she raised her right foot and allowed her shoe to cover it. Keeping her head down, she began inspecting her nails. The bus arrived. Bending down, she plucked up the five pound note that had very carefully been folded twice into four squares. Holding it loosely in a closed hand, she followed a woman with shopping bags onto the bus, found a seat and sat down, with her handbag on her knees. She shook her fist gently at what she saw as her good fortune, a good half- week's wages. As the bus pulled away, a woman's voice said: 'I saw that.'

Looking straight at her, with the slightest tilt of her head in challenge, Jess responded: 'So?'

Then tuned abruptly away. Morals were an unaffordable luxury she neither cared nor concerned herself about.

....

As Jessica's late teens rolled away, she became more self-reliant, more confident, and probably more selfish. She was determined to make the best of life's chances, twisting them in any way, as long as she they were to her advantage. She had been renting a studio flat for a while now, had a small group of friends and was gradually learning the way the world worked. Every spare penny was saved towards driving lessons.

Just before her 21st birthday, her grandfather collapsed and died. Her grandmother had found him crumpled on the floor of the old garden shed, wedged between his bicycle and the lawn mower. He had reached out in a last movement, catching the fingers of one hand in the creosote-stained fruit nets.

The funeral was held on an overcast day at St Andrew's church, about a mile away. Michael, Jess' father and her grandmother's only son, was supporting, both emotionally and physically, the thin, ageing woman who had helped her when she needed it.

Jess acknowledged her mother with a nod. They had never reconciled, and had rarely spoken over the years. Jess turned away abruptly before any conversation had a chance to develop. The undertakers carried in the coffin and the ceremony began. The hymns and the usual prayers were played out, with the vicar leading the small group. His clear, strong voice sounded as though he was speaking and singing directly to God. After the service, the coffin was borne to the graveside and lowered carefully by straps to its last resting place in the ground.

The symbolic act of taking a clutch of earth from a small neat pile that had clearly been covered in case of further rain, seemed very odd to Jess. The queue shuffled past in slow silence, then it was her turn to look upon the open grave with a polished box at the bottom. The sound of the contents of her hand rattled briefly over the box, and she too moved on. This scene was to remind all in attendance about the brevity of personal time and of their own mortality. But being so young, this unspoken message wouldn't stay with Jess much farther than the Lych Gate. Standing some way off, with his back to the walls of the knave and watching the proceedings, was a middle-aged man with mid- length curly hair. Most people didn't notice him. His boots were still muddy, and his next job - after spading out that grave - was yet another backfill.

There was a gathering at the Parish Hall alongside the church after the burial. Jess noticed a woman wearing the floral dress with a large dark brown leather handbag dangling from her arm. She steadied a full plate, levering its contents with her free hand towards her mouth. She was still shovelling in food when Jess later squeezed her grandmother's arm and kissed her cheek with the quiet words:

'I'll pop in next week.'

Jess' grandmother wore a blank, weary expression during the proceedings that had been laced occasionally with a bewildered smile. Jess wondered whether she'd be OK, and more particularly, which of her relatives would be close enough to support her in the coming weeks. By the time she got home, Jess was tired. She skipped the mug of coffee she'd been thinking about, went to the bedroom, removed her dress and lay down on the bed. The sprung mattress eased a little with her weight, her body felt that momentary lightness. Letting out a deep breath, she lay still thinking about her grandparents. They had been the only firm posts in the sand that didn't shift. Now, one was washed away and the other was leaning precariously.

Starting to think about her own life, Jess acknowledged how much she had progressed in a relatively short time. In her job, she was now taking clients' instructions, measuring buildings to place on the market and acting as a commercial negotiator, earning a great deal more on commission than any wage, when the market at this time was just beginning to be driven by inflation and was starting a slow but steadily upward trajectory. Passing her driving test had widened her world massively, giving her the freedom to broaden her work and social opportunities. She was constantly observing and copying people around her that she considered her betters and, so far, it had paid off. She slipped into a short sleep.

Barham's opened a satellite office in a nearby large market town, on the main road to London, in the spring of the following year. A new partner was absorbed into the firm, and Jess became directly responsible to him. It took little time before the afterhours meetings were anything to do with work.

Outwardly, she had the signs of success. A small, rented flat of her own, a firm's car and a growing social life, but Jess instinctively knew there might be an easier route to improve her life, so she cultivated carefully any men that might be useful. Peter Stoneham, a client, was such man. The party he staged that summer of 1969 was just outside the M25 ring road, on the edge of a village of little merit, but with easy access to both London and the West Sussex downlands. The large Victorian house with its clay peg roof and part tile hung exterior had been left to decay silently since he had bought it. Jess had been invited by Peter, together with Barham's partners, but on the day, she was the only one from the firm, and she was happy with this.

Jess was in no doubt that her original invitation had been purely as decoration, but this didn't upset her, it only amused her. Peter Stoneham was comparatively young, already rich through a property company based in London. He had bought many investments over the years to chuck over his shoulder, into an unseen bag, his company reaching like the tentacles of a jellyfish across the southern counties. This man though, had no physical stature whatsoever. He had little to no hair, and a deeply unattractive pot-marked face. These, Jess thought, were possibly some of his better points. What he really cared about were deals, as many as possible, and the cash they brought enabled him to wear his money like an iron waistcoat, not for pleasure but for protection. This time it was the party, other times, it was Epsom or Henley or the rugby at Twickenham, even a personal box at the Albert Hall. Lush knew no boundaries.

That Saturday was both hot and still, with a heavy over-riding closeness. Jess left her flat in plenty of time to arrive for a late start, no one, she reasoned, wanted to be the first among the few. Sitting back, relaxed, she was allowing the car to lead her. After a few minutes, she turned on the radio using her forefinger to stab at the row of buttons to change the station. Hovering for a moment on a burst of news about the nation's trade gap widening, her concentration was quickly dulled by the subject when she was further distracted by the fuel gauge nearing the red reserve marker. She turned off the radio.

The filling station was not too far away, but this situation always made her uneasy. Later, pulling onto the forecourt and gently breaking, she manipulated the car directly alongside the pump. The attendant was already walking out to serve her: 'Hello, what would you like?'

'Super please, it should take about four pounds worth.'

The attendant quickly skirted the car and flipped down the rear number plate to reveal the petrol cap. First, Jess heard the thump of the tight spring, then a thin tuneless whistle began, but she had already fixed on the turning dial, pence were turning to pounds and halves spun to gallons. Finally he hung the pump with a smack to its housing, and they both checked the dial. With the recent budget, petrol had just reached the seven shilling a gallon mark.

'.. 'fraid that's four pound eight and six.'

Was that really a smile or some sort of an apology she wondered, as she passed over a five pound note, and waited for what she thought was longer than necessary for her change. When the attendant returned, he placed her change in coins in her hand, his fingers seeming damp to her palm. As she started the car again it occurred to her that perhaps, occasionally, people forget their change. She pushed the car up through the gears to a steady 60, then turned on the radio again, this time to a music station, adjusted the volume and relaxed into the drive.

There hadn't been much traffic on the main road and within an hour she was among the lanes, following instructions in the proximity of Cranston. It wasn't too difficult to find, turning her car with a deft flick of the wheel between the gate posts, she drove slower up a curved driveway that disappeared behind a long laurel hedge, immediately blanketing both the house from the road and the road from the house. Parking on the wide gravel apron among many other cars, she turned off the engine. Making a small adjustment to the mirror, she ran her tongue across her top row of teeth, lightly re-did her lipstick retrieved from her small shoulder bag, before opening the car door and swinging herself out. She cursed quietly at the thought that the stones might damage the edges of her shoes, then, bending slightly, she locked the car door. The wide, gently-sloping lawns surrounding part of the old house had been cut neatly, but the edges grew over the gravel and the flower beds looked poorly attended. A tall row of oversized Douglas firs had been allowed to grow high decades ago to blank off the house's neighbours on two sides, giving the air of calm and privacy.

The sound of music came from a large marquee that had been erected on the flat area of the hard, dry surface of the middle lawn at the side of the house. Jess guessed that the house, with it shutters drawn, was empty and at some later stage it would be part of a larger acquisition package, possibly with its neighbours, to be torn down for redevelopment.

Moving closer, the cacophony of voices from the marquee lifted towards her, wavering slightly on the light breeze of music. Keen now to be among this throng, Jess quickened her pace. In front of her came a man in black with an outstretched arm, pointing like a sign post to the open flaps of the party. She walked purposefully on. A few people stood on the outside. Passing them with the briefest smile, she moved into the mouth of the entrance. Her height gave her an easy view of the crowded marquee.

The farthest side was wide open. Many guests had spilled to the tables and chairs outside, overlooking the lower lawns. Clutches of people stood in small groups earnestly talking, heads jerking to the speaker's tunes. The band were playing to an empty dance floor in front of them. The interruption of her visual appraisal was by a voice of a waiter, again in the same black uniform, holding a tray.

'Good afternoon, Madam'

The offered tray held several drinks. With nothing more than a 'Thank you,' Jess reached for a white wine, the glass clearly showing it was cold. The waiter moved away, glancing from side to side as though looking for someone, which she was too in a kind of way. Moving slower, drifting to the music, she felt a touch to her elbow.

'Hello, Jessie.'

A short conversation followed with a small group of known agents from another surveyors' practice, then moving on she raised her hand and waved at a few faces father away that she vaguely recognised. This could have been to keep them at bay, or to set them up with a mischievous smile for their wives or girlfriends to question. Taking a sip of the cool wine, she knew that her decision to dress in a simple, short summer dress was already paying a dividend.

Using the forefinger of her free hand as a comb, Jess brushed a few errant strands of hair over her shoulder. Someone called her name, and swinging her head to the left she saw the pale, bald head on the white open-neck shirt of her host. Playing the entertainer to a gathered audience, he was waving her over. She raised her hand to a wave and started to move in his direction.

Sooner or later she would have to make her mark and thank him, so she might as well get it over with. Appearing to be keen to see him, she crossed to the group. Peter's arm stretched out and swept around her waist briefly. It occurred to her that they must look odd, as she was a full three inches taller than him. 'Jess, how lovely to see you…' The words fell from his lips. He carried on: 'Let me introduce you to…' And he did. Jess played the part and played it well, and he left that group shortly and wandered over to other guests. As he went, he leaned to whisper in her ear, while slipping his arm around her again.

'Ring me next week, I have something interesting for you.'

His hand had purposely brushed against the area lower than her waist. Her smile was compliant, but she was thinking that he hadn't got a chance of getting more than that. After a respectable amount of time, Jess made her excuses and headed for the bar. Respite and recharge, she thought. The barman approached her attentively. 'What may I get you?'

'A large glass of cold, white wine please.'

'Certainly, we have a medium, or a dry …. which would you prefer?'

With tired resignation, she said:

'Oh …I don't mind, I've been either interviewing people or being verbally battered for the last half an hour and really I just need a large dose of alcohol.'

The laughter didn't come from the barman, but from two younger men further along the bar who had overheard. The nearest was taller with a simple composure. Moving the hand that held his glass very slightly, as if to indicate his invitation, he said:

'Would you like to join us?'

Jess didn't move or respond immediately, she just looked at him, allowing a smile to widen on her face, and in that moment he smiled too. She took a few slow steps, with both hands holding her glass of wine, as though giving the matter more thought, before moving to join them.

'Hello…'

His word just hung there… alone, suspended, before he continued: 'My name is Derek, Derek Firestone.'

He offered his hand as the simple confirmation of this introduction. She reached to shake it. As she did so, he went on: 'Oh, I'm sorry, and this is Simon Johnson.'

'Well… hello to both of you.'

But she was only really looking at one them when she said it. 'I'm Jessica Howard, my friends call me Jess.'

It was Simon who spoke first.

'What a gathering, how do you know Peter?'

Looking at him first, she sidestepped this punt for information, with: 'Does anyone really know Peter? I'm not sure I do really, how about you, what do you do?'

Trying to sound amusing and relaxed, Simon started again: 'Planning consultant at your service,' and with a flourish between finger and thumb, produced from the top pocket of his sports coat a card. With a theatrical 'Da …Dah', he passed the card to her.

'Ah…'

The small inflection injected to that single syllable, showed total enlightenment of the situation as if it was unfolded to her. Her face, though, reflected only momentary interest. Turning her attention back to Derek as she dropped the card she was holding into her handbag, she realised that he was watching her with both hands pushed deep into his trouser pockets. Standing straight, with his legs a short distance apart, he had a certain casualness about the way he wore his clothes. He seemed to belong where he was, and with confidence, an immeasurable asset that so few people even know they possess.

It was later, after the buffet and the dancing, that the first hard flutter on the canvas arrived. The first sign they were aware of was the wind under the unseen cloud bank that had been building steadily from the south west. The stewards had lowered the flaps to the open sides, pegging them securely as the light dropped away an hour or so before. The first raindrop fell to the canvas like a small pebble, its continual echo followed, turning to a pouring of sound. The wind increased, tearing at the heavy canvas. In such circumstances, there is an always a period of time between awareness and movement, and it was the growing sound of the wind that made people look to the roof of the marquee with more than a trace of unease. The depression passed within a span of time, but women were already edging cardigans on and people had started to leave.

Derek, with an arm casually draped around Jess's shoulders, looked at her with the unspoken question of: what now?

'Don't worry, I've got an umbrella I'll be back in a minute.'

While he headed for the backstage area, Jess looked about at the tables that staff were doing their best to clear and noticed a flattened salmon sandwich that lay discarded under a seated woman in a rather too tight dress. The woman was clearly drunk and the sandwich had been trodden on.

'OK then?'

Again Derek was at her shoulder, now holding an umbrella not by the handle but by the middle of the folded section. It was one of those large, coloured umbrellas with a sponsorship logo slapped on. It was wet, giving her the distinct impression that it wasn't his. Stepping outside the marquee, the ribs of the umbrella buckled the moment the wind caught. They laughed together as he discarded it close to one of the guide ropes with no more than a shrug of the shoulders. When they crossed to the car park at a quickened pace, both of them were still laughing hard. They sat in her car talking and, later, running their hands over one another for a while, eventually parting and each disappearing separately into the evening. He said he'd phone, she hoped he would, but then, they all say that.

The car's head lights worked their way through the lanes and back onto the main road with no wrong turns while Jess replayed the day in her mind, like a silent film. The thunderous sky gave no warning, turning again from a brooding quiet, to heavy drops falling large and fast as if to blister the surface of the road before its wash.

The silver poplar trees at the roadside were bending to the tune of the strengthening wind. The visibility was dropping and the condensation was rising. Feeling a moment of anxiety, Jess pulled into a lay-by. Keeping the engine running, she lowered the driver's widow briefly then took a cotton duster from the door sleeve and wiped the windscreen with several long swipes, folding it each time. Revving the engine and leaning slightly over the steering wheel, her fingers tightened slightly. Urging the car back onto the road, she drove on. The storm passed on its oblique trajectory, leaving only the rolling sky with the road beneath it taking her home. Early the following week, she called Peter Stoneham, hoping to squeeze some new instructions out of him as well as to thank him for the invitation to his party.

'I'm so pleased. You looked as though you had a good time, it all went well didn't you think?'

'I had a great time, thank you…I met some very interesting people.'

But he had moved on, she had given him the chance to comment, but he just walked by it. Reverting to his subject, she got what she wanted for Barham's: instructions to act on his behalf for a rent review of a shoe shop which was one of a national chain, and its disposal in the investment market afterwards if it reached his perceived rent level.

'I want a good Zone A rating and lean on the upstairs storage, that lot will be mortgageable separately for three flats one day, mark my words. Get

Charlie to sort the review out and we'll have another little chat then?'

Sounding grateful and enthusiastic, she took the name and phone number of the manager. The original lease, which he was sending to her in the post, had been let on a 21-year term with a rent review every five years. This would be the last one, but inflation had made this the biggest rise and, with it, the biggest gain. After the phone conversation had ended, Jess sat for a moment thinking how there were times with him when she felt an undercurrent that made her squirm, and his suggestions of 'little chats' were heavily laden with innuendo.

Derek phoned her while she was out at lunch. He didn't leave a number, but said he would try to call back at the end of the day. She felt that rising rush, the expectation that comes at a beginning. Staying in for the rest of the afternoon, she waited for the call, and right on 5.30, it came. Swinging on her swivel chair pushed slightly back from the desk, she took it.

Derek had been invited to the party because Peter had used his small, but growing, site-finding consultancy. Derek employed Simon Johnson on a sub-contract basis as a planning expert. He was, in fact, moonlighting from the neighbouring County Council. Jess would later come to understand the relationship of the two men - a front man and a stooge. One looked up to the other, while the other almost – but not quite – looked down to the former. Both had something to gain. It was an unequal partnership, but it worked.

Simon, the stooge, was solid, clever, reliable, but tepid in some secondary way, always a follower, never a leader. These were the qualities that both Derek and

Jess saw quite separately in him. Not bad-looking really, Jess thought, with his straight, mid- length hair lying thin, but he was the sort of man that would always be in the second row of a bank of people, hanging back, peering forward with a weak smile.

Both men registered with her for completely different reasons, but it was Derek she was casting the fly for. Like a skilful angler, she would lure this wily fish to take the fly, to wriggle, even fight on the line, but eventually he would allow himself to be landed.

That was exactly what happened over the next two weeks. Each thought they were the hunter with a prize within reach. It was her flat that they returned to on another wet Saturday afternoon and slept together in her bed for the first time. The only things that lay between them undisturbed were their untold secrets.

He told her his working history had no path. He had moved through sales to self-employment and he spun stories that were made of dreams. There was a future here, she thought, believing that she had spotted a rising share in a crowded market. It took several months before work commitments and gaps in his evenings were explained with a lie that became less concealed with time. When Jess found out Derek was married, her period was late and she thought she could be pregnant, again.

What had started with fire ended with tears; and so the wheel turned and the coin dropped again.

The unravelling of her life was a pincer movement of circumstances. Her pregnancy fears proved false, but just two weeks after her relationship with Derek ended, Charlie announced that Barham and Company would cease to trade from the end of the week. Company debts were forcing the firm to close.

Charlie made the announcement at a meeting of all the staff, on a Tuesday morning at just before 10. The normally securely confident man appeared nervous and awkward when he entered the conference room, holding a sheaf of papers and a pen in one hand. They must have been a prop, as he never referred to them. Jess watched his other hand hang limply at his side, with his thumb flicking against his forefinger constantly, as though to remove the ash of an unseen cigarette. He spoke for only a few minutes, saying that he hoped to be able to honour the company's obligations to its staff, but his words bounced like a dud cheque. She remembered how he had then walked to the back office, to get something she thought, but he never came back. He left the building and wasn't seen again.

Jess's face was lined with anger, she had wanted to shout at him: 'You bastard, you lied to us all, dumped us like trash onto a tip.'

She wanted him to know that it didn't stop there, but he was already gone, unaware of the despair and ongoing damage he and his partner had caused to the lives of others. Now Jess had no job, and no income. She found out soon enough that when you're at your lowest, the people that offer to help are very often not the ones you expect. She tried to be strong, but was crumbling. One of the few phone calls she had at the flat after she'd been made redundant was from Simon Johnson.

'Thought you might like someone to off-load on? Would you like to come out for a drink? I could meet you in The Crown tonight, come and join me?'

'Simon, you're so kind, I need a friend, but I'm nearly broke.'

'Oh, don't worry about that, I'll treat you. 7. 30 be ok?'

'Thank you, lovely, I'll see you then.'

Still holding the receiver longer than normal, she was left with the lonely continuous buzz of the dial tone. Hanging the receiver back in its cradle, she sagged back on the green corduroy sofa, thinking that at only 22, a door was closing and she was on the wrong side of it. It was 2.30. Five hours before she would meet Simon. Leaning from the waist, she picked up the paper from the low coffee table in front of her and looked with no enthusiasm at her two circled adverts. Folding it, about to discard it again, she changed her mind and folded it back to its ordered pages. The main story on the front page was the ongoing coverage of The Troubles in Northern Ireland - the murders, the knee- capping, the marching, and the guns. It seemed to her like a war in a neighbouring backyard that might spill onto the mainland.

A small paragraph announced that Lulu had been chosen to represent the UK in the Eurovision song contest with 'Boom bang-a-bang.' Jess considered this entire competition to be housewives' music, orchestrated for the masses. She far preferred bands like The Move, Fleetwood Mac, or Jimmy Hendrix.

Bringing both her hands together and thumbing the pages to turn them, she saw that British Leyland was launching a new range of cars, the first of which was the Austin Maxi. The car's lines were sleek and ahead of their time. This new range, the article suggested, would help the company spearhead its drive for exports as well as the home market. This held her interest just long enough for her tongue to snatch between her thumb and forefinger to dampen them and separate the next two pages. Her eyes scanned from top left to bottom right like a Labrador locates a downed pheasant in the grass, and in the bottom right corner she was held by the words:

EMIGRATE TO AUSTRALIA

Arc of Doubt

2

Jessica, England. 1969

The £10 assisted passage.

Underneath the strapline was a picture of a family on a beach, playing with a ball. Superimposed over part of the picture was a row of smart, suburban bungalows with neat lawns and driveways, one with what Jess thought Australians called station wagons parked outside. There were two phone numbers at the bottom. Dropping the paper to her lap, she thought the ad could have been written just for her.

She thought how this series of these adverts, encouraging people to move to the other side of the world, had appeared throughout the national press for a considerable amount of time now. They were run by the Australian government through Australia House in London. Occasionally, she had heard about friends of friends who had applied, and large numbers of people seemed to be taking up the offer. Was it possible that they would consider her? Was she serious, and what could she offer them?

Stretching an arm at first, without looking, she found her colourful woven shoulder bag and pulled it towards her by the long strap. Its contents moved towards the open end, revealing the bottom edge of the red and white packet of Embassy cigarettes. Its very presence, just showing from the corner of her bag, was if to taunt her. How many times had she wanted to quit? But it was never the right time. She plucked out the packet and flipped back the lid, only to feel a vague disappointment at the few that were left. Taking one and putting it between her lips, the match flared at the end of her finger and thumb, the cigarette glowed at the first draw and then she tossed the matchbox onto the coffee table. Bending forward a little, she used her forefingers to draw the strawberry red ash tray closer. The smoke drifted upwards to her face, then taking a long drag down, she removed the cigarette from her lips and put her elbow on the arm of the settee before finding a more relaxed position and expelling the smoke through her mouth.

The previous year, she had gone on holiday with some friends to Minorca. It had been her first time abroad, and it was the warm scented air, and the shared laughter that filled her memories. So, she already had a passport, removing one obstacle. Could this advert just be the piper's tune she had been subconsciously waiting for? Stubbing out the cigarette in the ash tray, the heat on the end of her finger brought her back to reality. Time was running, there were just two weeks before she had to either pay another month's rent or leave the place she was living in. There was always work of some sort somewhere, she just had to find it.

The empty hours of the afternoon were filled and lost. The crossword, the ironing, and the last chapter of the novel she was reading, A Burnt Out Case.

Picking up the folded paper on the sofa, she moved it to the edge of the table then stood to cross the room with a few short paces to draw the curtains. There came the familiar rattle of the curtain hooks on a steel rail from somewhere inside the pelmet box and then her hands crossed, as did the curtains. The closing darkness was now outside. She headed for the bedroom, then opened the door to the tiny, windowless bathroom. Retrieving the rubber plug with its broken chain from the ledge, she pushed it into its place in the bath. The geyser fired the moment the hot tap was turned on, and the bath started to fill.

Stripping off all her clothes and leaving them strewn on the bed, she stepped into the bath, leaving the door open to allow the steam to escape. The shallow water was not much more than the depth of a puddle, so hair-washing would have to wait. This exercise held little pleasure. Quickly, she snatched the towel from the back of the chair as the first shiver moved over her and wrapped it around herself while wondering what to wear. Now her enthusiasm for meeting Simon was in danger of evaporating. Finally, she chose a pale ribbed polo necked jumper with her jeans, and added a little makeup. She was ready.

Hoping she wouldn't need a coat, she twisted the key in the lock of the front door, the bolt shot and she descended two flights of stairs to street level.

Turning to the left, she had walked no more than a dozen paces when a male figure came out of an alley that ran like a horizontal bore hole through the buildings. He brushed past her, without slowing his step or moving his head. Drawing up like a hare in headlights she stopped, startled, and then started walking again. The cold damp air of the November evening pressed up against her, and she regretted not bringing her coat, but it was only a few minutes to The Crown. The brass door handle was cold to touch, but opened easily, and she moved through the gap. The door closed itself, and the pub's welcoming warmth was on her. She was hoping she hadn't arrived first, when she saw an arm raised among the bar line of stools. There was that timid face, smiling, under fair hair that fell straight from the crown of his head. It was Simon.

He slid from the stool, walked up to Jess and, opening his arms, gave her a hug. 'I'm sorry to hear about your job….'

Then he stepped back, waved an arm. 'Come and have a drink, what would you like.'

'Um….may I have a …a glass of Liebfraumilch, please?'

Simon looked at the barman and was acknowledged with the slightest of nods while he was finishing serving someone. He then promptly served the woman alongside his previous customer. Sensing his own embarrassment at this, he nervously glanced at Jess. She appeared distant in the act of drawing smoke to her lungs for the hidden hit with a newly-lit cigarette. Turning back, the barman was in front of him: 'What can I get you?'

'A glass of Liebfraumilch and another pint of Red Barrel please.'

While the beer was being drawn, he swallowed the last of his first pint and edged the used glass over the bar to be cleared away. Paying with a ten shilling note, and barely checking his change, Simon lifted the two glasses and said: 'Would you prefer that table in the corner?'

'Oh …Yes…..'

'It's a bit quieter. So, how is everything really going at the moment?'

Jess launched into an outpouring, encouraged by this willing audience, and ended with: 'I'm not sure how I'm going to make it. Actually, I'm thinking of emigrating, going to Australia.'

'Wow, that's far out, but too far out for me...'

She told him of how she had seen an advert for the £10 assisted passage scheme, and how she could save enough to start a new life by leaving her flat and moving into a cheaper bedsitter. The more she talked about it, the more the idea of emigrating seemed to fix itself in her mind, like setting concrete. By the end of the evening, Simon had treated her to a pub meal, and offered her the spare room in his flat, to help her out financially. It was nothing more than Jess had hoped for from the onset. She decided to accept his hospitality, but he would get nothing in return. The pace of her life over the next few months changed radically. The first action had been a call to Australia House. A form was sent, completed and returned, and then the waiting began for the interview date.

She then found a job with a car hire firm that had just opened, and became one of the front office staff, checking cars in and out, taking calls. It was easy stuff for her and no responsibilities beyond that of her hours. Jess continued to save everything she could, and living at Simon's had helped. Poor old Simple Simon - he had charged her no rent and paid for most of the groceries in exchange for intermittent cooking and cleaning. He had walked about with his tongue hanging out like a faithful dog most of the time.

But after six weeks at Simon's flat, she had to get away from him. He irritated her with his foppish hair, his silly face that could never quite make it to a proper smile and she started looking for somewhere cheap to rent. Jess decided on a small room in the back extension of a large Victorian house owned by a thick-set man in his 50s. He had an annoying habit of shouting to her up the lino-covered stairs, rather than climb them. He was divorced and lived downstairs with a cat in the front part of the house, while her room was on the second floor. It was unlikely that you could swing his cat in it.

Somehow, a single bed and chair and what passed as a small wardrobe had been levered in to fill the space. The door could open to 45 degrees to allow its occupant to pass, but had to be closed in order to move about the room. At the end of the windowless hall was the bathroom, shared by several other tenants. It was grim, with its monstrous gas geyser fixed above a roll top bath with a coin meter alongside. The kitchen was the same standard.

It was on a Tuesday, coming back in from work, that Jess saw the envelope on the heavy carved table just inside the front door. The tenants' mail was always laid out alphabetically in a neat row, showing the landlord's orderly mind. Snatching up the single envelope, she roughly opened it using her key to make the initial tear, then sliding her forefinger into it sufficiently to rip it open. The letter was short and simple. It gave her the appointment date and required her to bring her passport and school certificates with her. Medical and chest X-ray reports were also needed and these could be arranged – and paid for – through a local GP.

The two weeks seemed to pass slowly, but the calendar turned. Jess had gone to bed the evening before her appointment tired, expecting to sink to oblivion. She drifted though the 4am zone with some scattered sleep around 5, then finally got up just before dawn, exhausted. Coffee was the only breakfast and later, using a girl's oldest excuse, she left a message on the firm's answer machine, telling them she wouldn't be in that day.

Taking the 7.20 train and changing only once onto the main line, she joined the commuters to Waterloo. The quieter, new diesel electric train was crowded, but it didn't bother Jess in the slightest. She loved the closeness of the unfamiliar people and she was excited. The day would be a brush with the world that lay ahead. When the train arrived at Waterloo, all the passengers got off, as though poured from a bottle. It was like a continuous flow of humanity, seeping into every orifice that the station had to offer; down the stairs deep into the underground, or out and onto the roads, where they thinned to mingle and mix with the throng of London. Starting to cross Waterloo bridge, carrying a small, coloured map of central London for guidance, she could clearly see, away to the east, the dome of St Paul's and the city beyond.

Reaching the end of the bridge, she was about to take the stairs to The Embankment when a gust of wind pulled hard at the large sealed envelope in her other hand. She stopped it flying into the water below, and gripping it tighter, pulled at the zip on her jacket to let in cool air before continuing down the iron stairway. Looking down, she turned the paper map in her hand, having lost her place. She realised it wasn't far on The Embankment before she could cross the road and cut through to The

Strand and find Australia House. When she got there, she had to ask for directions. The first 'excuse me' went unanswered in the passing rush. At a second attempt, she stopped an older woman: 'Can you tell me where Australia House is, please?'

The woman pointed directly across the road, and said, with a short laugh: 'Just there.'

Then the woman drifted back among the flow of people on the pavement, and was gone. Jess looked again across the continuous stream of slow-moving traffic, then at the huge, majestic building. It was built and finally completed, she found out later, just after the First World War on a triangular site of Portland stone over a 900-year-old sacred well, drawing from the River Fleet, a subterranean London river.

The water in the well was still clear and apparently has been tested as safe to drink. Most interior materials of the palatial, Regency-influenced building were imported from the mines and forests of Australia. Crossing the road with extreme care, she stood at the main entrance, overawed by the moment this all stood for in her own life. If there was a threshold for her, it would surely be here and now.

How many people had gone through these doors with such hope, just like her? The massive outer doors were pegged back, leading to an inner porch with swinging doors that opened into a magnificent hall. Its height seemed to reach up for ever. People crisscrossed the veined marble floors, making a low echo that blended with the babble of voices. A broad, winding staircase was set deep in the hall, flanked by two sets of cage lifts with brass concertina doors topped with a series of thick, oily cables standing ready to pull the cages to the sky.

A long mahogany desk seated several receptionists, and alongside them was a sign on an easel, a black arrow pointing to the West Corridor with large bold letters: **Immigration and visas**

Standing still, Jess removed her jacket, revealing a simple blue dress that she had worn when she worked at Barham's. She had chosen it because the hem was not too short, nor the neckline too low. Checking her bag, she took out the appointment letter and looked at the time on her watch. She had 40 minutes to spare. Following the arrow, she first heard the voice then saw the uniformed concierge instructing loudly:

'Immigration appointments, wait until called please.'

A small mass of people partly filled the waiting area of the inner hall. Hesitating, she watched two women disappear through a door marked Ladies and followed them. When she returned, she stood clutching her possessions until her name was called. It was much more informal than she had expected. Her medical report and X-ray print out were passed over, then her savings account and passport were examined. Almost without looking up, the man said:

'What line of work are you hoping to follow when you arrive?'

'I am a skilled and trained commercial property sales woman as you can see from my references. However, I will do any work, no matter how hard or dirty in order to gain a foothold in Australia.'

He looked up with the indifference of a man who had seen a thousand faces before him and cared little for any of them. The questions he asked first qualified what she had written on the application form, then randomly probed personal issues.

'Have you got married or started a relationship since the application?'

'Do you have any children?'

'Do you know anyone in Australia?'

'Your first choice is Sydney, for your second choice we would suggest Melbourne.'

He stretched one arm across the table, as though struck by some momentary cramp before withdrawing it and carrying on: 'The boat passage will take about four to five weeks. It leaves, conveniently for you, from Southampton.'

Looking up from his notes, she thought he was going to smile at her, but he didn't, he just carried on in a tone that seemed as if he was reading from a board behind her. '... All the food on board will be included and your sponsor will meet you when the boat arrives in port. His job will be to settle you into the immigrants' hostel where your first two weeks would also be included. The sponsor will help you find work and see you established.'

He then stood up, with the clear indication that the interview was over. With a handshake, he added, this time with what appeared to be genuine warmth:

'Don't worry, everything will be fine, we will be in touch with all the details very soon.'

'Thank you'

Jess turned and left the room, leaving the door open. Starting to retrace her steps to the main entrance she checked her watch, and saw that she had been in there less than 20 minutes. The loud speaker split the air with another name, but she didn't hear it, she was far away. Later, walking westward down The Strand towards Trafalgar Square, the red Wimpy Bar street sign invaded her thoughts and on impulse, she veered towards the doorway. Stepping on the escalator to the first floor and raising her head towards the uphill journey she stared at an intermittent line of stationary people, as though time had just passed over them. Then she too was spilling from her own position, catching her heels as she almost fell over.

She bought tea and, holding the cup and saucer, found a stool at what could best be described as a wide shelf facing the wall. Peering down at the expensive liquid, with its limp tea bag semi- submerged, she then dropped in one of the two sugar lumps from the small paper wrap. Using the teaspoon, she worked the tea bag until the colour became darker, then deftly squeezed it and removed it before adding a little milk. Her thoughts were on what had just happened. It all seemed so matter of fact, done, boxes ticked, forms signed, ticket on its way. They must have checked her for any criminal record, but that wouldn't have found anything. Surely it couldn't be that easy?

Raising the cup to her lips, she tilted it slightly to take a first mouthful when a single droplet left the bottom of the cup to land in the middle of the front of her dress. Cursing lightly, she fished about in her handbag to find a small handkerchief, then attempted to dab the mark. Giving up, she pulled her jacket closed. The sweet, rich aroma of the Wimpey burgers being flipped on the hot flat iron by the short order cook was almost too much.

Finishing her tea, she headed down the escalators and back to the platform for the homeward train.

It was 30 days of counting before the letter of letters arrived.

Part Four

Arc of Doubt

1

Nat, Sydney, Australia. 1971

The Poseidon nickel strike at Windarra, north east of Laverton, came at a time of colossal demand, coupled with extraordinary speculation on its future share price. Nat had, with only luck alone, bought in at the optimum time at the very beginning of its rise at 12 cents a share, and sold at practically the peak five months later, for $271.03 per share in early January 1970. He was now a millionaire. He couldn't stay where he was of course, and with the boot coming off his injured calf that week, he bought a second-hand truck to melt into any background and headed for Darwin. While he drove, the surreal dream of his present reality turned over and over in his head.

The first stop at Halls Creek was two full days of driving and from there he pressed on, jarring his way across the Top End until he finally returned to Darwin, and began his life there, again. No conspicuous show of wealth, no boastfulness, just another man amongst the crowd. During the next couple of years, his fortune grew further, built on land holdings and city office investment buildings. He achieved what he wanted; financial security, an uncomplicated personal life, and he was completely unchanged from the way he had been before, leaving him free to learn to sail, and embed himself among others in what he now felt was his community. He made a trip to Sydney and bought a flat overlooking

West Bay with a berth for a 12 metre boat right outside on the marina.

Nothing ostentatious, smart enough for the same pick-up to look out of place, but not the driver. He had used a city legal firm for the flat's conveyance and had met a young partner who he quickly came to regard as a friend, as well as his legal advisor. At the time he had no inkling this man would become the primary link, responsible for the first brick to come loose in the wall, the first irrevocable force of fate that, together with a cluster fuck of timing and natural circumstances, would accumulate to his personal nemesis.

That particular day was the start of it all, the lunch at the Boulevard Café, a purposefully understated relaxed space. Nat was casually dressed, his new friend Andrew Mason wore a smart lightweight suit, and they sat at a quiet table at the back, with a long view of the room, air conditioned but not too much.

The waitress, who had an American mid-west accent, was attentive before taking their order. Both of them chose a one course lunch, without alcohol. The talk started with Nat's plans for finding a company, or companies, to invest with further. Andrew suggested he should meet various people, including a wealthy property developer his firm acted for by the name of Frank O'Hagan, and said he could arrange it. Their conversation shifted to mutual interests, sailing and traffic congestion among them, then converged on politics and the economic outlook. After lunch, they took a short walk together across the wide avenue into a park, and parted with a handshake in the middle of the open grasslands.

Andrew headed back to the gate through which they had entered the park, while Nat watched him for longer than he might have done, before raising his head slightly as if to confirm his own direction. He then continued on a perpendicular route of the park into a thin belt of pine trees, to emerge at the high main gates. The burst of traffic noise became incessant, the scent of pine was left behind as the lights changed. Completely relaxed, with his hands in his pockets, Nat strode on. Two days later, returning from working on his boat's diesel engine, the red light on the answer phone blinked hard at him. Four calls, two were notifications from Darwin regarding accounts, one was from the cleaning agency who would call at the house the following day at 10am, and the last was from Andrew Mason.

He didn't call Andrew back immediately, but went to the downstairs shower room. He reached in through the open door, turned the water on to run warm, withdrawing his arm smartly as the cold water hosed him. Shutting the shower door temporarily, he removed all of his clothes and the band from his hair, stretched to flex his body, then, extending a hand though the part- opened door, he tested the temperature. It was now warm. He stepped in quickly, closed the door and allowed the water to cascade onto his head and down his entire body. Slowly, he moved his head backwards, shutting his eyes. Then, leaning forward, he took the soap from the tray and thoroughly washed himself. After shampooing his hair, he stood motionless under the falling water, watching the rivulets and water beads dancing on the clear Perspex shower panels. Then, with the jerk of a wrist, he turned off the shower, put a towel around his waist and went to the basin and soaped his face to take the long strokes of the razor.

The briefest smell of shaving soap reached his nostrils before dissipating. Glancing only briefly for the inspection in the wall mirror, he quickly dressed, brushed his hair to hang loose to dry and moved like a foraging animal to the kitchen to cut a doorstop sandwich. He could see the boat from the window rubbing gently on the fenders, secured safely by the warps. Life was good and he knew it.

Picking up the trim phone receiver, he pressed a series of numbers. It rang twice before it was answered and he was put through to Andrew.

'Hey... OK Nat? I've sorted it for you with Frank O'Hagan.'

He continued:

'I gave him an outline of your history, he seems keen to meet you, either at his offices, or if you feel more comfortable, on neutral ground. He recommended The Round House next Monday at 12.30. What would suit you?'

'I think...,' began Nat, 'That as a first and introductory meeting, this place The Round House might be best. What is it and where is it?'

'Oh sorry..... It's a bar with useful separate rooms for meetings over at Highland Street, near St James subway station.'

Nat decided to arrive early so he could walk around The Round House, to feel the shape of its bones. Before him was a two-storey, stone building, with a rounded gable. High up above the first floor window was small doorway with a haul post above it. He thought it might have been some type of grain store when it was constructed originally.

Tilting his head slightly, he noticed the brickwork high up was slightly perished, giving off a softer orange colour alongside the deep red of the main swathe of face bricks. Using the steel hand rail, polished by a thousand hands to a dull gleam, he guided himself up the four steps, through the doors wide enough for two horses to pass, and passed through open glass doors into the bar. To his left he saw a staircase to the wide, galleried restaurant area upstairs, guarded by a young, smartly-dressed woman in black who greeted him impeccably.

'Good afternoon sir, may I help you?'

'Hello, yes, I'm here to meet Mr Andrew Mason and Mr Frank O'Hagan, my name is Nat Gibson.'

She turned her head slightly, signalling with a raised finger to another young woman dressed in the same neat black attire.

'Would you show this gentleman to Mr O'Hagan's private booth?'

Turning back, she gave him a natural, confident smile of welcome, which he returned. 'Thank you.'

The door to the booth was opened for him. Two men rose from the table, one quicker than the other. A warm casual greeting followed. 'Hi, Nat.'

Andrew spoke first, then showing an open palm in the direction of the other man continued: 'This is Frank O'Hagan, you two have a great deal in common.'

His voice tailed away, giving O' Hagan sufficient time to lower his glass to the linen tablecloth and step forward with an outstretched hand. In a firm voice he just said: 'Frank... Frank O'Hagan.'

Everything else just followed.

Later, when Nat recalled that first meeting, he remembered not a booth but a private suite of rooms with long reaching city views, centred by a staffed dining table and, more particularly, that handshake. O'Hagan's hand was large, and had wrapped around and almost enveloped his. O'Hagan's forefinger and thumb clamped his hand, creating a firm handshake that, on reflection, seemed almost symbolic.

O' Hagan was about a decade older than Nat, with dark hair, shavings of grey touching his ears and the nape of his neck. He was very smartly dressed, in a sober style that gave him an old school air, but not quite. His face was slow to break into a smile, while he talked about various deals, returns, and general opportunities yet unconquered. He was keen to show Nat a site he was putting together, and enthused about companies and stock options like a man going fishing. He dangled the bait, while not discussing the hook. They had other meetings after that, and eventually a company was set up, Mainstay Holdings, with a large lump sum from Nat. The shares were equally held by the two men, while a development freehold was supplied by O' Hagan. Things went well from the beginning. The returns were spectacular, other deals and flips took place with assets being acquired along the way. The balance sheets shone like torches piercing the darkness, and with this optimism, the loan ratios grew higher.

Nat would later inject his office holdings into his own wholly-owned subsidiary of the company for tax reasons, leaving only long- term land holdings and his house in Darwin and flat in Sydney in his name. It seemed to be working well with O'Hagan, who was the driving force, as CEO and Nat as director of a growing number of limited liability companies. Nat spent more time in Darwin, staying in touch mainly by 'phone, with occasional visits. O'Hagan had worked on the pitch of rising inflation, higher borrowing and more deals with more profit. What followed had flowed into wealth creation, like a continual, glinting waterfall.

The election of 1972 changed everything. The coalition government, which had enjoyed 23 successive years of power and was the longest running government in Australia's history, gave way to an unexpected win by Labour, who took power with a slim majority of nine seats. Gough Whitlam and his party had felt the mood of the country, and with his humour and oratory prowess, squeezed into power under the banner of quality of life issues; health care, education, and urban development. The cost of such wide-ranging changes, both economic and social, were to have unforeseen consequences.

There were times when Nat wondered about the full depth of Frank O'Hagan's business interests and what his partner was really into. He had found out more when, on one of his visits to Sydney, he had taken O'Hagan's girlfriend, Jessica, a tall, blonde woman, out sailing. He had invited them both out for the day, but O'Hagan was far too busy and seemed completely indifferent.

Nat remembered how Jess had arrived in a German-branded sports car, with the hood down, sunglasses balanced on her head, the radio giving good and loud, and with a smile that would hit a camera. She had no idea about sailing, but seemed just happy to be out on the water with him. She talked a lot, giving trailers, hints, stories, all creating a kaleidoscopic image of Frank as an acquisitive, driven man, who collected assets like a boy collects cigarette cards. Nat, in return, told her how he was teaching his neighbour and his disabled son to understand and sail the boat, and how much pleasure they all got out of sailing in the harbour. The conversation between them was easy, fluid and enjoyable. Nat made her laugh and encouraged her to talk about her life, and how she had come to be living in this part of Australia, but he was carefully vague about his own. They talked about the 'old country' and how much better their lives were since they left. It seemed only natural that they should arrange another day out.

Nat's association with Frank continued, even under difficult and changing economic conditions. Then the oil crisis forced the early recession of 1974 and unemployment doubled during the year. It must have been a struggle for O'Hagan to hold it all together, just to stay afloat with wages and prices out of control, but he kept most of the bad news under wraps. Nat took these times in his stride, believing that the essential framework to the business was sound, and like a ride on the speedway track, they would skid their way over the rough corners.

But he had not counted on the cyclone at the end of that year. The newspapers, at home and across the world, were full of it.

It was probably that first weather forecast most people had remembered, maybe for its bland almost monotone delivery on the Territory TV and radio station. People there have a subconscious take of the Territory and its people.

Most of them weren't born there, but came to see themselves as frontiersmen and women, compared to their city- dwelling countrymen from the other capital cities. Up there at the Top End it may have been its geographical isolation that bred the 'I can take it, I can do it' attitude. The message by the forecasters earlier in that fateful December of 1974 was that cyclone Selma would hit the outskirts of Darwin. It did, in fact, pass to the north and brought no more than extraordinarily heavy wind and rain.

When the next forecast came around with the announcement of cyclone Tracy on December 20, people were caught out, thinking of Christmas and, as it had not been too bad last time, most people just prepared as best they could.

It was late on Christmas Eve when the rains and the winds came, growing to its full destructive force overnight through into that fateful Christmas Day. The cyclone was forecast to pass some 60 miles to the west of Darwin, with the eye of the storm expected to pass right over an unoccupied area known as Rum Jungle, further west. It was not accurate enough. The wet season brought its share of hard rains, driven by thunderous winds lashing the area, but shuttered buildings always prevailed in the past and even those strong winds didn't seem to upset the rhythms of their existence. This time it was different. The screaming force built upon the initial thunderstorm seemed to arrive like a wall falling on a single person, but this monster covered the city with its destructive force wrapping it in a maelstrom of ferocity.

That evening, Nat had been at the home of neighbours at Fannie Bay, near the sailing club. Had it been a summer's day, they would have enjoyed an open, beautiful view, but as the winds increased in the early part of the evening, that view was closed out by the recently locked shutters. Just one window was left open at the back of the house, to act as a ventilator for air compression. His friends suggested he should stay over. They had a basement, which would be useful if the weather became much worse, but they all thought this was unlikely. Alcohol and bravado were more evident than nerves, but that all changed by the middle of the evening, when the sound of the wind lifted to another gear. Other noises interfered, the drifting of trash bins and loose items that hadn't been put away. Later, the building shrieked as the wind really started to flex its muscles, the living room shutters tore away and the large glass pane was sucked out, its sound was on them, only to be instantly drowned by the scream of the wind.

It was Bob's voice, giving a command that his wife and Nat heard before the wind took them too.

'Basement, now. Crawl.'

They made it to the hall and the steps down, just as the power faltered, flickered, then went out. A flashlight beam cut across the single room.

'Don't worry, we're well stocked down here. Batteries, flash lights, tins of food, water. Not much comfort, but we'll rough it out.'

Nat could see Bob was grinning, but it didn't fool him. Bob was scared, his wife Joanne was already petrified, her face was off-white like the under belly of a squid. He looked round the large room, there wasn't much there;

an old sofa, a table littered with essentials, two deckchairs and a battery operated transistor radio. There was a large pile of wet-weather sailing gear on top of folded sheeting and assorted junk.

Bob picked up the radio to turn it on, only to hear massive interference on the airwaves.

'Where does that go to?' shouted Nat, pointing to a bolted door.

'Outside steps, up to a second set of flat doors, then out....' The rest was lost. 'I'm going to check upstairs...'

They opened the hall door at the top of the stairs, the air seemed to suck Bob through the gap.

'When I bang on the door, you let me in, OK?'

'Stay here, it's too dangerous to go out.'

'It's my house... it's all we've got.'

The door slammed shut, the bolts were rammed home. That was the last they saw of Bob.

Holding out a set of wet weather clothes to Joanne, Nat said:

'Here, put these on while we can, we must stay warm.'

She wriggled into them silently, then curled herself into the foetal position on the sofa and as the minutes passed and the hours turned, Joanne took on the quiet terror of a woman on the edge.

The radio signal was poor and intermittent. It was of little use anyway, as they knew by now that this maelstrom was very close. Nat did his best to wrap the throw from the sofa around Joanne, preparing the plastic tarpaulin so it could be pulled over and round them quickly if needed. She pulled it over her own head, trying to isolate herself from what was happening. Nat put an arm around her, continually leaning close to talk to her, trying to keep her calm.

The batteries ran out around 3am, and the darkness intensified the other noises as the cyclone reached for its own intensity. The smashing, the grinding of metal, and the terrifying shriek of the wind - it seemed ever louder when the low flat doors to the outer steps were ripped away. The outside cellar door held as the wind forced its way through every gap to whistle and screech at fever pitch in the basement.

Nat looked at the luminous dial of his watch again. It was 4.25, he reckoned the hurricane must be reaching its height. It had to break, and break soon. Without any warning, the deadening of a tumultuous crash immediately above them happened, like an intensified car smash in a split second, cut off by further orchestration of the winds and rain. It was a new noise, so loud to start, but in a second, it seemed to be cut off, before water began to seep through the floors into the basement.

Then the torrential, hammering rain began draining steadily into their prison, covering the entire floor. Nat presumed the roof had gone, he would later discover the whole story. Water was continually running in rivulets through the floor joints and the light sockets. Holding tight to Joanna, he heard her say: 'We're going to die…' It was a statement, not a question. He leaned close to her wrapped body, and said:

'I'm with you, I will keep you safe. We will make it. Hold on.'

By the time daylight came, the main force of the cyclone had passed, leaving the butt and the teaming rains. At just after 8, Nat crossed the basement with water splashing round his ankles and unbolted the door to the outside staircase. Pushing it hard, it partially cleared some of the concrete step before jamming. An aluminium step ladder had buckled itself behind the door with others debris. Raising and bending his knee, he lashed out through the narrow gap, kicking the steps before again forcing the door with his shoulder. It gave more space and he was through. The rain and wind slashed and tore at him as he ripped away the debris from the steps. Climbing slowly and nervously until his hands were on the edge of the parapet, he raised himself on tiptoe, not knowing what he might see. He was confronted with a scene he could not possibly have imagined; a landscape that had been smashed, and thrown away by a force as powerful as the very hand of nature. Nothing other than the road itself, as far as he could see, was left unscathed. The scattered remains of what had been his city lay before him. He stared without blinking with his mouth falling slowly open in absolute disbelief at nature's own cataclysm.

The heavy rain fell monotonously, soaking his hair and running down his face, making him spit water at his feet. His hair fell across his face and with the flat of his palm, he brushed it away and continued to stare. This time, the shock was less but the full realisation was stark. Every single building he could see had succumbed to the monumental force of the cyclone. The entire area had disintegrated and was littered with building debris. The road was impassable, power cables and phone poles were askew or down, sailing boats from the marina were piled in heaps like children's toys. Cars were smashed and dinghies, flung from the sailing club pound, were crushed and scattered in hedges and gardens. Trees were up- rooted. Everywhere he looked, a giant hand had shattered its path through the city, taking with it his house and possessions. He shivered as a sweeping sense of good fortune came over him. He had survived. Returning to the basement, he pulled the hood of his jacket over his head and secured it with a single yank of the toggle. Taking Joanne gently by the elbow, he eased her upright from the sofa and gently put his arms around her.

'It's OK, it's OK now…. It's over, we made it.'

She gave no response, the look of terror had been replaced with a confused and blank expression. She was sweating heavily, and had at some stage completely lost control of her bladder and wet herself. Nat steered her towards the steps.

'Don't be frightened by the devastation, we are the lucky ones, we made it…' She turned her head towards him. 'Where's Bob?' Nat paused:

'I don't know, I don't know where he is… yet.'

They made their way out of the basement, and stepped past the remains of Nat's house. They stopped further down the road to pick up a sodden photo of a young family, laughing and entwined in each other's arms. It was from another place, another time. He had no idea who they were but, for some reason, pushed the photo into his inside jacket pocket. The wind was on their backs now as the gradient of the road decreased slightly. There was no reason to look back… to what was.

Nat eventually found refuge for them both in a rear store of a partially damaged clothing shop. They were among other survivors, and they were dry. Later, the scavenging started for water, tinned food and any means of communication.

80% of city devastated – population evacuated

The records show that winds were officially recorded at 217 kilometres per hour and cyclone Tracy was among the most destructive ever to hit Australia. Records have identified the 71 names of individuals who perished as a result of the cyclone and many more were injured. Around 80% of Darwin's buildings were destroyed or suffered severe damage, and all public services – communications, power, water and sewerage – were severed.

Rescue, recovery and reconstruction were organised by emergency committees established to deal with items such as clothing, communications, evacuation, food, law and order, sanitation and health and social welfare. The defence forces played a major role in cleaning up the city and suburbs. With essential services all severed, and with food and shelter at a premium, many Darwin people were evacuated.

In the week that followed the cyclone, Darwin's population was reduced from 47,000 to little more than 10,000. Many of those injured and traumatised by events never went back, and for the next six months, access to the city was regulated by a permit system. The Whitlam government established a reconstruction commission, which helped to rebuild the city within three years.

Arc of Doubt

2

Nat, Sydney. 1975

It was almost two weeks before the full realisation of Nat's position became abundantly clear. He had decided to decamp to Sydney from Darwin on the resettlement evacuation programme, offering to share his home with an evacuee family. These plans had fallen through at the last minute, when they were offered help by a family down the track at Katherine.

His priority was to arrange a meeting with Frank O' Hagan, to assess the current status of all the companies they were involved in together. His interim calls from outside Darwin had first met with concern and the repeated message: 'Don't worry about anything, we're in touch with the insurance companies and mortgagors down this end, it's all in hand.'

But as he found out on his arrival in Sydney, nothing happened. No loss adjusters had contacted him at his home there either. His first call from Sydney to O'Hagan, when it was finally answered, produced only prevarication. Finally, a call was not returned, which felt like being stranded at low tide with the growing panic of an incoming sea.

Nat was awake early, having slept badly. Just before 6 and, without a shower or shave, he left the house quietly. As he walked, he stuffed his shirt tail haphazardly into his trousers before tightening his belt, his mind by then focusing clearly on his course of action. On his signal, a passing cab turned circle in the already growling street which was starting to fill rapidly with the city's journeymen. The back door was level with his thigh as he reached to open it and slide in on the bench seat. The cab driver had already hit the meter.

'Where to, pal?'

'Ah, corner of Sycamore and Corinth Roads on the city edge.'

Settling back, he felt the pull of the vehicle, 15 minutes should do it.

'Well, what do you think of Whitlam's latest daft idea then…?'

Nat shut the driver down.

'Today of all days, I have a lot on my mind, thanks.'

He shut his eyes and pulled his briefcase close, to be sure that he wouldn't forget it. The taxi pulled up outside the office campus block. Nat paid with a note, and thanked the driver; barely seeing him. He walked up the steps to the plate glass doors. The lights blazed, but the doors were securely locked. The noise of his turning the polished steel handle brought a stout security guard from another quarter. With a flick of the wrist, Nat saw it was just on 6.45.

The guard stood before the glass doors, saying: 'Yes?'

'Hi. I'm early, to see Frank O'Hagan'

'He got in early today. Around six. If you hang on, I'll ring up. He might take the call. I'm only doing night watch, not day staff.'

Nat saw the guard flit around the edge of the desk, lift the phone and start talking almost immediately. He waved an arm gesticulating while he listened, then the phone went down. He opened two locks and let Nat in before re -locking the door. 'His offices are…' He was cut off.

'Yeah, thanks, I know my way.'

Striding fast towards the staircase, Nat's words fell away behind him. In under two minutes he was standing in the foyer, in front of Frank, who was attempting to greet him with an outstretched hand.

'Hello Nat, come on in… .'

He wasn't smiling and Nat avoided the handshake.

Nat walked down the broad corridor and into the large office on his left. The scene that greeted him was a confusion of papers, files, documents and unopened mail covering the desk and a large part of the floor. There was a stale smell in the office, that unwashed, unventilated odour that clung heavily to the edge of your nostrils.

Nat stood in front of the desk, turning sideways a little: 'Frank, what the fuck is going on here? Insurance for the wipe out in Darwin, that cyclone, why haven't we heard anything yet? Where are the list of schedules for your group policy? Let's start with that, and why didn't you call me back? You've been avoiding me, haven't you?'

There was no immediate reply.

Then Frank started quietly: 'There is a problem with the cover. They are saying the portfolio has been over-valued and under-insured and they are holding back. They are in discussions with our lenders about other matters.'

'What?'

Incredulity had crept into Nat's voice.

'There's no reason for them to do that, unless… what is really going on here, what have you been doing behind my back?'

The tempo changed as Frank said: 'When the going was good, you took the money. Lots of it. Well, times have changed. If interest rates continue rising as they are, and we can't find buyers in this rapidly falling market, we're all fucked.'

Nat's mind was racing now. He was feeling unsteady. This was a bigger mess than he'd thought.

'God, what about my personal holdings. All the figures I sent down were kosher, professional valuations....'

He was met with another silence.

'… You bastard, you tampered with those figures as well?'

Frank wasn't looking at him. He turned to retrieve a file from among the many on the floor.

'It's in there. Check for yourself.'

He dropped the file onto the crowded desk, spilling its contents as he did so.

'You told me it was on a block policy…?'

'Yeah well, it wasn't, it's more complicated than that.'

Frank's lies, deceits and half-truths looked like they were heading for a tail spin.

'You're like a floating mine. You've destroyed me haven't you?'

Frank stood ready, feet and arms braced, and more than ready to handle the outburst he was expecting. Then he took another tack, and started moving again, talking faster this time and waving his arms about as he explained.

'The oil crisis did it, and that bloody cyclone canned it all. Whitlam doesn't have a clue how to stop this spiral. Your assets, land and all. Now the arse has fallen out of all of that. Insurance… huh…. they'll hold that up for years. Our joint stock holdings in the companies have run out of funds, they're illiquid, we can't service the loans now. Very soon they'll fold into insolvency. If you were half sensible, you've already taken a load of cash out and put it somewhere safe. In your case, it's just been luck – good and bad – and a few years. For me, shit....it's a lifetime's work and struggle. I've got too much to lose and I never had, or wanted, a plan B. I'll fight with everything I've got to hold on and I'll never let this go, so help me.'

His voice had raised its pitch until he was almost shouting. Then he finally stopped. Nat felt there was little point in carrying on with this. He was angry and completely unprepared for the cover up of a catastrophe that had exploded like this.

'Best thing is, I'll take some independent advice and we'll be in touch.'

He didn't trust himself to say more. Picking up the file and its spilled contents from the desk, together with his briefcase, he walked out, stopping only to speak to the security guard who was just finishing his shift.

'How many of the floors and suites in this block are occupied now, other than Mr O'Hagan's enterprises?'

'Ah, that's easy enough … just one. Campions, behind us on the ground floor.'

He jerked his thumb over his shoulder.

'I started here last year, when six floors were occupied. Now there's only two.'

'I have been up with Mr O'Hagan, how many people work in his office? A dozen or more?'

'Oh no, three. There used to be many more... but things are getting bad around here.'

Nat smiled as best he could, to look encouraging, then left the building. It was almost two years later when the dust started to settle. Nat had tried everything to hold the business together, but he was facing bankruptcy. On his last evening in Sydney, having taken a late bus south to Sydney Cove Passenger Terminal, he set about walking the last mile and a half to Gregson's Boatyard. A black sky held ready with rain, the dark evening dark was tinged with artificial light. He stopped at the edge of the yard and sat slouched on a street bench.

Sliding his shoulder bag off and placing it on his knees, he rummaged around until he found the paper bag containing some sandwiches. He looked up to see a woman with a young man not ten paces from him, her grocery bag had started to split, spilling cans and packets into the street. The young man stood helpless and slack armed, like a child, as she scrabbled with her collection. Nat saw her eyes moving like a wary animal, frightened for her mistake and its possible consequences.

'Can I help?'

The woman nodded.

Nat carried on: 'I have another a bag here. You can have it.'

He produced one from the side netting of his small backpack. A weak smile appeared across her pale features as Nat walked towards her. It was then that he saw the man had tears escaping from his eyes, and he was smearing them with the sleeve of his sweatshirt.

'Are you ok?'

'No... not really, got dumped by my girlfriend about two months ago. Yesterday I was told I've got stage three lung cancer. I don't even smoke, do I? Where's the fair in that? All the love and money in the world won't change a thing. I've been served notice. It's more certain than death row. Without my sister here, I would have done myself in already.'

Shocked, Nat watched him as the distance between them lengthened a little. The 'thanks' was said without a look, an emptiness seemed around them all. Then the pair walked away towards the Edinburgh Road junction, opposite dock gate four. He could just hear their quiet utterances. Their story, their lives bore such a contrast to his own.

Straightening himself, he drew a deep breath, allowing the air to escape slowly. His salutary lesson over the last few months had a sanguine effect on him. After checking the time on his watch, he quickened his pace. He didn't want to be late. The sailboat skipper would leave on the turn of the high tide, whether Nat was there or not.

Arc of Doubt

Part Five

1

Jessica, Melbourne. 1969

The Fairsail was one of the Raymac line's last vessels to be contracted to take immigrants on their assisted passage route from England to Australia. The older troopship, nearly 23,000 tons, had been extensively converted 12 years earlier. It had been given a new diesel electric engine to power 1,500 passengers and 400 crew at up to 16 knots to transport another generation halfway around the world. Gone were are the old, cramped dormitories and in came comfortable cabins, air conditioning throughout, with a swimming pool on the stern deck among many other improvements. It was luxury that a generation of people, having grown up with post-war austerity, could hardly believe.

Travel was something people only read about... and here was Jessica, having a cruise that had already called in at Naples, Port Said, Colombo, Fremantle and the next stop was Melbourne. She sat on the bottom bunk in the cabin she had shared with three other single women for five weeks, fingering the last cigarette in the flip top packet before clicking the chromium lighter for the leaping flame. She took a long draw, then dropped the lighter into the open bag beside her and idly scratched her thigh. She had realised for some time that this new start was not going to be the honey spoon it had been made out to be in the adverts. Fortunately, the monotonous round of deck walks with hide and seek thrown in, to avoid 'those that had to be avoided', were over. Sitting in a striped canvas deckchair with matching sun shades, reading yet another book, only to look occasionally between the white rails at a flat blue sea had soon begun to get through to her.

Leaning forward, she took the last draw near the filter, coughing as the heat from the smoke changed. When the coughing died back, she reached to crush out the stub in the wall ash tray, leaving only scattered sparks. The door handle turned but didn't open immediately. She heard a raised voice, and when the door opened, the full view of one of her room mates, Jen, was filling the door frame.

'God, if I see those two Hanson brats after I get off, I swear I'll strangle them...'

'What have they been up to now?'

'Oh you know, rude little devils, calling names. The smaller one just called me Miss Fat Legs. I tried to give him a thick ear but he was too quick, the little sod just stood there poking his tongue out at me.'

Jess laughed, as Jen slightly screwed her eyes up as she talked.

'Hardly surprising, when you see their Mum and Dad. They don't care about the kids… give us a fag will you?'

Perhaps it was the smell of Virginia tobacco that hung in the cabin that produced this request, but it made no difference. Jess just smiled, showing the empty packet, inwardly pleased that she was out of cigarettes, because Jen was always on the cadge.

Brushing her hair behind her ear with a finger, she stood up, then looked at her watch, moving it slightly with her other hand to adjust it on her wrist. It was 10.20.

'Sorry, Jen, I've got to go. I've not done half the things I'm supposed to have done.'

She slipped passed her roommate, down the narrow corridors, past endless cabin doors to the stairs that led to number two deck. When the representatives of the Commonwealth Bank had come on board at Fremantle, she had been one of the first to open an account. She had transferred the 170 English Pounds into her new bank account with confidence, knowing that having food provided on the voyage, she had spent very little of her savings.

Reaching the deep alcove at the bottom of the stairs, Jess joined the queue for the immigration cards, shuffling forward among the couples and families until she reached the Immigration Officer at the round, Formica-topped table. He seemed to rest up a bit after the family in front, by leaning back on the long upholstered bench that ran round the alcove.

He leaned back, folded his arms briefly, then removed his glasses and polished the glass with slow deliberate movements on his handkerchief, before returning them to his face. As Jess looked at yet another grey-suited man fingering forms, it occurred to her briefly that a woman could have done this job just as well. But they were never given the chance.

She slid her passport towards him slowly, while waiting for his response. He lunged forward with a swinging motion, sweeping up three forms. Then holding them together between his fingers and thumbs, tapped them gently on the table to bring them neatly together.

'Just fill this in here, passport number and answer some straightforward questions,' he said, smiling at her.

She noted his fleshy fingers as they slid the form towards her across the table, covering some light, straight, slicing knife marks, no doubt left carelessly by some long- gone sandwich maker.

'… and pop it in the box … '

Extending his right arm, with the biro wedged firmly in his writing fingers, he pointed at a varnished box that had been fixed temporarily against the bottom handrail. He pretended not to be looking too closely when he handed her the blue and white luggage label…but he was.

'Name on that one, it's got your hostel address on it, make certain it's firmly fixed or …'

His voice dropped away, leaving the obvious unsaid. She slid the blue patterned label with its waxen string deep into one of the front pockets of her tight jeans. Again he was watching her over his glasses, although he tried to smother his interest with a vague smile. Moving on towards the ship's theatre, she heard a door slam. It registered, but she didn't look; and weaving between the loose groups and stragglers, Jess passed towards the aft of the ship where medicals for those leaving the next day were being carried out. Being captive to the low ceilings in the corridors and function rooms, the sounds of voices all joined in amplification. There were more queues, and snatches of conversation came to her, blown over the heads of others.

'Will the doctor make me take my clothes off?'

'What about the X-Rays I had done?'

'How long is this going to…?'

Eventually, she stood before the doctor. The cold pressing mark of his stainless steel stethoscope dabbed against her in several places. He asked:

'Any infectious diseases while on board? May I just look at your arms? Let's see, ah, yes inoculations all done … negative on chest X-Ray, just your blood pressure then.'

Jess sat on a single folding slatted seat. Details went against her name, as the pen moved on a clipboard, and then she moved away, finished. The tannoy clipped in, a two tone bleep with its announcement. 'Good afternoon, Ladies and Gentlemen. The ship is cruising at around 16 knots south of Portland Point with an estimated arrival in Port Philip Bay late morning tomorrow. Those leaving the ship at Melbourne must ensure their baggage is packed and labelled and deposited in the baggage department at the rear of the ship before disembarkation. Stewards are on hand to help. The canteen is now open for lunch until 2pm.Thank you.'

Something gave, far away in her mind, into auto suggestion. Jess diverted in the direction of the canteen, following the herd. The aromas came before the vista.

More queues. Taking an aluminium tray, she placed it noisily on the rails in front of the hot food cabinets. Shuffling forwards, pushing the tray, it slid easily making only a low rasping sound, before stopping in front of the heated plate glass. Behind this lay large aluminium dishes, sunk into a holding position and colour filled with a variety of food. Chips were always hard to pass, so she didn't.

'What can I get you today?' chimed the woman in front of her wearing a white apron. Only a measured, single smeared finger wipe lay on the crisp, laundered apron, near its centre. The smell of the culinary mix was heavy and full. Dabbing her finger at several items, Jess asked:

'Sausages, chips, gravy and peas please … and, oh tea, a large tea please.'

The movement of the serving spoon held her attention, as it swept the sausages with the onion sauce onto a heavy white china plate, then the other items joined it. They were placed with a short swinging motion, tapping first then with a fuller sound as the plate was put on the glass shelf above the open cabinet. It banged the glass with a scratching sound.

Jess retrieved it.

The plate felt warm in her hand as she moved towards the tea urn, vaguely wondering again how uncomfortable and tiring it must be working in the galleys. But even before she'd reached the urn, her compassion for the kitchen staff had vanished. She placed her cup under the spout to take the gush, stepping back quickly as it splashed up in the bottom of the cup.

Turning, she surveyed the rest of the café, stopping at an elderly couple. The woman had her glasses on the end of her nose, and she scoffed at some remark from her beleaguered husband, then, using her middle finger, she shoved the glasses further up the bridge of her nose and returned to her reading. Jess moved on to a heavy, middle- aged, balding man with a thick beard, wearing a black T- shirt bearing The Barbary Coast on it, and a long tattoo on his forearm. What was that about, she thought, perhaps, it was a mid-life cry for attention, or for the last threads of a vanished youth.

Then she saw a vacant table and moved quickly towards it. Placing the tray on a table for two, she put her laden plate in front of her. Picking up the knife and fork, and with the blade of the knife on one of the sausages with just enough pressure to hold it, she pierced the skin with the fork, watching the sight of the clear juices escaping. She angled the sausage to enable the knife to slip between the prongs of the fork, and with a deft movement she slit the sausage open, end to end. English mustard was liberally applied using a tiny spoon. Raising her head like a grazing animal, she began the refuelling process. Then she deftly wiped her mouth with the paper serviette.

Johnny Manners was one of the few men about her age on the boat, other than most of the stewards, who claimed they weren't married. He slowed to stop at her table. 'Hi Jess, may I join you?'

'Be my guest.'

The chair grated as he drew it back, then after placing the tray in front of himself, he leant forwards to speak. But that didn't happen, because his elbow turned the plate's contents straight into his lap. Jess's open hand covered her mouth, trying to conceal laughter.

Finishing her tea with a single swallow, she stood, touched his elbow saying: 'Poor old Johnny, next time....'

She made her way back down the corridors to her cabin to finish her packing and preparations. Down two decks, the air conditioning was fighting the engines and only just winning.

She could feel the dampness spreading between her breasts, and her scalp was starting to prickle with sweat. The sooner she was done with packing and depositing the suitcase, the sooner she could shower and have the luxury of washing her hair for the last time on this boat.

Opening the door, she was immediately aware of the cramped activity of Jen's and 'old Margarine's' voices, with the thin tinny sound of a cheap transistor radio pumping out pop music. Marge was much older and rounder. She was about 40 and Jess thought she would be single forever, having seen her climb up to her top bunk for the past five weeks. It was a sight not to be forgotten. The cursing, the heaving, plus the occasional accident. How the bunks remained fixed to the bulkhead she didn't know.

It was Marge's round, red face that turned to greet her with her mop of unfashionably wiry hair that reminded Jess of Jinks, the long- haired terrier that lived at the end of the road where she grew up. It ate, slept and lived in the yard and looked like it, no kids went near it. Marge was kneeling on the floor in front of a large, pale, speckled suitcase with reinforced corners and with a stretch band around the lid, struggling to get it shut. She was about to speak when Jess said: 'Oh, you two are hard at it ... I'll give you more space and be back in half an hour or so. It'll give you both more room.'

With that, she reversed into the corridor, closed the door and let out a slow breath. Putting her arm through the loop of her handbag and pushing it casually to her shoulder, she headed up the stairs, making a direct course for the main reception on A Deck. There was, as always, a crowd of people in the reception area, milling about talking. She joined the queue and eventually approached the sliding glass windows of the reception office. It doubled as a small shop selling toiletries, tobacco, sweets and other small useful items, as well as an office.

'.. 20 Rothmans and a packet of Dr Whites please.'
The receptionist turned away, picking up first the
cigarettes from a back cabinet and then, with a rustle,
the sanitary towels were put inside a plain white paper
bag. While she was doing this, Jess extracted a dollar
note and some loose change from her purse and
carefully placed the money on the counter. As she did,
she took in the picture of The Queen and what
appeared to be rather poor drawings of a wallaby and
an emu that looked as though they were dancing
around a coat of arms. The sweep of a hand broke her
view, then looking up, she heard the receptionist say in
what seemed a rather patronising tone: 'Well done,
correct.'

Jess turned away, clutching the paper bag and her
cigarettes. Heading out through the heavy door onto the
narrowing deck-space at number two life boat station,
she found a slatted bench out of the breeze. She had
spent months looking forward to arriving in Australia, and
she was now so close. Scanning the sea, she saw how it
carried its deep, dark blue on the roll, giving the illusion
of gently running towards her destination. Her two
closest friends on the trip had left the ship at Fremantle,
leaving their forwarding addresses, but time would
probably be its own eraser.

Using her nail, she picked at the thin red edge of the
cellophane around her cigarette packet before pulling it
off from around the centre. The wind whipped it from her
fingers and took it on an uneven drift. She removed the
silver paper inside the packet, screwed it to a tiny ball
between her finger and thumb, and dropped it into her

handbag before extracting a cigarette. This was smoked in the quiet of her own thoughts.

Using her thumb and centre finger, she flicked the glowing butt of her cigarette over the rail, watching it go, until it caught the breeze. Leaning forward a little, gripping the edges of the bench alongside her, she breathed the sea air deep into her lungs. Tomorrow was the day. It was very close now. Turning her wrist, the white face of the Timex watch showed it was ten minutes to three. She made her way back down to the cabin. This time it was cleared and empty. Taking her suitcase from the end of the bunk beds, she opened it in the middle of the room and filled it quickly and efficiently, leaving out just her shower stuff and the clothes needed for the next day.

She closed and locked the case with a tiny key and firmly attached the baggage label to the handle, and set off to take it to the baggage area. It was heavier than she expected, and she managed to carry it along the long stretch to the central gangway before allowing it to drag to the floor. Stopping for a rest, she briefly wondered if one day suitcases would have their own wheels. After checking the label was secure, she waited in the baggage queue. She glanced down at the label again, and the single word leapt up to her... AUSTRALIA. She had made it. After just one more night's sleep, she would be in this new country.

The voice of a steward brought her back to now.

'May I take that for you?'

'Thank you'

She fell away from the queue, and he moved on.

Up on the central deck, she clutched the colourful shoulder bag she had bought in Port Said. It contained just a few overnight things, her personal items and documents. Finding space on a bench, with her back to the steelwork, she looked past the row of people at the rail to the narrowing distance across Port Philip bay. Then she noticed an overweight man in a tight jacket nearby. She watched him only briefly as he screwed his forefinger into his nose scraping at the contents surreptitiously, wiping it on the underside of the rail.

Like the animal he was, his head then swivelled in both directions as though to be certain no-one was watching his compulsion. Opening her bag, she found the lighter first, and with her head lowered she scrabbled in the deeper regions for the cigarettes. Before she could locate her packet, the man said: 'Please, have one of these?'

He was a few years older than her, an open face, happy looking in a lopsided way, with a hair line that had started to recede. His smile lasted.

'That's very kind, thank you.'

She lifted it to her lips, swept her hair from her face and cupped the lighter for him. Their heads came close briefly.

'Nearly there now.'

He looked at her first, before starting to talk.

'If I'm honest, I'm bloody nervous, I suppose it's the unknown … leaving the ship... lack of confidence...I'm wondering if this was the right decision after all.'

'Nerves. Once we get going, it will all be different.'

'After that discussion with the Good Neighbours welcoming group yesterday, it sounds like it's all primroses and pineapples. It makes me deeply suspicious that a brutal awakening is not far away. Perhaps we'll find out at that migrant camp we'll be shipped off to, half- way to Sydney. I think they called it the Surmina Migrant Training Centre or something. There's talk leaking back about that place.'

'What do you mean?'

He carried on, skidding over her question.

'It's north of Melbourne, a fair way north, we'll all be herded on trains. I'm not sure I like the sound of it. And then there's the White Australia policy. They've been taking only white Europeans since the War, but I heard it's going to end. Asia has started knocking on the door asking if they can come to the beach too, and we could be swamped.'

He paused, this time with his head tilted sideways as though to invite response.

'You're crazy… for Christ's sake this is 1969…'

Jess stood up, realising she had made a bad judgement call by talking to him. Waving an arm towards the direction of land, she said:

'Look out there…it's our future. I have every intention of being among the front runners one way or another. The waves may break over us, but I'm going to keep on swimming. I've come a hell of long way in my life so far, and I'm not going back, or down. I'm going up.'

She went back to her cabin and, after a last meal with her room mates, slept in her bunk for the last time. She woke early, put on a floral print dress, picked up her wash bag, towel and underclothes and headed out down the corridor to the ladies' washrooms. One of the three showers was vacant, and with three neat steps she was inside the cubicle with the door bolted.

Dumping her bag and towel on the pine seat, she removed her dress and hung it carefully on the wire hanger that had been left on the back of the door. The wooden duckboards beneath her feet were still wet from the last occupant.

A flick of the chromium handle was all that was need to bring the warm water to a light spray. She tested it with an upward palm, then stepped under the water. Standing absolutely still for a short while, she allowed the water to cover all of her body. She used her fingers as a comb to flick her hair over her shoulders, and grabbed the Vosene shampoo; then soaped and rinsed herself.

Eventually, and almost reluctantly, she got out the shower and dried herself carefully, before putting on her pants. Then, looping her bra around herself, she did the clasps up and with a swift, well- practised movement, twisted it around. Somewhere, from the depth of her bag, she located a red plastic brush and tilting her head to each side in turn brushed away the tangles and swept her hair over her shoulders to dry.

She was aware of the soft smell of the deodorant as she rolled it on with a quick, double stroke. The dress followed, and she felt back for the zip. With her shoulder bag re-packed, she drew back the bolt, allowing the door to swing open. Breakfast in the canteen was busy and noisier than usual, as the sense of excitement spread among the passengers. Later, a crackle broke in on the tannoy, like the sound of rustling paper, and everyone stopped talking to listen.to the announcement.

'Disembarkation for Melbourne will begin soon,' said a clear voice with an English accent. 'Those leaving the ship will be directed towards Station Pier Terminal. All baggage can be collected after customs clearance.'

The voice went on. Immigration papers, contraband, taxable goods, quarantine, animal products... and finally it stopped.

Jess made her way to the gangplank, descending steadily and pausing part way at the significance of these few steps. She felt she was diving into a vibrant coloured world of opportunity. It reached for her, enveloping her with the blanket of optimism, washing away her nerves and sweeping her along the same path as hundreds of thousands before her. During the next few months, reality struck hard. The migrant training centre was housed in accommodation blocks that had originally been an army base during the war. There were multiple rows of very basic timber framed huts, and although they were lined now, they were sparsely and cheaply furnished, with communal washhouses and shared latrines.

Both the smell and the flies were memories that would stick with her like those very same fly strip papers that hung from the rafters. The food there was slush, cooked as though it had been held over the heat until all the goodness and form had given up and departed. There was constant tension, as most of the so-called residents were Italian, Greek and German, and were unable to speak the language of their new country, English.

All their frustrations turned to demonstrations against the authorities, and on one Tuesday morning it spilled over into violence. Police beat people down with truncheons, indiscriminately trying to take out those they saw as ringleaders.

Then things got completely out of hand, a small group of men splintered into a classroom and set it on fire. Several people were injured, some seriously. Fire trucks had difficulty in accessing the area before they could contain, and then extinguish, the flames.

Until then, Jess had been drafted in to help with the English tutorials while waiting for what she hoped would be a good starting job in Victoria. This episode changed her mind. Using her own money, she bought a one-way train ticket to Sydney, checked into a women's hostel and took the first job she could get, working as a receptionist at a garage. Within 12 months she was selling cars from the lot like a pro, her progress helped along by sleeping occasionally with the boss's son, Neil. In no time, this married man was like a yoyo at the end of her string. Somehow though, she never seemed to get it right with men. He could guarantee her promotion, but little else.

Her new life had taken on a settled base. She rented a flat on the North Side, she felt good about this new county, and there was a sense of optimism that came up with the sun.

Arc of Doubt

2

Jessica, Sydney. 1972

The first time she saw Frank O'Hagan, although only briefly, was as the winter of 1972 was beginning. It was a wet day, heavy with thundery showers. She had no umbrella, so she turned her collar up and wore a newspaper for head cover as she ducked into Lorenzo's sidewalk café. He was talking quietly at end of the counter to a grey- haired man she took to be the owner, and was dressed in a smart Italian suit. He then turned and walked confidently out of the café, holding his trench coat.

She asked the woman who brought her coffee who he was. The reply was simple. 'That, is Mr Frank O'Hagan. He owns every other building in this Street.'

Every day for five days, at the same time, Jess came in for coffee - hoping she might see him again, but she didn't. It was the strangeness of fate that, in a city so vastly entangled with life, their paths should cross again three weeks later. That was the day they all went to the races. Jess was with friends, couples mainly, and they had two tables roughly pulled together, covered with the remnants of lunch. Voices were loud, bottles discarded in the middle of the table and there were smears and spills blotching the tablecloth. She had passed around a pack of cigarettes, lighting her own with two others then tossing the box to one of the men at the other side of the table in a playful gesture.

Laughing, while turning her head towards the others, she stopped when she saw that same man from Lorenzo's looking straight at her from the far end of the bar. He was holding a tray of drinks, he stopped mid stride. For that long moment they were locked, her laughter cut out, and his smile started. She responded, then turned back to her celebrating party. But she couldn't resist another look.

He was watching her too, looking up from his group of male friends. All of them were too loud to be sober. Later, when she went to the ladies with one of the other girls he crossed the room and tried to talk to her as though he knew her, positioning himself to split her away from her friend.

'It's OK,' said Jess to her friend.

'I'll catch you up....' And then she turned to face him.

'Hello... It must have seemed rude staring at you like that earlier.... I thought I'd met you before but I was mistaken. My name is Frank, Frank O'Hagan. I wonder if you would like to join me later for a drink, we are going to the members' enclosure soon.'

He spoke slowly, as though he had no doubt she would agree. She didn't reply straight away, she just held him with her eyes. His face was set on the edge of a smile again. He then shifted to a different tack.

'Maybe if you're busy now, perhaps an evening next week?'

She could tell now he was stumbling with his words a little, were his friends watching? Or was it the alcohol she could smell as he leaned a little towards her. 'Um....perhaps...' Jess hung a silence out. Then gave him what he wanted: 'Maybe, as we are both with friends, it would be easier if I just gave you my phone number and you could ring me.'

That was the beginning of it.

He was full on with his chase. Three dates, all at expensive restaurants; picking her up in an Aston Martin, paying her a waterfall of compliments on the way she looked, her style and her sense of fun. He washed away her defences, wore her down. Then, after a night in the casino, he took her home to his penthouse, high above the office quarter of the city.

She took the hand that fed status and wealth, it appealed to her basic instincts. What started as a taster of how the wealthy lived very quickly became addictive, until she thought this was how she wanted to live her life. Frank was absorbed in his business most of the time, working long hours at his office and travelling frequently to meetings.

He seemed capable of negotiating a path with architects and surveyors for the construction of a vast office block in the city and a new house being built on several acres near the sea, while still overseeing everything else. His many staff, or lieutenants as he like to call them, covered many companies, mostly involved in property management.

There were joint developments as well, with complicated deals being done almost daily. His enthusiasm to finish a house for her, after she had moved into his penthouse, was self-evident too. He talked in ever bigger circles. It was a material extravaganza and she surrendered. The forfeit, of course, for her was that intangible thing called love. So far, Jess had never experienced it.

There was a whirlwind of designers, landscape gardeners and builders, as they created a gym, a cinema, a pool, a games room, and all the other rooms. There were endless trucks and deliveries, but Frank left her to it, more and more, and she was exhausted. Once they had moved in, his appearances became more infrequent, and gradually she came to realise the friendless state she was inhabiting with a man she barely knew. He was drinking heavily now, constantly. His mood swings were becoming more erratic, shouting at her and the staff. Then, one day in a particularly vitriolic argument he stepped closer to her, raised his arm and slapped her hard across the face.

She stumbled, shocked; welts rising on her face instantly. Her ears were singing, and she clasped her head. His voice took a pleading note: 'I'm sorry, I'm so sorry … look at me, I didn't mean to do that, I am so sorry please forgive me.'

He reached for her, stroking her and apologising again and again through his tears. She forgave him that first time, but their relationship was like milk on a warm day, it was going to turn sour, sooner or later.

Frank promised to clean up his act and make a real effort to cut down on the booze, but he struggled and he soon slipped back into the same old habits. During the following year, his businesses took on more flow and less ebb. It was around the time he had been introduced to a new investor through his lawyers. Frank told her that they had met at another male-only evening that she would not have wanted to go to.

When this new partner was down from the Territory for a business meeting, Jess was drafted in to add the casual decorative sparkle at lunch the following day. A table had been booked at a restaurant with a striking design that had been crafted around the view, giving it a feeling of space and purpose. Today as always, she had chosen her clothes to please Frank rather than herself and she arrived a few minutes early. She went to the ladies' room, and after touching up her lipstick, she stepped towards the door before giving the mirror a last look.

She decided to take a seat on the small sofa in the foyer, and then looking up at the sound of a familiar voice, she rose to greet the two men. Frank made a ridiculous show of endearment towards her as an opener, and then introduced her to Nat Gibson.

The new investor was unexpectedly young, about the same age as Jess. He was tall, fit-looking and had the slightest hint of a limp. He wore his long hair tied back and had a casual air about him. It was obvious that the lunch was really just a continuation of their earlier business meeting; she was there just to soften the corners from time to time.

The food, of course, was exemplary; the views of the harbour and opera house were outstanding and the table was naturally the best. How it had been booked at such short notice, she had no idea. Nat was engaging, trying to bring and keep her in the flow of conversation. He didn't know Sydney well and when she suggested he saw more of the city before he went back up north in a couple of weeks, he took it as a personal invitation. He looked at Frank, saying:

'I would love that, if of course Frank wouldn't mind. Perhaps he could take some time off too?'

Frank didn't mind at all, or care. Anything that furthered his business interests was acceptable to him and he had no wish to join them. It was already clear to Jess that Frank was the sort of man who just wanted to buy the 'it' of everything. The very act of ownership overpowered him, consumed him... but only until it was brought within his grasp. Then he lost interest. Perhaps it was the same with her. He was insatiable when it came to doing deals. But what was it that drove him on? Was it a deep-rooted sense of failure, or a lack of self-worth from his early life? Jess could never get him to talk about his childhood or his teenage years. She wondered what he was hiding beneath all his acquisitions, which included her.

Even during those early months together, his initial delight in her body had quickly evaporated. Now, he just climbed on and fucked her. If she tried to talk to him, rows quickly escalated and the fear of physical abuse made her feel sick. He had told her, several times, that if she left him, he would find her. He was, and always had been, a bully, who used his power to subdue by fear.

'Well then.'

Jess had been lost in her thoughts and it was Frank's words that brought her back. They were the closure words, lunch was over. A bill was never produced, there must have been an arrangement. Accompanied by the Maître D' they walked out, down the stone steps that left the building and onto the pavement. There were handshakes and the niceties of social convention, then they parted to get into two waiting cabs that had been called.

The relationship between Jess and Frank wore thin after an unexpected pregnancy. The surprise news was at first celebrated, but as Jess grew larger, Frank's interest in her faded. It returned briefly at the birth of a daughter, then disappeared. They lived separate lives, with occasional spats, outright arguments or bouts of violence, which she took silently for the sake of her small daughter, Jamie. The money Frank gave her became irregular, and Jess realised she had to find a way out. Her focus was directed solely to ensure Jamie thrived, and the safety and security of the child became paramount

Eventually though, there was no reason to stay. Jess didn't see Frank for days at a time and when he did come to the house, he was listless and morose. It was clear he was losing a sense of reality and his business affairs were getting complicated.

Callers often came to the house, looking for Frank, but she had no idea where he was most of the time. His staff, complaining they hadn't been paid, began filtering away, and the house and grounds became neglected. One evening in spring, just as the darkness covered the day, Frank arrived back at the house, and during the evening he picked a final and pointless argument. This time, he was too burnt out to raise a hand to Jess, he just went from the house, too drunk to drive but not drunk enough to fall, and drove away.

Within half an hour, Jess had packed two hold-alls, collected her hidden jewellery and checked her purse for cash, then finding a pair of scissors, she cut up the charge cards, throwing the remains into the large white fruit bowl. She found a pen and paper and scribbled out:

'Frank, I have taken Jamie and the keys for the bungalow at Bulli. Don't contact us. We're finished. I want nothing more to do with you.'

The note was left protruding from under the same bowl. Jess couldn't shake him off completely, though. He would turn up at the Bulli place now and then, worn down, then disappear again. He seemed to have lost his passion for business, and for life. Eventually, he stopped coming. What happened to him? She neither knew nor cared.

The next decade, for Jess and Jamie, was calm. Although there wasn't a great deal of cash around, it was a simple, easy way of life. Jess got a job at the nearby canning factory, and Jamie enjoyed going to the local school. She was clearly an intelligent child, and seemed popular with her classmates. There was no hint of the hurricane to come. The teenage years came as a shock, and for Jamie, the rails ran out. Behind the bad behaviour, the anger of youth, and the slamming of doors when she disappeared until morning lay a far greater problem.

Drugs.

Jamie refused to talk to her mother, and would walk out of a room the instant her mother walked in. The school called Jessica in several times to discuss Jamie's difficult and disruptive behaviour, but Jess felt out of her depth. She didn't know how to deal with her daughter and conversations about the importance of passing exams were met with sarcastic laughter or a slammed door. Just how bad things had become really sunk in when Jess returned to the bungalow late one evening after a shift at the factory. Tired and unguarded, she opened the door to be pushed aside by a boy in a black leather jacket, who was shouting:

'Come on, let's get out of here….get out the way Gran…'

And he shoved Jess with the flat of his hand. She stumbled back, arm outstretched to stop a fall and fell over the arm of the sofa just as Jamie emerged from Jess's bedroom. Alarmed, Jess called out:

'What are you doing? Jamie….Jamie..?'

Jamie didn't look in her mother's direction. Her face was taut and desperate as she followed the boy quickly out of the door. Later, Jess realised her precious jewellery box and her watch had been taken from the dressing table.

Most of the jewellery was worth nothing, it was just cheap glass from her life before Frank, but it was the intent that scored the deep furrow. Over the next year, Jamie only returned to the bungalow to take fresh clothes and raid the fridge, and Jess had no idea where she was most of the time. Long sleeves had covered the truth about Jamie's addiction, but finally that came out too.

The sky fell the day the police arrested Jamie, who was seriously injured and in hospital after a horrific fall. Jess was at her daughter's bedside night and day. The damage – physical and mental - was already done, she knew that. The long haul back, if there was going to be one, was going to be incredibly hard.

A sense of helplessness hung from Jess like a heavy overcoat. Where had she gone wrong? Why hadn't she intervened long ago, when things had started to slide? How had she let her daughter sink so low? She never imagined this was the way their life would pan out, and she was a long way out of her depth. Jamie was later charged with robbery and violence, as well as breaking and entering. There was a lesser charge of possession of drugs. Maybe because of her age, and because this was a first offence, she was given a suspended prison sentence. The relief was palpable to them both.   Jamie was also instructed to attend a drug rehabilitation course, and she would be under supervision for the next couple of years.

A local doctor advised Jamie on both her physical and mental rehab programme and she joined a therapy group that met weekly.

Everyone there was a recovering drug user, which gave some support initially, but Jamie only stuck with it for as long as she had to. She soon splintered away into a loose friendship with a much older man she had met at one of the group sessions. This friendship helped to balance her in some way. His name was Paul, a tall, physical man who was well-educated, and had enjoyed a professional career before losing his way through drugs. He had fought his way back, but at a price. They became close friends, supporting each other. He had a shaggy-haired dog that farted and smelt of damp grass, but how Jamie loved that dog.

It took some time for Jamie to lose her walking frame, and she gradually moved from two walking sticks to one, which she would probably need for the rest of her life. After a few months, she got a job in a local store, and a sort of normality, if you could call it that, returned. The summer helped the healing process and it was time spent on the beach, with long swims, that eased mother and daughter closer again.

One time, Jamie, Jess and Paul took a picnic up on the headland. Jamie had idly pulled two long stalks of the dried grass and began folding them and snapping them at intervals absentmindedly. Slicing one palm on top of the other she brushed away the seeds that had stuck to dampness on her hands, the dog at her feet. They decided to walk the shorter way home, doubling back towards the railway cutting, or what was left of it. The walk to the beach was always filled with the sense of expectation; the return took away some small sense of joy.

As soon as the path entered the gap in the trees, the temperature dropped and the density of light changed. 'The half mile' track, as it was known, was wider, with thick undergrowth on either side and was pot-marked with dog shit, discarded drink canisters and the detritus of urbanisation. Their conversation drifted over several observations, intermittently there were passing hellos to a handful of other dog walkers. They arrived eventually at the junction. Emerging onto a side street, with a rusting chain link fence down part of one side, Paul let out a quiet, high-pitched whistle through closed teeth and his dog, Lurch, just stopped on the pavement.

Turning his head, he waited. He knew the call of the lead. With him loosely tethered, they moved on through the remaining streets before Paul split his own way and the two women continued towards the bungalow.

That evening, Jess decided to make a chicken salad. Starting by getting the large off-white chopping board from cupboard beneath the worktop, she then chose a wide blade knife, which was blunt, to slice the tomatoes. Opening the lower shelf draw, she found the steel with its polished mahogany handle. The act of sharpening a knife with a steel always gave her a practical sense of achievement, honing the blade against the steel , the sound that it made, the drawing curved downward motion to the guard, and finally to test its sharpness by rubbing the edge of her thumb one way across the blade. The job done, she dropped the steel back to the drawer.

Holding a knife in her hand feeling the weight of it, she had a flash of thought back to those last couple of years when she was with Frank. Then, with a knife like this in her hand, her emotions might have driven her over the edge. Thank God she had left when she did. Turning slightly, she could see Jamie watching TV, occasionally laughing.

. . . .

Years later, when their lives had settled into a normal rhythm, Jess had woken up early one warm weekend morning and left the bungalow, with Jamie still asleep. She slung her small swim bag over her shoulder and set off towards the headland and the beach. Neither of them could possibly have known what that day would bring.

Part Six

1

Jamie, Sydney. 2010

The doorbell responded to the lightest touch, ringing only briefly across the small bungalow. Jamie turned her head in acknowledgment of the sound, put the open magazine face down on the side table, so as not to lose her place, and picked up her walking stick beside her. With a well-practised heave, she stood upright. At the same time, she shouted: 'Hang on, won't be a minute.' She walked to the door, flicked off the chain and turned the catch to face a postman.

'Special delivery for Miss Jamie O'Hagan. ID needed I'm afraid.'

'That's OK, not a problem.'

Turning in the narrow confines of the hallway, she propped her stick against the wall, and walked crookedly to the hall table. Using the edges of her fingers, she swiped gently among the small pile before picking up a bank statement.

'This OK? A bank statement?'

'Yep, fine.'

Returning to the door, she signed on the allotted spot, took the buff-coloured envelope and shut the door. Then, standing still, she looked closer at the printed name and address, with its franked stamp, and bearing a red and yellow special delivery sticker. Turning it over, there was still no clue as from who it might be from. Slowly, with growing curiosity, but in no hurry, she tapped the envelope on her other hand, then went to the kitchen and put the kettle on the stove for a mug of tea. Turning back without any hesitation, she opened the letter using the edge of a teaspoon, ripping the envelope to a ragged edge to reveal a single sheet. It was folded neatly in a way that meant the heading would be seen first. Printed in a crimson red block was:

Hobson and Healy Lawyers,
141 King William St, Adelaide.

Trying to find a comfortable position against the edge of the worktop, Jamie withdrew the letter to reveal its contents. Beneath the firm's address, with the centred reference in bold type was:

Frank O'Hagan deceased

She raised her head… so, it had finally happened. The bitterness of her chaotic childhood. The man that caused it had gone. Looking back at the letter, she read:

Dear Miss O'Hagan,
This firm is conducting matters of probate and has been appointed executers of the will of the above named.   Your name is mentioned in these matters. Please contact the lawyer named below,

The letter was signed with a name that was also printed below in bold blue-black ink.

Robert D Miller

It had given no hint of what, if anything, was to come. Reading the short text again, she noticed that the signature had three dots underneath it, rather than the bold confirmation of a heavy line. Putting the letter behind her on the worktop, she folded her arms and, looking at a spot towards the ceiling on the wall opposite, took a long breath in, then expelled it slowly, along with her thoughts. Fingering the switch on the kettle, it crackled on the beginning of the boil, then belching steam from the spout, it turned itself off with a soft click. Turning to face the cupboard, Jamie made a series of quick moves to complete the tasks for making tea, the speed of her actions was the first release of anger towards the man that had gone.

It was difficult for her to carry through the day's tasks, knowing that the letter was there where she left it, waiting for a response. The very mention of her father's name brought back the memory of those broken years. The misery endured by her mother, and all the pain, fury and sense of dislocation. His idea of a family and what it meant were far removed from reality. Her overriding memory of her father was of a man who had, in his obsessive quest for money, done anything and everything to benefit his business, sacrificing anyone to reach the elixir of wealth. According to her mother, acquisition was everything for him. Once he had bought, or owned something, he quickly lost interest. Jamie had done the washing-up and ironing already today, but the desire to finish the other household chores just evaporated. She felt the slow building pressure give way to anger, and said to the wall facing her:

'I… need… a… drink.'

But she shut that thought down. Instead, she decided to go for a walk, and set off to the headland beyond the beach. It was after 4 when she returned, and she picked up the letter she'd left propped against the hall table light. She took the phone from its wall-mounted cradle, and called the number on the letterhead. It rang three times before it was answered: 'Good afternoon   ... ..Hobson and Healy.'

The sing-song voice changed pitch at the end of the last syllable. 'Hello, can I speak to Mr Robert Miller please.'

'May I ask who is calling?'

'It's Jamie O'Hagan, I have letter here in front of me from him. It arrived special delivery to me today.'

'He's on the phone at the moment, and he might be a little while… can I get him to call you back on this number?'

'Thank you.' Then Jamie put the phone down.

Moving slowly, and with the usual difficulty, her body sagged the short distance before dropping to the wicker basket chair. Using her arms, she positioned herself squarely, then adjusted the back cushion. Leaning back, she placed both hands together as if in silent prayer and lowered her head so that her chin was resting on her outstretched thumbs. It was a position of concentrated thought.

This was finally the end, she reasoned. Nothing much would change, but even his slightest shadow over her life had now been extinguished. She tried to recall her earliest memory. It must have been when she was around four, it was the sound of waves thundering on the beach, probably a storm. She remembered incessant rain and she was holding her mother's hand. Her mother had been frightened. It was a memory of panic. Her memories formed woven pictures, some of which she could replay like an old cine film. She could vaguely remember moving out of the big house overlooking the bay, which her mother called the mausoleum, or could she only remember her mother talking about it? They had rarely seen her father after that.

Work and money had been his preoccupation, and, as she later learnt, he had accumulated a fortune, but that had all but evaporated. Back in 1974, the cyclone that had ravaged Darwin had taken out a business partner of his, which had resulted in financial panic.

Years later, he would still rant about how he was cheated by this man, his anger frothing like a bad pour in a beer glass. Yet while her father had survived, having ring-fenced certain operations, rumour had it that his partner had lost everything. After the Darwin catastrophe, finance that her father had thought was finely balanced had see-sawed in a growing market. The business had stuttered, then heaved as the expected market growth faltered, leading to a chain reaction of loans being called in, then the insolvency of one company after another. Last they heard, he had gone bankrupt.

Jamie didn't know for sure how old she was when she moved with her mother to the timber bungalow down at Bulli, about an hour south of Sydney, where she lived now. The property had been acquired by him, either in part exchange, or in lieu of a debt, who knows; but its ownership had been transferred to her mother at some stage. They were never married, so it was just a 'kiss off' without the kiss.

It wasn't much, a timber- framed clapboard, single storey house with a tin roof on a small plot in Hill Street. The paint was peeling now, the tin roof looked the colour of a peach that had passed its best, but it still held good, shooting the winter rain through the gutters to the house-high tank beside it. Inside, when it rained hard, you could barely hear yourself think, let alone hear other people's conversation, but it was home. It was a place she felt safe.

Her father had appeared occasionally when she was young, always without announcing his arrival. He may have looked in her direction now and then, and ruffled her hair. Sometimes, he had persuaded her mother to let him stay overnight.

He always had plans to resurrect the business, but they never went anywhere. His appearance became more dishevelled and he had a lingering stale smell of unwashed clothes and yesterday's beer. That smell hung around the bungalow like a low mist on a damp day. When he was there, he was sometimes noisy, sometimes morose, occasionally violent, but he never added anything to their lives.

For years, all Jamie wanted was for him to show some interested in her. She dreamed about having a dad like her friends, to feel what it might be like to be part of a family. His visits grew less and less through her early teens, finally ending altogether and she never saw him again. In time, she turned against his very existence, blaming him for everything that went wrong. But of course, he was never around to take the bile that she spat out. Everyone has sharp spikes of memories that are covered with layers of dead leaves. It shouldn't come as a surprise when the wind blows from a different direction, and the past reveals itself.

The shack, as she liked to call it, with its small veranda, had a few redeeming features. It faced east, catching the morning sun as it lay across its boards, then, when the sun gained height in the sky, the southerly slant would just clip the far end of that veranda. This was where she and her friends used to lounge around on a worn- out sofa in the evenings sometimes, listening to music, talking about all the stuff that teenage girls do talk about when they are grown up in everything except their years.

At the end of the street was a cut through over some scrubland, which led onto a pathway dotted with gums and mimosa trees. The trees gave way to the long grassy slope to the southern end of McCauley's beach. That beach was their back garden, a free range, the promise of exploration and a natural environment. She had an open childhood with no formal boundaries. Secondary School, though, provided no engagement. A good deal of what was covered during class time was easy for Jess, so boredom quickly crept through the cracks of her wandering imagination. First, she skipped the odd day, then it became more frequent until bad-tempered truancy became her normal behaviour. She avoided talking to her mother, and would disappear without saying where she was going.

When she was 16, it was a bit of a rollercoaster, then her life started to slip like a slow land slide. It got much worse when she met Gene. It was in the Mall over at Woonona on a Saturday morning. She was on her own, wandering past the shop windows, vaguely thinking that she might steal something. It must have been the noise that made her turn as three boys, shouting as they ran through the shoppers, turned a trolley over and sent the contents across the tiled floor. They were laughing and acting like clowns when they came alongside her. One of the boys stopped and said: 'Now, that's a great jacket, red leather… tasty….'

He moved closer and said:

'Hi… I'm Gene. I've not seen you around here before. Have you just moved here?'

Looking as relaxed as she could, she smiled:

'Na... I just hide when I see you and your mates coming….'

'Ha, that's a good one ... what's your name?'

'Jamie'

'Well, Jamie, we're off for a wander and a smoko, want come along?'

That inauspicious meeting took her into the shallows that would eventually become very deep, dark waters.

He was a couple of years older, and they felt an immediate connection when they realised both their names could be used by boys or girls. Gene said he liked the actor Gene Wilder, and joked he might change his surname, as it suited his character better than his own. She had laughed and he took her hand. She didn't let go. Gene talked her into going with the others to the rock festival over on North Side, it was a three-day beach event. The idea was to crash it somehow.

It was a downward path, at first a few joints, harmless gatherings with music. Then the pink pops turned to tabs, the acid trips were frighteningly strange and over the next couple of years the road reached the final dip. The tailspin came in a cramped flat, stinking of damp and loss. Heating the 'loving spoonful', then the warm rush of the shoot up, and the rush of relief. It marked her decent into addiction.

By the time she was 20, Jamie had fallen so low; she started breaking and entering homes to get money for drugs. She became more and more brazen, taking part in robberies, and it was only a matter of time before she got caught. She only went back to the bungalow to grab a few clothes and take some food from the cupboards, and always chose a time when she knew her mother would be at work. When it happened, she was off her head.

Following an elderly woman home, Jamie knocked on her door then forced her way through the house, pushing the woman to the floor while shouting at her to tell her where she kept her money and jewellery. The woman pointed upwards to the bedroom, in fear of what might happen next.

Jamie took the stairs so quickly, she fell forwards, with her face and specifically, her eye, smashing into the stair riser. Her skin split open, with more blood than a slaughterhouse floor. This brought some sense to her, and crying with frustration, she turned back, stumbled in total confusion, and fell over the woman's prostrate body before making the door to the street.

The woman was convinced she had been kicked, and was clearly terrified when a neighbour found her on her way back from work later in the afternoon. She swore she had been robbed. Jamie's fear, returning to the flat empty handed, was not the police but the man she was now living with, who was expecting her to return with supplies. A few weeks later, she was found at the bottom of the stairwell, having fallen through both flights.

She was found semi-conscious by an elderly tenant coming into the building. For some peculiar reason Jamie had a strong recall of the smell of salami. She remembered little and didn't know if she had she been shoved over the rails, or had climbed over. In hospital, the full extent of her injuries was clear. She had a badly fractured hip, with multiple complications of smaller injuries, including a ruptured spleen. She didn't realise it at the time, but she was incredibly fortunate to have survived.

Waking in that hospital, in a small ward of four beds - all occupied - it had been dark except for the small area of light surrounding a desk at the end of the room. The sound of two night nurses talking was just audible.

The sound of a sub volume continuous moan reached her from somewhere in the ward. Moving her fingers across the sheets she located the buzzer hanging on the side bars of the bed and pressed the red plunger with her thumb. The figure advanced quickly, the blue and white uniform spoke calming words, a water refill, and then she fell back to the pillow and the induced sleep came on to her again.

The police had put the case against her together quickly enough, her swab for DNA - in its infancy in Australia - was a perfect match for the break in. She was duly charged with robbery with violence, and other lesser charges. The initial hospital tests revealed Jamie had a powerful cocktail of drugs in her body, an amount that would have supercharged her actions. Her mother's reaction wasn't what she expected. She closed ranks and did everything she could to support and help her, blaming herself for not challenging her daughter's behaviour when they still had some kind of relationship, or for asking for help when they needed it.

The trial went Jamie's way, maybe because she was contrite for her actions, perhaps because it was her first offence. Plus the extenuating circumstances put forward were that, as an addicted user, rehabilitation and supervision were considered the most suitable course. The early days of mending, even with help from prescribed drugs, were like a cold war being fought against an unseen enemy. One day followed another, linking the days to a week and beyond. The hot, the cold, the shaking, the feeling of internal destruction gradually passed, leaving a cavernous space of emptiness; a void of loneliness that reached right into her being. Her mother was the only family she had, and, even though there had been signs of drug abuse when Jamie was at home, her mother had been clearly shocked when she realised the state her daughter was in.

Something her mother had said when she was in hospital on one of her visits struck home: 'Is this the way you're choosing to die?'

The crying turned into a river of remorse, and with it came the simple realisation that this was the only chance she would have to change.

'You have choices,' Jess had said: 'I should have taken one years ago with the only man who really cared for me. He wanted me to start a new life with him, but I didn't, I was too scared. Think carefully about the choices you're going to make now. For your best or your worst, these will be with you forever.'

Her fingers touched Jamie's arm, sealing that moment with clarity. Once the points on the rails had changed direction, Jamie found the going became easier. There were three further operations, and then she was eventually discharged from hospital, and started to rebuild a life at home. After a slow start, she was out of the wheelchair and using a frame to get around. Then it was two crutches, then just one stick.

She didn't go out much, but just a few steps would reach the peeling picket fence, the gate jammed open off its hinges long ago, then down the stony track. Taking a left at the tarmac brought her to a small corner shop run by a friend of her mother. Sometimes, she would lean on her sticks and read the postcard adverts placed at the side of the big window: pink floral dress, as new. BSA 250 motorcycle, sky blue, runs but needs work. Occasionally, looking through the glass, she would see Mary, who always raised her hand and waved, smiling. It was uplifting to feel human contact.

A short walk further on, there were steps up a grass bank to higher ground with a bench that would have had a view down towards the bay, but the overgrown hedge on the opposite side had become too high years ago. Sometimes, she would sit for a while on the bench, fingering the initials scratched into the wood, wondering where these people were now and how their lives had gone. Soon, Jamie was walking with just one stick, and then she could sometimes manage without it. Eventually, she could drive again.

A couple of months later, Mary gave Jamie a job in the shop for two mornings a week, cash. It suited them both, as Jamie didn't want to upset her benefit payments and it got her out of the house with purpose. One day, Mary fired her morale with some positive remarks. 'You're a bright woman, Jamie. If you believe in yourself, anything is possible. If you have the courage to lean on the door, it will open for you, just remember that.'

Her mother had remarked on Jamie's change of attitude and how much more compassionate she had become with others. She saw her help an elderly customer one day in the shop, load her trailer bag and help her get safely through the self-closing door.

At the time, Jessica had been working in the offices of a meat packing and canning factory down off the Chinoa Road. The *slash and can* it factory, as she called it. It was conveniently close, the hours were cut and dried, and she was always back in time to cook for Jamie in the evenings. Nothing much happened, they just lived the days as they turned.

Before that December was out though, disaster struck Jamie to the ground, as surely as a hammer drives a nail.

. . . .

It was a warm and bright Sunday morning. Jess had said she would be meeting her friend Alice for an early swim on the high tide. She left the bungalow around 8 with a red and white striped beach bag that had been packed ready and left in the hall the night before. By the time Jamie got up, she realised her mother had already left. It was a glorious, windless day and Jamie decided to take the old Holden out. She drove off with the windows down and the radio full on; it was mood-lifting.

She took in a burger at the hilltop view park pull- in, then called in to see a friend on the way back.

It was well into the afternoon when Jamie parked up with two wheels on the edge of the higher ground on the roadway. The old V6 engine hiccupped twice, still trying to run as the engine was turned off. Swinging her legs out first, she pulled herself almost upright, levering herself out with the car frame and locking the door. Crossing to the bungalow with a now painful leg, she stopped for a minute and leaned on her stick. A dark cloud passed over, covering the sun only briefly. The slightest involuntary shudder rippled over her, as she recalled the forecast she had heard on the radio earlier for possible light afternoon showers. The front door key slid easily into the lock. Twisting it gently, she used her shoe to edge the door open and removed the key again. The lock, she thought, was only really capable of keeping out the weather, but there was little of value inside to tempt others.

She gave a shout, but it was answered only with the emptiness of an echo. Lifting the lid from the bread bin, she took two pieces of wholemeal bread from the cellophane wrapper around the loaf before twisting it slightly and replacing the lid. Just as she dropped them into the toaster and pushed the spring loader down, there was a loud knock. She made her way to the door, releasing the catch and opening it wide against the wall. Standing on the step were two women in uniform. One of them asked, gently, if she was Jamie O'Hagan. She confirmed that she was, instinctively realising something was badly wrong.

'May we come in?'

Her jaw slackened before falling slightly.

'Of course...'

Then winching herself down the short hallway to the living room, she bent to sit, dropping her weight to the armchair and pointed towards the sofa.

'Thank you.'

The police officers sat down on its forward edge. One of them took her cap off, placed it beside her. Her hands touched the top of her thighs, then slipped back to her lap, she let the silence last just a little longer.

'I'm afraid I have some bad news.

'I'm so sorry to have to tell you that a woman we believe to be your mother has been found in the water. We haven't had a full report yet, but it seems she probably drowned at Ballade Point this morning. Her body was brought onto the beach by the beach patrol after it was seen in the water by a member of the public ...'

The woman stopped talking to let the gravity of what she had just said sink in. Jamie's face dropped in disbelief. Her mouth opened, but no words came. This statement had collapsed her, her body sagged and she began shaking. The other woman, who Jamie would later discover was a family support officer, moved to the side of Jamie's arm chair. When Jamie lifted her face, wet with tears, the senior officer carried on:

'It appears that she was on her own. Her clothes and bag were recovered some way further down the beach. We believe she was caught in the rip just on the point. Judging by her injuries, probably from the outlying rocks, it would appear that these may have caused her to drown. Fortunately, her body was recovered quickly.....'

All Jamie could do was nod.

'Do you have a friend or neighbour who can come and sit with you? Would you like me to make you a mug of tea..? Will you be Ok?'

Jamie just sat there, stunned.

The officer told her they would need her to confirm the identity of the body at the mortuary. She took a card from the pocket of her jacket, and gave it to Jamie. 'When you're ready, in your own time, just give me a call on this number....we can collect you. We will contact you again in any case as soon as we receive the coroner's report.'

The front door closed with a solitary hard click. Silence. One hand went to the wall to steady herself as Jamie walked to the phone. She pressed a number, with tears still streaming down her face. She muttered 'please be in' as it rang several times. Just as she was going to give up, a male voice answered: 'Hello?'

'Paul, Paul, thank God you're there. Please help me....'

'I'll come right over, OK?'

'Yes... thank you...'

Paul was the man she had got to know through rehab, when she had first come out of hospital. He had become a close family friend and he had stood calm, like a tower, for her when the wind blew too hard. The next few months were desperate. When anyone loses their mother, it's the final and brutal severing of the umbilical cord. That lifeline has gone for ever, and with it goes the closest relationship of life...birth.

The funeral was at the crematorium, an ugly modern place, with electric bells in the tower and a miniature organ in each of the three chapels. The polished newness of it all made Jamie wish it was over almost before it had begun. It was no place to say goodbye, but it had surprised her just how many turned up to do just that. People her mother had known from different areas of her life were there, and they spoke to Jamie, offering the same hand of friendship. When it was over, she drove home feeling weary and washed out in a way she never had before.

It was the finality of it all... the reminder of our temporary place in this world.

Jamie didn't make a conscious decision to leave the house exactly as it had been when her mother was alive, but it was several months before she could face going through her effects. Eventually, after the clothes had been sorted and gone, her mother's life came down to a few pieces of jewellery and her sandwich box, as she had called it. Pouring a large glass of red wine, Jamie set the small pine box on the table and unclipped the brass eyelet catch. She opened the lid fully to rest on its black and white webbing strap. It revealed little. Two bank savings books, with a few hundred dollars in each, a hand-written will, properly dated and witnessed as far as she could tell, leaving the debt- free bungalow with any money and chattels to Jamie.

A large, loose bunch of photographs, of various quality, many black and white; the car papers with its current insurance certificate, and an odd assortment of newspaper cuttings. At the bottom, lay her own birth certificate, and that of her mother. In a separate envelope were her mother's immigration papers. Fanning these out across the table, Jamie put the empty box on the floor. Then, sitting back with her arms folded, she stared. What was spread out in front of her was a life, without a being. Picking up a handful of photos, she passed the first few hand to hand, giving the unknown groups a long glance, fingering some with passing thoughts. These were snapshots of a life that was gone. Then she stopped at one.

It showed a gently-shelving beach of white sand, with a few sunbathers in the distance before big blue rollers. It was the foreground of the picture that piqued her curiosity. It showed the lower part of two pairs of sun-tanned legs, almost touching. One set were clearly male, they were strong and muscular. There was a tattoo and a distinctive pale scar on the inside of one of the man's calves. The other legs were obviously female, and she guessed this must have been her mother. The photo must have been taken by one of those two people while lying prone on the sand.

Using her other hand as a rest, Jamie deftly flicked it over with a vague feeling of anticipation, but on the back there was nothing. Other snaps showed Jamie's first day at school, a group of kids in the backyard larking with a hose, one of Jamie with her first bike talking to someone out of the picture. Who could that have been? There was so much about her mother's life she now wished she knew. As a child, or a teenager, she had never thought to ask her mother about her own life and how she came to Australia. Her own life had been rushing forward, and like all children growing up, she was focused on her place in her own universe. It was too late now.

Jamie had been distracted by the noise of the lightest of rain that was falling briefly. Then, with the rattle of it on the old tin roof, she raised her eyes to the low clad ceiling, and thought yet again - would the roof hold, and if so, for how long?

Arc of Doubt

2

Jamie, Sydney. 2010

The shrill tone of the phone distracted her. It could only be the return call from the lawyers, who else would call?

'Hello.'

'Good afternoon, is that Jamie O'Hagan?'

'Yes, speaking.'

'This is Robert Miller from Hobson and Healy.'

There was a pause. She thought she heard the sound of the intake of breath, fearing interruption, she waited briefly. Then he continued.

'I'm sorry I was unavailable when you called earlier, as I mentioned in my letter to you this firm has been appointed executers of the estate of one Frank O'Hagan, whom we understand was a direct relative of yours?'

'He was my father, if you can call it that,' she interjected.

He carried on. 'It's a somewhat unusual situation, and as you have been specifically mentioned we would ask you to present yourself at our offices...we have an office in Sydney in Hunter Street, which makes this more convenient for you, obviously. You will need to bring full identification, including a passport or driving licence , a utility bill from your current address, not more than three months old, and a copy of your birth certificate, if you have it.'

With an acid edge to her voice, she said:

'This seems a lot of effort for a man who left me and my mother years ago. Last time I heard of him, he was well down, and nearly out. Did he win the lotto then?'

Miller didn't answer directly.

'As I've said, this is an unusual case and I would strongly advise that you call in at our offices. I have briefed my colleague, Gordon Williamson who will be able to see you in a week. That gives us time to send the package, which is on my desk at the moment, to him.'

'Thank you, I will call him.'

Replacing the receiver, Jamie leaned against the wall, wondering how such a wound - the one left by her absent father - could get infected again so quickly. Using a blunt stub of a pencil, she wrote in clear bold letters the name Gordon Williamson on the edge of a pizza flier. Then she headed back to the kitchen, realising the rain shower had given way to sun again. Taking a mug of tea, she moved to the veranda tucking herself into the corner of the sofa allowing the warm dampness of the shower to reach up to her with its sweet soft scent of the early evening, telling herself that nothing in life should be complicated. It was people that made it so. This lawyer would no doubt tell her that tying financial knots, the way her father had done, was easy; the hard stuff is getting them undone later. She reflected that our lives are a bit like that. Later, much later she got up, checked the doors were locked and eased herself across the bungalow to her bedroom and fell to an uneasy sleep punctuated with mixed dreams that seemed so real on waking in darkness. The next day, putting curiosity behind her, she diligently went about other tasks trying to keep busy but finally overcome, she made the phone call and made the appointment at the lawyer's office for the following week.

Reaching the main highway, 40 miles away, by bus was a slow burn. Then, it was faster to the city, and the bus station. From there, it was a local bus route to the office district, right to the place she had to go. The first bus was on time, it stopped with a long hissing sigh of the airbrakes and the doors slapped back. Using the rail she hauled herself up the entrance platform onto the Routemaster for two stops before waiting in a short queue for the city flyer. By the time it arrived she was aching and pleased to be able to find a seat towards the back of the raised level.

She had a clear window view of an elderly man reaching with open arms to a young woman. They came together, locked for a short while in an embrace. Not the pat, pat; there, there type of hug: but the all-encompassing moment expressing love. The young woman's arms then fell away from the body of the man – maybe her father - while his slid upwards to her shoulders momentarily before he kissed her lightly.

Jamie watched that moment of joy, and had in some very small way shared it, then shifting herself on the seat settled for the journey. There weren't many stops to pick up passengers and so after the first few, she stopped looking at the new passengers boarding.

It took a further 20 minutes, and a third bus, to arrive within walking distance of the address at the top of Jamie's letter. Unsure of which way to go, she turned her head first to the left and to then right as though some sign might be forthcoming. The buildings all around her were seemingly reaching for sky space, floor upon floor, brick glass structures, piled with architects' dreams of legacy.

Jamie felt small lost in the wind vortex that shifted in the heat at ground level. The lights must have changed somewhere as the crowd on the pavement suddenly appeared to be sucked forward. Her hip was aching badly now, leaning on her stick she edged near to a lamp post which took her out of the stream. Two people she asked just shrugged, shaking their heads. Then a voice close to her said: 'It is… literally behind you…

Turning to the voice, she saw briefly a young man with a drawn face.

'Thank you'

But he was gone, all she saw was the back of another head in another crowd. Threading her way across the pavement and up the two polished marble steps, she was funnelled to the secure space where a positioned door entry microphone was directly in front of her. Pressing the button with more than a little trepidation, she drew her breath and said as calmly as possible: 'Jamie O'Hagan to see Gordon Williamson for an 11.30 appointment.'

Catching her off guard, the opaque door opened after a few seconds. Walking towards her was a smartly-dressed woman in her early 20s.

'Hello… before we go up, may I ask… have you got your ID?'

As if in confirmation, Jamie rummaged in her bag to produce her birth certificate, a recent phone bill and her driving licence.

'I don't have a passport, as I've never been outside Australia.'

She felt no embarrassment at this admission.

The woman's smile showed all too clearly her lack of interest at this point before moving on.

'I need to take a copy of these for Mr Williamson, is that OK?'

Jamie nodded in confirmation and, pointing at a couple of sofas, said: 'I'll take a rest for a moment.'

She didn't wait for a reply, she just limped over and sagged down. The receptionist went over to a long desk, pressed a button on a phone, and said something Jamie couldn't hear before turning to a photocopier. Jamie noted there were three other women, all young, front-office types. She thought they looked like replicas of one another, and they were sitting in similar poses in the rather clinical space. Before she had time to recover from the arduous journey in, the first receptionist came over to her, as one of the two lifts noiselessly slid its doors open and waited as though expecting a response. Jamie hadn't seen it arrive, had it been summoned? She pulled herself up on the arm of the sofa, and walked over to the lift. It swallowed the two of them before silently taking them up to an unknown floor, stopping with a quiet suddenness. The doors slid back to reveal a much smaller reception area, more of a wide corridor.

'I'll leave you with Sarah then …'

The receptionist returned to the lift and was gone.

Jamie wondered whether her escort personally knew Sarah, out of all the people in this vast building, or whether she just read the name Sarah Winters on the plate on her desk.

'Mr Williamson won't keep you a moment.'

This time, the chair Jamie sat in was more upright. It was somewhere to perch, rather than relax into. She was still tense with nerves, but thankfully, a lot cooler thanks to the efficient air conditioning. It was probably five minutes before a door further down the corridor snapped open. He just stood there for a moment before removing his glasses, and holding them in his hand, raised his arm in invitation for Jamie to come into his office. While holding the door for her, he said: 'I do hope I haven't kept you waiting too long…. Please…'

Indicating a chair, he added: 'Do take a seat'.

The informality of two modern, easy chairs facing one another in the comfortably-sized office did not escape her, neither did the view from the floor- to- ceiling window. The details of the city lay far below them.

'Well, this is indeed a most unusual case, Ms O' Hagan.'

And, reaching down to a small gilt-edged table between them, the lawyer picked up the large expanded manila envelope that lay on it. Sliding his hand into the envelope, he brought out several well-worn exercise books. Bunched together with string, they were an assortment of colours.

'As you know, we are the executers of Frank O'Hagan's will. We hold strict instructions from him to see that these books are placed in your hands, and I can confirm that you are the sole beneficiary of his last will and testimony. Unfortunately, his assets at the time of his passing, such as they were, barely cover the cost of his demise.'

Producing a smaller white envelope from the larger one, he carried on: 'This is our invoice and also the estate's final account.'

Part Seven

1

Frank O'Hagan, Adelaide.
2010

Hello Jamie.

My name is Frank O'Hagan. I know that I saw very little of your childhood, and then your later years were difficult; but this doesn't excuse my absence from your life. Now, I have the certain knowledge that I am dying, the big dirty capital C. The one that invades, pervades, consumes and eventually lays you down like a grey shadow. It's like turning down an invitation to a party that you would have liked to go to: 'It is with regret that I shan't be able to … etc.'

This is the end of my story, you see. This short explanation is only the beginning. If I start here, you - wherever you are when you read this - will know the whole story, the truth, and your judgement will be my trial. You will, I hope consider other extenuating circumstances during my life that have shown me in a different light. I have done my best to remember it as it all happened.

So, where to start? I have no idea where I was born. I was found, as my foster ma was keen to tell me many times … 'at the end some poor girl's nine months,' in a box wrapped in a dirty, blue, ladies' rain coat, left in a doorway of an ironmongers in Kings Cross Sydney.
It was the back end of September 1934.

In the coat pocket, written on a scrap of paper torn from an unknown source, was *'My name is Frank O'Hagan'*. The faint pencilled name was barely legible. It is still the only connection to a lost heritage that I have.

Just think about that for a second, a name is highly personal, it is ….you. But, to attach it to a blank history can bring both depression and strength at any stage of your life. At the time, exhaustive inquiries were made with regard to the name, which turned up nothing. It was almost as though the name had been made up in the moment. I was raised initially at the notorious Row Side Children's Home in Sydney. As a young child, I was put with several foster families. Maybe I got the wrong ones, because by the time I got to Maisey and Bill Heron, I actually thought they weren't too bad.

When I was about nine or ten I suppose, I 'borrowed' a small bike. How I loved that bike. Someone took it off me eventually, which was the same way I got it in the first place. I had kept it always covered up in the lockup in the yard. One weekend, I decided to go out on the bike, leaving the lad I shared with sitting on the bed reading a Victor comic. Coming out of the room into the corridor, I carelessly swung the door behind me.

I would like say the wind caught it, but it didn't of course. From the open scullery door came the heavy, malice-laden tone of Bill's voice.

'Shut that fucking door.'

It was Bill in one of his usual rages.

I then opened it again quietly and slammed it hard as my response. Then it started.

'That's it, the door to your room is coming off. I warned you.'

But I was well down the hallway by then. I reached the hall door and flung it open, slamming that one too hard as well on purpose, just to wind him up a bit more. Panting a little, I jerked the bike from the leaning timber shed just outside the back door. Swinging it forcibly from underneath the canvas cover, the back wheel caught the smaller empty dustbin, and its lid fell clattering along the concrete path.

Fuck them. Both of them, they don't care, why should I - how could a nine year old understand the anger of adults? Reaching the back gate, I wrenched it open, mounted the bike, bumped the kerb and rode off down the road. Leaning well over the handlebars with my chin jutting forward, I fired the pedals down, increasing speed for 50 yards or so before sitting upright and breathing deeply. Allowing the bike to freewheel, the speed slowly started to drop again.

I resented the defected attention I received. I felt I was at the bottom of the chain of events, usually to be hit or shouted at by someone. Like a boxer, I tried never to get too close, unless I wanted to strike back.

It was always my fault, they all had it in for me.   'Watch where you're going lad.'

The handlebars shifted in a sudden movement, the bike skewed, brushing up against an old man. His backward avoidance failed and he slipped over. I hadn't actually looked before starting to turn into the narrow pathway between the old block-built garages, so I hadn't seen him. He seemed to fall with fright, sort of sideways; first trying to break his fall with an outstretched hand. Snapping on the brakes, I pulled up dead and dropped both feet to the ground to look at the man, who was by then on his hands and knees trying to get up. I was already flicking the pedal with my toes, bracing a foot against it to ride away, when the man shouted at me:

'You little sod, can't you see the sign up there, No Cycling.'

It was the mud smeared over the old man's hands and trousers that started me laughing. Then, to finalise the insult, I raised my hand slowly and gave the two fingers to him before pedalling away at speed. The narrow passageway acted as a wind tunnel, my senses were alert and I felt the thrill of the adrenaline. Laughing aloud, I didn't even look back. The stoned path, tracked by weeds, widened before coming onto Little Park Lane.

Staying on the pavement, I then cut through a narrow gap in the hedge into the park, taking a swipe on the mouth from a stray branch. I didn't falter, pain was a colour I recognised. Crossing the football pitch at an angle, I headed towards the allotments. The grass surface of the pitches were bumpy, harder to pedal on, sending minor shockwaves up through my body. Aloud, I would emit that same vibrated broken sound from my mouth, a-a-a-ah-ah-ah-oh-oh- then laugh and talk to the tall football posts.

'You think you're tall, well I'm clever see? … you saw me back there … you did, didn't you, trees ..?' At that age, I babbled away all the time. Joining the path again, I cycled hard down its gently falling gradient for a short way before confidently taking my hands from the handlebars. Sitting back in the saddle, I would whistle to the birds with folded arms. I was good at that too. I was drawn towards the allotments, they were my wrecking grounds.

I had secret ways in, under, over and through the boundaries. I lived a game inside my head and this was my playground with imaginary friends. Mooching about, I would silently plan my campaign of revenge on the unknown adult army. Perhaps pulling up stuff on a single plot and leaving it all in a neat row to be found later, or opening sheds out of curiosity, sometimes trying a spade or rake before throwing it to the ground. I used to wriggle through tunnels in the hedge using my elbows, imagining I was escaping from a prisoner of war camp. The brambles cut my hands, like the barbed wire wounds of war. The sweet taste of my own blood was in my mouth.

Today, it was stoning. My routine for stoning was to check first that there was nobody working on the three plots in the row I had in mind. Then I would choose six good- sized stones, not pebbles. They had to fit easily between my finger and thumb. I stopped at my 'point one', selected two stones and threw them over the bushes one after another. Nothing.

Pushing the bike further up the road, I stopped level with the lamp post with the small sideways sticker on the lower panel door, my 'point two'. Resting my bike against it, with my hand turning the remaining stones in my trouser pocket, I looked up and down the empty road, then again lobbed two stones in a curving arc over the bushes. Nothing.

Turning very slightly, changing the angle, I took the two remaining stones and, bending my arm to a cricketer's stance, I arced them in quick succession. The sound of breaking glass lifted back on a rebound. One stone had found one of the three greenhouses. That moment for me, that tinkling sound when the impact caused shards to fall through the air glancing off themselves was the pinnacle of delight.

Picking up my bike, I cycled on in the direction of the town, full of joy and amusement with no concern at all for how my actions affected others. Passing the news stand at the front of the bus station, the wind blew in gusts, curling the edges of the newspapers held down on the shuttered shelves by long spring wires. It was well after five now, and the smell of chips from the chip shop followed me on the downwind.

I walked past the lower end of the high street, all now closed up, leaving the Red Lion to soak up the drinkers. Abruptly, I turned and headed back to the chip shop, my hunger inflamed by the smell. Shoving the bike onto the front wall of the shop. I turned and let go of it at the same time. I looked back at the dragging sound, as the bike slipped down the wall, stopping only when the handlebars caught on the rainwater down pipe. The poorly-painted door was opened by the only customer coming out and I went straight to the counter. The woman I was looking at was a similar age to Maisey, my foster carer, and was wearing a white coverall topped by a white apron, covered in grease stains.

'What can I get you?'

'Uh....'

Then, leaning my head a little, I lied: 'My mum never left any food for me today, can I have some scraps? I have no money.'

The woman looked at me and said: 'I'll pop in a few chips as well for you.'

She picked up a greaseproof bag then fetched a large slatted spoon from the rack, spooning around in the hot fat to collect the waste batter. She slid back the roll-top on the hot chip compartment and placed a few chips on the pile of scraps. While her back was turned, I lifted a pickled egg from the open jar on the counter and shook it lightly once before dropping it into the pocket of my shorts. Then taking the offered bag and mumbling my thanks, I went out to retrieve my bike.

Finding a dwarf wall behind the precinct, I opened the bag and started with the egg, shuddering a little from the heavy backbite from the vinegar. Fingering the first of the greasy chips, now only warm, I heard voices. Two boys, much older than me, were closing the distance on me, and recognising that this was an occasion to roll over, I, with a little hesitation, offered the bag.

The taller of the two stretched out his arm as if to take it, then he flicked the backs of his fingers under it to spill the contents onto the pavement. Laughter came from both of them as they walked away without a word. Staring at the scattered mess on the pavement, I could still taste the vinegar on my lips.

In a loud voice, I called after them: 'Bastards.'

But they were long gone.

The puncture came crossing the space between Bantham Road and the old railway track. I took the slope at speed, expecting to jump, and flicked the handlebars as if riding a wild stallion. But at the last minute, the back of the bike sank, deflated with the intrusion of a splinter of glass or a thorn, and the momentary escape to a dreamland adventure went with it. It took both hands to push that bike home, and I soon got tired. I knew that I would be late back, and that would mean a belting - at best- from my loving foster parents.

As I grew into my early teens, I came to realise that Bill and Maisey were just like all the others. Greedy, violent, selfish and mean- spirited. But that's just the way of it. I learnt that you have to take, before you're taken. So, directly or indirectly over the coming years, that's exactly what I did. In some ways, I was fortunate as I only had one short spell at Amersham, after The Sydney Children's Court sent me there.

I was then 14 and had been held for theft after breaking into a house near the bridge. It was by no means the first; the owner had come back and caught me emptying the drawers in an upstairs room. I thought I had been clever, leaving the back door and the yard door open for my escape route. He was a big fella, stout and strong with it, in baggy trousers held up with braces. I literally walked straight into him coming through the gate. He gave me a murderous slapping, then told the police I'd fallen over trying to run away. They just laughed and took his statement, then took me down the station. I was cocky, my defence mechanism had kicked in. I'd been done before for similar things, but had never been caught red handed. It made no difference, the result was just the same.

After my court appearance, I was sent for 'correction' at Amersham Court Reform School on the outside edge of the city. I had reported at the station early that day. If I hadn't, they would have come and picked me up. They drove me to the reform school, locked in the back of a black police van. That journey was the beginning of a trip into the unknown, without any of the familiar structures around me. Amersham must have been a private residence once. It was down a long winding drive, hidden from casual observers. There were trees of all types that had been planted when the house was new. Now the trees were full-grown and the grey stone building bore the marks of change. Bars scarred all the windows and rolls of razor wire were piled onto lower reaches.

Its large gates opened as if to swallow me whole. If I had been weak and vulnerable, I would have been broken forever in that place. It bred gangsters, drug dealers and all kinds of thieves and perverts. I learnt quickly that there were only two types of people. The strong and the weak. I'd been there only three days when an older warden, a big, fat deviant of a man, cornered me in the indoor wash house, saying:

'You're a nice looking boy Frankie... … I want you…..
I will be coming for you..., you're mine....'

Frightened? Oh yes I was, but I was not scared. I set my mind singularly for survival. The next time he was on nights, he came into our dormitory and shook me awake with the simple command:

'Come with me.'

I got out of bed, and by then he was outside the door, leaving it open. I bent under the bed with both hands for my shoes, and with one hand I pulled out the home-made spike I had fashioned from a metal biro casing. The blunt end I had sunk into a small wooden block, about as big as a cork. I secreted it into my palm and the sleeve of my pyjamas. Standing in the semi- darkness, and pushing my feet into unlaced shoes, I slid and shuffled over the bare boards towards the door. I heard the shifting sounds of bedclothes and the creaking movement of bodies in beds. The other boys knew what was happening. It had happened before many times … the chosen one was being called for.

Trying to make out I was compliant, I felt that electric tenseness you feel before a fight, when you're positioning yourself for the first, unexpected strike and you need to make it count. He was further down the corridor, opening a store room door. The click of the low voltage light seemed louder in my head. Then, with his arm very firmly around my shoulders, he closed the door. He was in a hurry, I saw it in his face.

I looked up at him as if to encourage him to kiss me ….. he lowered his head towards me, and I raised my hand as if to stroke his head. Then I stabbed the bastard right in the eye, and for good measure stabbed at him again in about the same place. He crumpled to the floor screaming.

I was out of there fast, but before I got back to the dormitory, all the lights were on and the firestorm started. I remember him in that storeroom even to this day, with his belt undone and his trousers down, with blood all over his face. I had really hurt him. That made me feel supreme. The rush I got at the moment of delivery gave me instant gratification. He lost that eye you know. Sure, I got a bad beating afterwards, but like all the things that happened there, it got hushed up. Nobody would have believed me, even if I had spoken out, which I tried to do. No one bothered me there after that though. My reputation for violence was established.

I spent a year at Amersham. In a place like that, you make connections, not friends. Being together in small groups is the only illusion of safety you have. Like the animal we all are, at heart, we are on our own. The day I came out, it was wet and dreary. All I had was what I had gone in with, one old hold-all. But I was also carrying a load of bitterness and revenge and a determined desire to get my own back on society. There was, of course, nobody outside waiting for me. I had been given enough for a bus fare, but I walked those miles back to Roeallan Avenue to find no-one in. I waited on that cold stone step, miserable and hungry before Maisey showed.

Bill, she told me, had been sent to prison for drugs, but not before violence had become an everyday event in that house. The last time Bill was inside, Maisey was so terrified the beatings would start again when he came out, that I heard she had tipped petrol over herself and set fire to it. This was way after I had left that place, but I heard she didn't scream. I didn't cry.

By the time I was 16, I had learnt all sorts of lawbreaking habits, but I was quick with money and never wasted it. I had opened two savings accounts and I fed them with regular lumps of cash as I 'acquired' it through my various schemes. If the cashiers asked, I told them that I sold hot dogs off my stall, or I sold cheap shirts -anything that had a ring of legitimacy about it. It all came to a head when I took a lorry load of cigarettes. Well, I say took, it was opportunism. We stole them from a driver who had stopped for a leak, the daft fella was bursting. We guessed that because of the speed with which he got out of the cab. I was with Jimmy Sproin in his long wheelbase carpet van, going back from one of his jobs. I told him to pull in for a look when I first saw the lorry. When I nipped up to the cab, the keys were just dangling there. Well, what was I to do? I started up and drove away, with Jimmy hot on my tail.

I drove off, laughing fit to bust, and after about a mile, I turned onto a side road. Then we stopped and I backed up to Jimmy's van. With the same keys, I opened the rear doors to see what was in the back, and there they were. No-one was more surprised than me to see the boxes and boxes of cigarettes. Jimmy's courage nearly failed him at the last moment. He may have been three years older than me, but in life it really comes down to how big your balls are, doesn't it? Anyway, we filled his van tighter than a cork in a claret bottle with those boxes, then wiped the wheel and handles for prints and we were gone. Jimmy started to leak nerves when we unloaded them into the large, empty coal store at the back of the outside dunny at home.

Jimmy was happier not being involved, so he came cheap. Bill was still 'away' at the time, Maisey, the lazy cow, only went into the yard once a day with a fag and maybe a newspaper, so I knew it was a safe hiding place. It took almost two months to clear the last box of cigarettes, and that was when I realised I needed to step up to something that did at least look legit.

All of this coincided with my 17th birthday. When the cigarettes were gone, so was I. I took a small single room in large house in Strathfield, with a shared kitchen and bathroom. It was here I met Cindy on the stairs. She was older than me by a few years, and I think she felt I was young and lonely. Well, I played the game and got the prize. She took my mind off work on a good many occasions during my time there.

For years, I had watched and emulated the people I saw and mixed with, mimicking them all, first for humour and the way they talked, walked or carried themselves; and then with the realisation that if I could copy them, it would open doors . I studied them all, the senior office workers at their lunch breaks were my favourites. The way they dressed and acted - so confident, so absolutely assured.

I remember very clearly the day that changed everything. I had stopped outside an insurance broker's office in Parramatta, listening to two men discussing the prices of houses. When they moved away, I saw the notice alongside one of the pictures. 'Junior staff wanted. Must be presentable and personable.'

That day, I bought a dark blue suit with a very pale blue shirt, a wide- striped tie and a pair of black toe-capped, highly polished shoes; rounded not pointed like the fashion of the day. These purchases didn't even dent the money I had made as a runner for one of the loan men, not to mention my side-lines. I got that job, and I never looked back, but why would I?

The pittance they paid didn't matter. I learnt quickly how the selling of insurance worked, then moved very smartly into property. The market was just coming out of its downswing and the feeling of real optimism was out there. Banks were out to loan money, it was just a question of sorting a few details…. like my still being a minor for one.

Our (I often talk in the third person about the business, it seems to shelter me somehow) first house went well. We split it into two houses, and it took a while. It was hard, dirty, heavy work. I learnt a few lessons about dealing with people, but I wouldn't take any shit from any one, shoddy work was not paid for except with bruised knuckles. That took a year to sort and sell, and although the profits could have been better, the learning curve was steep. We went on to new-build apartments and we were steaming.

But we would never have really got off the ground without our friendly bank manager, George Benstone. He was old school with cash flow problems of his own. His tickle was gambling, and like all lovers, he couldn't leave it alone. I first saw him coming out of a casino very late at night, looking miserable. One of the girls who worked there was comforting him, gently holding his arm briefly before going her own way. I never forget a face and I recognised her. By pure chance, she happened to live in the same block as me. I knew her just casually to talk to you understand, and one day I asked her about George and she told me all about her regular customer.

I targeted him, deciding on the very direct approach. It all seemed so natural to me to make an appointment at the bank to request a loan, but when George faltered over the details, I told him I knew about his gambling problems. I didn't want to turn him in to his employer, I just wanted a mortgage. He hesitated, of course, but when he saw the bundle of dollars I put on his desk, he came round. That fat fish was then firmly on the hook and that suited me fine until we grew bigger, then we left George to his own devices. He wasn't going to be the anchor chain that dragged me under with him.

Over the next decade, I concentrated on more straightforward stuff, moving completely clear of my previous lines. I no longer got my hands dirty and I took to wearing smart suits with waistcoats every working day. It was an image I was cultivating, but beneath the surface it was the same old me, gunning for what I wanted. Bribery was the tool of choice. Any personal information was always exploited. Gifts to my contacts were common – whisky, cash in various amounts, entertainment in its many forms. I paid for girls mostly, that always gave me more leverage, anything that might ease someone to my side of the table - agents, planning authority's information suppliers. As more deals were struck and new companies opened, I started ring-fencing individual developments.

My cash flow was different now and I needed a big cash injection to grow fast on the upward market cycle, but this would mean selling a chunk of equity. The banks are canny, and slippery. They were always trying to wave greater loans for equity in front of me, promising better gains for better leverage. If they thought it would benefit them, they would hang you out to dry and then chuck you to the dingoes.

I trusted no-one. My way had always been to 'cream off' where I could. One little business that earnt well was when I 'invested' in Paul Skinner, a small stocky boy I met in the early days of secondary school, which neither of us completed for different reasons. He wasn't so much a clown, just acted like one. But it was a camouflage for his calculating mind. It was always his voice that could be heard orchestrating and cajoling situations in the playground where he could round up a group of people like a sheep dog, and get them to bet with money they didn't always have. He kept his 'book' a sort of diary, with a worn, red felted front and two thick elastic bands around the cover and the current date page in the inside of his coat pocket.

I watched his face quite often when he fingered notes, the collection of his winners always made him sweat with excitement. Like all the others, he had a weakness. He liked to splash the cash, so he was never far from being broke at any stage of his young life. I bought one of my early shops, a secondary location in a parade at the foot of the low rise community housing over on the growing east side. Nice it was, as I remember, on the end of the block, with three useful lock up garages (you never know what you might want to put in those later, do you?).

It was with Paul in mind, not as a tenant but as a minority partner, that I set up what quickly became P and A Racing. His name of course was best suited, but it couldn't possibly be used. I was more than happy to put his initials upfront, never my own. It grew well under my watchful eye to eight shops and became a good cash cow over the years. Eventually Paul became too greedy, and I sold the majority share, along with long leases on the shops, to a national chain. They turned him over soon enough, squeezed him out like a septic spot ready to burst.

Years later he was found dead in a smart condominium. You remember that don't you, Jamie? You saw it in the morning papers, you even went as far as trying to contact me to ask why I was named in the article and how was I involved. The police interviewed me because of our business connections, but that was years ago, and I swear to you I had nothing to do to it, I was not involved at all. I know someone beat him up very badly, so badly that he died from his injuries. Your ma was very upset by it, she was convinced I was involved. Well, I've directly or indirectly been responsible for a few enforcements as a 'stand-over man,' doing a favour for someone, but, just remember, under the right moment when all the stars are aligned, anything is possible. A human being can sink to any level. Causing pain is just another way forward for a single- minded man such as myself. It's all part of the human condition.

By the late 1960s, my hands were tied really, and any hope of further expansion had to be put on hold. We had loans out on industrial investments we had bought in a separate company. They were very highly geared to enable cash to be extracted for other parts of the business. We were banking on higher growth in the rents to resettle the loan ratios, which in turn would rebalance the investments - but this took time. It was frustrating, for all the wrong reasons.

As you realise from reading this, all my life I was driven by acquisition and money. They were the only goals, other fleeting desires never lasted long. It was relentless. It must have been about this time that I had a blow up in our offices out at Chatworth. I don't remember what it was about, but I do remember I decided to go for a walk to cool off. The wide staircase had a polished stainless steel hand rail that, every time I descended, I rested my hand on it, allowing it to sweep around the bends on the landing. Descending at my usual fast pace, I was aware of its absolute smoothness. Was this just my habit, or was there something solid, giving me unconscious reassurance?

The offices were not showy stuff; just a handful of rooms above two shops with a staircase leading straight to the street. It was on the corner of Maypole Street and Wyche, with a church and steeple on the other corner. If they could reach for the sky on their corner, I reasoned that one day we could do the same. The tenants found by the agents took a long lease on the ground floor, providing another good income stream, and we grew into the rest of the building. Fine for the time being, but one day this would all be torn down for redevelopment, along with the neighbour's old garden and the land behind.

I didn't walk far before I got on a bus. Paying the fare for a few blocks, I sank into a window seat to empty my head. The bus came gently to a standstill at some lights alongside another that was making the filter lane. Turning my head slowly, I raked the row of scattered passengers in their window seats on the bus, passing over a few, registering neither movement nor colour, before resting on a stone grey-haired, unshaven man with oversize glasses.

Starting to focus on the detail of the man, I studied the life lines of his face and forehead. Then suddenly, the man looked in my direction, fixing me, holding me in unspoken contact. In my looking away, it was as though I was ashamed in some small way at having been caught out. The observances were broken, forgotten in the time it takes to turn your head.

Traffic moved, the bus was gone, and that inconsequential fleeting scene was in the past. Funny how such a small point of total distraction relieved my tension. I just stood, then walked to the boarding platform, waiting for the next stop. The conductor called out loudly: 'Endeavour Street.'

I got off. I knew this area well, the fledgling office area of the beloved city of Sydney, the name of this street summed it up. The street was named after the Captain Cook ship, The Endeavour. There was another, not quite so famous boat, a yacht by the same name that was commissioned by Sir Thomas Sopwith and built at Camper and Nicholson's famous yard on the south coast of England. It always struck me as odd that three minutes' walk away from Endeavour Street was Nicolson Street.

A large, framed etching by an artist named Wiley (I always liked that name) of this magnificent J Class racing yacht under full sail on a broad reach in a stretch of water called The Solent was hung in my company's reception. Behind it on the wall I had written in pencil 'keep trying, never give up.'

The yacht was 130 feet of the very best that money could buy then. It replaced Shamrock V for the 1934 America's cup challenge. It was fast, very fast, but not fast enough to win. It was the nearest England had come to wining the America's Cup. What was really needed though, was an Aussie with a heap of money to mount a challenge for that prize. That came later, didn't it? What a massive day for the soul of Australia in 1983, with Alan Bond and John Bertrand leading days of celebration.

But I've leapt forward a bit, let's go back to that office area in Endeavour Street and others nearby. One day, when I got things sorted, I had promised myself that I would move my business there too.

I walked back to the junction and, without thinking, took a left that would actually bring me to Nicholson Street, with the intention of crossing there to Beauchamp

Park. I first went there when I was a kid, on some adventure with the gang I grew up with. Those huge, wrought iron Victorian gates are still held open by angular stone cones. Those open gates seemed to beckon you in, like open arms, to the huge trees beyond, which were standing ready to shade, protect and lose you to another place.

Pausing for a moment, amused by the mixture of my memories and the actual view in front of me, I headed to an oversized bench that was unoccupied in the edge of shade. Lowering myself gently I sat back, allowing one arm to rest casually on the back of the bench and then I extended my legs and crossed them at the ankles. Sometimes, some things happen in our lives that have so many consequences that we might feel as if chance was actually in some way pre-set. My arms were folded and I was watching the sky, the noise of traffic was left behind, replaced by that of some small children a way behind me. As I looked across the open playing field that stood before the canopy of trees, I watched several people and a dog who entered the park from one of the small side gates on the northern boundary.

Barely more than dots initially, they grew bigger until I could just about see two men side by side, deep in conversation. What probably nudged my curiosity was that one of them was limping. One was waving his arms wide in expression, perhaps at something said. Then they stopped, isolated for a moment in the open space, and shook hands. The smartly dressed one angled for the main gate, the other then put his hands into the pockets of his shorts, straightened to his full height and continued on his perpendicular line in my direction.

The man with the slight limp, I could see more clearly as he got closer, was younger than me by maybe ten years, probably in his late 20s. He was taller than me though, over six feet, and had long, fair hair held back in some sort of a clasp. The way he filled his space was more rock and roll than hippy. How easy it is to pre- judge people. Our mechanism is rarely wrong, although when it is. He looked in my direction as he passed. We connected, he smiled, he raised a hand, and then he disappeared into the trees behind me. Later, I walked back through those same gates, and picked up a taxi to the office. Funny though, sometimes a face sticks in my memory and I see it bright, like a flash bulb in a mirror.

It must have been several months after that time in the park, if my memory serves me right, when I was invited to a dinner; you know, one of those boxing evenings. It was a fund-raising event with lots of testosterone flowing, mostly from men whose fancy footwork is now more metaphorical than literal. There must have been around 400 men sitting at round tables of eight or more, surrounding the raised ring side. A master of ceremony was controlling the atmosphere and the build up to the bouts. The only women present were those waiting the tables. They were dressed, well just about, in short black skirts, white T-shirts, stockings and heels and their tips ran higher as the evening progressed and the alcohol took hold. The bouts were fast, brutally furious with the bloody, short intensity of unrewarded gladiators. The tables were about mate-ship, money and business and there was a growing wave of voices beating upon the walls. It was power, driven by alcohol. I was always careful to limit my drinking, so I could watch what was happening and act on opportunities whenever they might present themselves.

It was a landmark evening really, at some stage the boxing was put on hold while a punch up started with minimal skill between an older man and another guy on the nearby table who he had seen touch up a waitress. She happened to be his daughter. With what appeared be perfect manners, he folded his linen napkin and placed it neatly on his side plate while excusing himself politely to his fellow diners. He then walked slowly over, tapped the shoulder of the younger man who turned, presenting his face for a volley of blows that were delivered in unison with:

'You asked for that … she's my daughter and she's just 18.'

Crockery started to fly about, others jumped up and got involved, but it calmed down fairly quickly. The attention left the ring for a while and focused on the fracas. It was then I came to realise that he was watching me. He was three tables back from us in the hall, sitting still, watching me. The beginning of a smile moved on his face, then died away. I knew that there was recognition, but I couldn't place where from.

I was to find out soon, as he pushed back his chair, stood upright and nodded to the man on his left. I saw the long, tied back hair, and as he started to walk in my direction with the slightest limp, the flashbulb inside my head went off. He just held out his hand introducing himself:

'Hello, my name is Nat Gibson.'

Everyone wore a dinner suit that evening, but not like the way he wore his though. He stood before me, toned, tanned and relaxed. The image held in my mind now is of the silver studs on his dress shirt and their swirling design, which I found out later to be in the pattern of multi- headed drill bits. He knew where I was going to be and simply placed himself in my path, in order to meet me. I was immediately suspicious, I needn't have been, as we had a mutual business friend in a common. That's how I met him - my Money Man. Although, of course, he might recall it differently.

How things might have been had I not met him? I don't know. He opened my eyes to land investment up in Darwin and I sucked him into my web for development in Sydney. But when the shit really did hit the wall, there was an almighty mess. Everyone near stank of it. He made a lot of money easily on the back of shares in the mineral boom somewhere, but having got it, he was not that canny with it. He was, in the end, just one more of the casualties. If he had spent more time on business and less time on the water, lots of things might have been different. At that time, he liked to sail in some piddling little catamaran called a Mosquito up in Darwin.

I had neither time nor inclination for sailing, although on one of my quick trips up there to the sticks he did persuade me to join him for a 'run round the harbour' as he put it. I'd gone to look at some land that he had got a hook on, somewhere south of the town. He'd already bought a good large slice outright, and we were talking seriously about swinging in at another large tranche of the stuff, if we could persuade the vendors their price would be via an option, rather than a lower straight offer.

It was set in a dirt dead place of well over 500 acres alongside a lagoon where a farm of some sort was barely operating. They came round in the end and we left the lawyers to get the due diligence sorted. I would have flown back to Sydney straight away, but it was too late in the day. The following day was Sunday and the only flight was fully booked. Maybe it was the euphoria of closing the deal that made me agree to his suggestion. I never understood why he didn't get a decent- sized boat, one that he could walk onto without getting his feet wet, God knows it wasn't the money, he could have bought the bloody club. That day he took me out was the first and final time I ever went on a small boat. I nearly drowned. We had sailed out a fair way, the hulls slapping, the waves jolting, bucking and lifting us as we headed close into the wind.

Then he shouted something, which was ripped away by the wind. Following him, I scrabbled across the centre netting, holding the trapeze wire, ready to follow his waving arm.

We'd gone about and the ride was smoother, much faster. The boat thrust a new course, as quick as a greyhound from a gate. We took a fast run with the stiff westerly wind bellowing the sail hard. Both us out were out on the trapezes, with one float lifting intermittently with the wind. We were heading up to go round a yellow buoy when the boat skewed.

Nat was shouting his head off at me, as I was still clipped onto the trapeze. I swung wildly, first round the mast, then, as the boat capsized, I was slung in the water underneath the boat. I panicked. It all happened so quickly. Did I black out? I'm not sure.

Then, and now, I can't be sure that he saved his own skin before even thinking of me. He told me later that he had stood on the dagger board and forced the boat to swing head to the wind and it righted itself with a smack so loud that it could have split the hulls. Somehow I got back on board and pulled him back on too. He was whining about jellyfish having stung him. I had that overpowering feeling of having no control over what was happening and I had to get back on dry land. This outing had really unnerved me. It wasn't long before we made the shore, covering the mile or so back to the Larrakeyan sailing club like an arrow. We weren't speaking much by then, unwritten blame I suppose. He drove the small cat through the shallows with both the dagger and centre boards up, then hard up into the tide line, it gave off a dry rasping sound as it lost some of its paint work to the beach.

Some bloke Nat knew brought the trolley over, then opened with:

'Could have been worse, you might not have made it back!'

He banged on about the sightings of crocs and sharks in the harbour. I realised then that jellyfish had been the least of our worries. Out there, a friendly hello from either of the other two would have been as welcome as a lit cigarette in an oil refinery.

2

Frank O'Hagan's notebook, Sydney. 1972

Far more interesting was how I met your ma. It was at the Binger Racecourse, Sydney in May 1972. Easy to remember that date, as I thought afterwards that I'd picked two winners. Bignor is a small track about 20 miles or so to the north of the city. One of our companies, Burbank Estates, was sponsoring the fourth race, The Thornbury Cup. It was the usual stuff, pay a lump sum, and in return you get your name in the programme and on the advertising boards around the park. You can have a suite for your clients and their partners, you bring along your star employees, maybe their wives, and there's good food and plenty of drinks. It's just a perk for your clients, but it's like axel grease, it's got be laid on thick, in the hope that the wheels turn easier....and, of course, it's all tax deductible.

It was a cool-ish day, perhaps 18 degrees with a dragging wind. I drove over in the Aston with the hood down, leaving plenty of time. I'd chosen to wear a linen suit and was feeling as though I didn't have a care in the world. It took a while to get there, the track was set in semi-suburban surroundings in the middle of a wide, sloping valley. I was greeted politely at the Douglas Gate private car park by one of the parking officials wearing the familiar red and yellow short- sleeved monogramed shirt. He leaned forward just a little from the waist at the side of my car, and I received a perfunctory:

'Good morning, sir'

I had already reached over to the glove compartment as the car slowed to pull out the numbered parking card and the ticket papers and was holding them ready. He made a big play at the inspection, exercising his grain of authority, then just said: 'After you've parked up, take the entrance to the west stand and follow the sign to the Members Only area and then on to the Dawson Suite.'

I drove slowly across the car park, making a couple of turns before slotting the car into the allotted space. I shut the roof and locked it, before sliding off the leather seat. I looked automatically at my shoes to ensure they were clean, before locking the car and heading back towards the staircase. The crowds of racegoers were pressing in as I walked those last paces upwards from Western Avenue.

You could feel the atmosphere, hear the hum of the crowds, and breathe in the excitement of the day. It took no time at all to push through and up the stairs to the Dawson Suite. I just raised my arm as I spotted Tony Varidker. He was dressed smartly, topped with the Turf Club blazer with its coat of arms on the top pocket. He was the fixer, the guide man and the event organiser. Reaching him, he nodded to me:

'Good morning Mr O'Hagan, all's on song for you and your guests.'

Respect and efficiency that's what I demanded, and that's what he gave me. The large room must have been three smaller rooms knocked together. The tall, corniced ceilings were in pale cream, and there were heavy, champagne-coloured drapes over three wide sets of French widows, held back with fancy cords and tassels. The bar was taking a hammering right from the start. The linen-topped tables were filled with people having a good time. I stepped up to some of the tables and welcomed people, with a handshake here and maybe a kiss brushed across a cheek for the few wives I had met before, then I headed out through the French windows onto the crowded veranda. The shade was on the long, mahogany, upholstered bench that ran its full length and the sun braced a blue sky. What a view. Dropping beneath to the crowded terraces and spanning the posted two mile course, the vista lay open to me, close enough that I felt I could reach out and touch the horses as they ran. It was exhilarating; I felt I owned the whole place. And so I did, but only for the day.

My thoughts were interrupted by a passing backslapper, then there were more handshakes. My colleagues, I could see, were doing a good job. They were important pieces in the chess game we were playing that day, I was just the guiding light.

The bookie in the corner was running hoarse by then, a lot of money had passed through his hands. I can tell you now, people who own betting shops don't go to Clark Island on vacation. Just for the show, I put money down for a couple of doubles and a monkey for a place on Bless My Wings on the Western Stakes Trophy. The smart money was on him - he was a cracker, coming in for that place at 4 to 1.

Our race was slotted in at a good place in the programme, at 2pm. At 1.40, the three year- olds were paraded round the 'bird cage' then after the sightings, took their places. The barriers went up right on 2. The rebounding echo from the loudspeakers conveyed clearly the quickening, rising voice of the announcer, who pitched faster as the tension built. The race was bunched up for the first mile, then the front three runners eased a gap and pulled ahead.

It held tight for the next half mile, then the whips flailed the air with urgency as the horses' hooves beat the turf. The power struggle raged among the colours, breaking into the final straight. At the line, the announcer's voice fell from its crescendo, slipping back to the slower, even tempo to confirm the finishing runners. The winner was Strike Run, a beast of beauty who won by a length over Black Pete. Third, but still leading the pack by some way, came Mighty Faith. I met the winning jockey, presented the cup to the owners, posed for the photographs in the winners' enclosure and then slipped away, looking for a quieter spot to melt into.

I ended up in a downstairs bar for a beer, and that was where I was when I first saw Jess, your ma.

I was with a couple of guests, she was laughing with someone near the long window that overlooked the track, and we made eye contact, her laughter stopped as though her power supply had been cut. I can remember even now the way her fingers touched her hair. Her lips moved, but I heard nothing. Later, bold as you like, she came over, smiling as though the world was hers. She was wearing white slacks and a cobalt blue T-shirt. She was stunning. She wore thin silver bracelets, lots of them, on her left wrist, but no rings on her fingers. She said 'excuse me' to my guests and handed me a note. It simply said: 'If you call… I'll answer,' and a phone number.

Anyway, that's the way I remember it. She may have told you a different story. I called her the next day. It's amazing now, when I look back. It all happened so quickly.

She moved in with me fairly soon, and then we started building East Winds, our home on that magnificent five acre plot at Shelly. It was a big place on the headland overlooking the bay, with vast lawns right down to the sea, you remember that don't you? That's where you were born and where you spent the first few years of your life. I threw loads of contractors at that house to get it finished for your ma. It was a massive project – it had six bedrooms, guest suites, a cinema, garages, flats for staff, a swimming pool – it was endless. And that path through the woods down to Shelly beach.

Maybe you can remember the time we were there together? Some days, if I had a day off, we used to play in the pool or go down to the beach, but I guess you were very young. Perhaps she showed you some photographs of the time we lived there? At first, Jess loved the idea of it all. It was such an impressive house, and she had staff on hand for everything. For a girl from the old country, arriving here with not much more than a bent dollar, she knew she had hit the jackpot with me. I did treat her well – most of the time. But things didn't work out with us. I'm sure it's hard for you to hear this, but you definitely weren't planned and the whole idea of becoming a father was an enormous shock to me. Deep down, looking back, I probably thought my best chance was just to ignore it.

I was working very long hours, I put everything I had into running the business, and when I did get home, your mother would nag at me. She irritated me some nights, said I was drinking too much and I admit that occasionally I lost it. You were so small, and she was wrapped up in you, and I can see now that I was jealous. Your mother grew further and further away from me, and I didn't try to change.

I guess it's difficult for you, or anyone else, to understand the pressures that I put myself under. I was a driven man, all my life practically, but it was all in the wrong direction. It may well have been clear to others around me. Anyway, that time with your mother seems so, so long ago now. I gave her all she had. The best tables in life were hers, but that wasn't enough. Eventually, she decided to trade it all off for that beach shack.

．．．．．．．．．．．．．．．．．．

The back part of one of the exercise books detached itself from the staples and slipped through Jamie's fingers. It fell past her knees to the floor. Leaving it where it fell, she stretched her body back on the chair, allowing her head to tilt to face the ceiling. This was not the way the story went, according to her mother. Was he a fantasist? How much of this version of events was true? What and who was she to believe? Shaking the very foundations of her life now would change nothing though. The light was beginning to fade. Jamie pulled herself upright using the arms of the chair, bent forward and picked up the notebook from the floor. A corner had been folded carefully then removed, leaving the bottom of an elaborate doodle that looked like a winged snake. Why had that corner been removed?

This book was thinner than the others, perhaps some pages were removed, if so, when had that happened and why? These questions were left without answers. Turning on the main room light, Jamie drew the curtains. Still holding the book, she went to the kitchen to make something to eat. The urge to return to the diary was compulsive, and once back in the sitting room, Jamie edged the tray onto the table, then re-arranged the cushions on the sofa before sitting again. Transferring a glass of orange squash to a cork mat on the table, she placed the tray with its plate of scrambled eggs on her lap and began to eat.

When she had finished, the tray was put on the floor. She eased herself lengthways on the sofa, resting against the cushions, then flicked the pages to find where she had left off.

....

I heard on the car radio a few years back, a song, well it wasn't so much the song that caught me, but the name of the song and its date when the DJ was talking after the record. It was from a double album by The Allman Brothers, hugely popular in the mid-1970s. Your mother loved that album, especially the track called Jessica. She called it *her* song.

That light shone in a dark corner of my head. Music, for reasons I couldn't understand, did it for her, but not for me. This particular album was played from her huge collection over and over. Dancing? She loved it. I had no time even to discriminate. One day, your ma told me she wanted out, and when I next came back to the house you and her had upped and gone to the bungalow. No nothing, just gone. Yes, I was upset for a while, I just let you both get on with it. I checked up sometimes to make certain you were OK, but not long after I had a lot of pressing problems of my own. My life's work was imploding, my wealth was evaporating, and it was difficult to see the sky, never mind think about weather forecasts.

Then, the cyclone hit Darwin. It was the blanket news story across every state. The place was torn up, thousands of people lost their homes and were evacuated. The funny thing about distance though was I didn't *really* feel it, what really cut deep was that it was the catalyst for a personal implosion. It was days before I eventually got a call from my partner up there. Anyway, as I was saying before I got side tracked, the fall was swift and had I not bought that place in Bulli for you both, you would have been homeless.

………………..

Jamie threw the book to the floor and screamed:

'You bastard, you selfish bastard, you still owned millions of dollars' worth of property and all you threw at us was a basic beach hut, far enough away so as to be out of sight and out of mind. You deserted us.'

The book had come to rest partially open with the pages creased and bent just under the loose cover of the arm chair. Tears of confusion poured down her face. It was about loss, she recognised this, loss of what things could have been, but never were. There was so much about her early life that her mother hadn't talked about, and now she didn't know which version of events were true – her mother's or her father's. Jamie lifted the book from the floor and slapped it down on to the coffee table with undue force. Then, using her sleeve, she wiped her eyes, smudging what little make up she had on.

Moving to the kitchen, she ran water into the kettle and, while it started to boil, found that there was no milk in the fridge. It's the small things that kick you when you're down. Defeated, she turned off the kettle. It would have to be a glass of tap water. Taking this back to the sofa, she lay slouched drinking it, while looking at the exercise book. Finishing the water, she placed the glass on the table and picked up the book again to find her place.

....

It was around then that the business blew out, as messy as a rotten pear dropped onto the pavement. As I said, it was chance that buggered everything - the cyclone that destroyed Darwin. My money man, as I called him, lost everything too. It was my fault. I arranged to inflate profits, bumped them way up, to get him to put his fall back capital into the business towards the end. I would like to share some of the blame with that bloody cyclone though – it came from nowhere. But of course, the reason the business imploded was because of the way I had structured the whole thing. I should have checked with him, but the clauses somehow got overlooked.

The insurances on a block policy up there in Darwin were not correctly in place, coupled with the financial wind shift that was happening. I was on the rocks. The only unanswered question at that time was how long it would take to be smashed to pieces. Still, he seemed a mug, greedy for the gravy like the rest, so I took him for his last dollar. We had well and truly overstretched, (well, I did the over-stretching, he didn't know too much about refinancing) buying stuff up there, then I borrowed heavily against all of it.

The bastard slipped away on a dark tide. Not a word to anyone, just disappeared. I heard much later he sailed away as crew on some yacht from one of the marinas…. skint. I never heard from him again. Can you believe that? I was about 40 then and thought I could rebuild, but no-one would touch me after the companies all folded one after another, it was the house of cards. The day the repossession order was slapped on me, the phone didn't stop ringing. I couldn't stand it, I just ripped it out of the wall. The sudden silence was so pervasive it seemed as if the panic in me disappeared, a fleeting calmness came to me. It was just like having a strong gin and tonic on a cool evening.

This didn't last though. A few minutes later the front door knocker went, the hammering was so loud it sounded like a jack hammer. The staff had already left over unpaid wages, so I was alone in the house. I practically had to run to get there and when I did, there were three men. Two in suits and one in casual shorts, with a khaki coloured shirt. One of the suits spoke first:

'Mr O'Hagan?'

'Yes,' I snapped at him.

This time he spoke in slower more deliberate way, like he was enjoying the scene:

'Mr Frank O'Hagan?'

'Yes'

And before that single syllable word of mine was dry on the wind, the flat of his hand shot forward and clapped me on the chest with the papers I hadn't noticed he had been holding at his side.

'Repossession order served by state bailiff on you for this property and its contents. This gentleman,' pointing to the other suit, 'is the representative from Standard and International Finance Bank.'

His economy with words was precision itself.

All I could think of to say was: '... and who's he?' pointing to the man with the khaki shirt.

'Locksmith. Please collect a small bag with some clothes and leave the premises. If you should, and I don't suppose you will, refuse, the police will be called and will arrest you for impeding a court's bailiff.'

I spoke only one word in the plural, which I don't wish to repeat to you. It was a long walk down the drive, the gates had been forced open, but when I turned around to look for the last time, I could see only one vehicle and a van parked just off the drive.

Hitching up the sailing hold-all in my hand, the fingers of my other hand closed around the self- locking keys of the new Aston in the garage, and in a childish gesture I threw them into the shrubbery. I had been warned of this event a few days before and it had led me to think about making arrangements, so I had already emptied the safe and put its contents in a secure place. At that time I was also paranoid. I thought I could somehow straighten it all out. But all too soon it became apparent to me, bloody pariahs. All the people I knew just evaporated. Doors were shut, I was completely turned over. I had that small stash of money, but it didn't last and so I started to slip back to the place I had crawled out of years before. You were the only lasting dye I had cast.

All the stuff we built never even bore my name. The next decade or so was unremarkable, lost, and forgettable.

3

Frank, Melbourne. 1991

The marker I remember during that time was the fire in 1991, in the residential tower block in Melbourne. What actually happened, how did the fire start? Well, don't ask me. At the time I hadn't the faintest idea, but it was literally the hand of fate that didn't just cover my tracks, it obliterated them. I was living hand to mouth then. I went to see Charlie Woodford in his flat number 92 on the 21st floor at Malvern Court about 8.30pm. As I recall...that stinking lift was stop- start, unreliable, the graffiti- covered corridors stank like pub drains.

I knew him from way back, from a pub we used to drink in. I had bought stuff from him occasionally, not for me you understand, for others. I don't touch that sort of stuff. He was a small time petty criminal, drugs mainly and loans. I had borrowed money, it had got awkward when I lost the job on the docks and got behind. I could see that I had got myself in a hole. Some holes are so deep that you need a ladder to get out, but who would pass you that without wanting something in return. Only someone who loves you probably, I wouldn't know.

On 3 March 1991, I intentionally killed a man.

In the simplest of terms, murder is murder. You can pare back, polish over, but never ignore the detail. There, I've said it, I have admitted it. Never before, nor since that day, have I said aloud or written those words. I carried around that knowledge locked in a space so deep that it made a grave look shallow. I was never caught or tried for this brutal act, but now at my age, it barely seems to matter. That must strike you as odd. Anyway, I asked him, Charlie, but he wouldn't even listen to my reasoning. He laughed, using phrases like 'dead man walking' and 'shortly your piano playing days will be over'. I'll admit I was nervous, but not frightened as such.

Sometimes, clarity of mind and calmness can come to you during moments of intensity. Charlie had got up from his leather armchair with that creaking sound as the cushion returns to its original state. He walked to the window. I remember he was revolving a pen in his left hand, jammed between his fingers and thumb. He walked as though weighing his next move, knowing he held the best cards. That was when I had this flash, this moment, this clarity of thought to strike him with the heavy glass ash tray.

I vaguely remember its contents, a pen and an apple core. They fell to the shag pile carpet as I picked it up. It was one of those cheap circular ones made to look like cut glass, but far too chunky. Somehow I knew my hand would clutch the rolled edge so I could hold it firmly in my fist as though it were a hoop, so that I could pound him.

Two strides was all it took and one powerful downward action. He heard nothing, he probably felt nothing much. I would say he was dead before he hit the carpet. As I said I was calm, I just looked at him as I stood over him, knowing with all certainty that my loan, together with others, was cancelled. I put the ash tray back on the table and for some peculiar reason picked up the apple core and the pen and replaced them.

There was blood, but not much, oozing slowly but steadily onto the carpet from the back of his head. But head wounds do bleed a lot, so they say. Well, it wasn't really a wound was it as such, because he was dead? I remember at the time thinking it reminded me of the very birth of a stream, you know that oozing of water from a crack in the rock before it becomes a trickle. I watched, it did turn quickly to a trickle. Was it premeditated? Not, really. If you can understand that. I thought about the vague possibility if it came to a struggle, that sort of thing. It didn't really occur to me that two reasonable men couldn't work something out. I sat back for a while on a shallow armchair with my arms on the arm rests, my hands hanging limp from the wrists thinking of nothing much, taking in my surroundings.

The wall clock over the mock fireplace was the kind that was strangely popular in the 1970s. The clock itself was the size of a small dinner plate, with brassy gold fingers jutting out from it, supposedly looking in some way like the sun. The time was, according to the sun, now 10pm. I'm not sure how long I sat there, maybe minutes or maybe nearly an hour, but I gave scant thought to Charlie, or indeed my predicament. It had occurred to me that I could catch the beginning of the news on his TV, but I didn't.

Ha... little did I know then that I would be part of it before the night was through.

There was blood on one of my hands, I got up and walked to the kitchen. Reaching over the sink bowl with its plates and pans unwashed, I turned on the hot tap leaving it to run while I glanced about hoping to find some form of soap. There was nothing and the water was cold.

Idly, I wondered whether his last meal, a curry of some sort, had been any good. I wiped my hands on the frayed corner of an old blue bath towel that passed as a dish cloth. It was damp, perhaps hanging in the vain hope of drying, and I then returned to the armchair. I was tired, it had been a long week of legwork, but I was due to start a new job as a yardman the following week. Even in my advanced state of weariness, I could see there was little future to be had from the job now. Deep breathing always did it for me, it was easier just to give in, surrender to it. I fell into a deep sleep.

I woke to what seemed like a metal object banging on the door twice, or it could have three times; louder than a door knocker but not a clean round sound, more of a dragging and bashing. Assuming it to be kids in the corridor messing about, and slightly resentful at this disturbance, I opened my eyes and the sun on the wall in front of me reflected its luminous dial. It was ten minutes past three. There was little light – had I turned off the lights? I couldn't remember. I gave Charlie a wide berth and went to the window to open it for fresh air, my hand was barely on the handle of that newly installed window when I thought I smelt the smoke. What confronted me almost stopped the very breath in my body. It was fire, leaping tongues of flame, clawing, raging at the outside of the building way below me. I was at a cross between terror and fascination. Then panic bit.

Grabbing the towel in kitchen, I threw out the plates in the bowl and plunged the towel briefly into the filthy water and then almost dragged it behind me in the rush for the door of the flat. Once in the corridor, I raced to the far end of the landing for the stairs I had come up earlier. I was through the double doors, swinging downwards on the rails when a fleeting thought occurred to me that I had seen no one on the landing as I left the flat. I covered three floors flat out before I entered the smoke zone. When I say smoke zone, up until then I was just running, then I was hit with the toxic smell of the smoke. It took me straight back to some job we were on years before, where all the rubbish timber was burnt rather than put in a skip. This was nothing like wood smoke, although that's bad enough.

No, this was like the day the idiot I was with threw two sheets of plastic corrugated roofing from a conservatory onto a fire. We had run up the garden in fear of burning our lungs with the hideous chemical rush. This was like that - except it wasn't just two sheets.

The wet towel was over my head in an instant, twisted around my neck. I used my right hand to guide me, running it loosely down the metal bannister and I covered the next floors at a much slower pace. It was still a headlong rush downwards, swinging round a corner while using both hands to steady myself. I felt a massive cross draught, which I took to be the next landing doors jammed open. God, this draught would fan a flame as surely as a match would light a fire. Now I heard panic in the shouts and mounting clamour around me. I sensed, as well as felt, this growing stream of human beings would fall like ten pins crashing over one another unless we came out of this soon. If a burst of fire were to lick upwards from the lower floors within this stairwell, we would be done to a turn, quicker than a sausage on a barbie.

It was about here I fell. Well, tripped over. I landed hard on my shoulder and the towel was ripped sideways from my face at the point of impact. Jeeze, it hurt. The blood was mine. I could feel it running from my nose and a cut to my cheek. That was when I swept her up as she lay twisted against me, not as a conscious thing, I just did it as an action. She was small. I don't know why I did it. Instinct maybe. How old was she? I don't know that either.

I readjusted the towel on us both, pressing her close to me with my left arm locked around her, and now with streaming eyes and a burning throat that seemed to extend right down my pipes, I just plugged on downwards. I remember the noise, a barrage of sound, wild and woven into fear, the volume bursting within the staircase.

The pace of movement, and the slower people falling. It was the instinct of survival, everyone for themselves; and yet still I held on to her. Then I felt the cold fresh draught, this time, miraculously, it was the main external door and a solid wedge of people were well through it and into the car park. How I covered those 20 floors I don't know.

That's when the coughing really started for both of us. Leaving the towel on my head, I put the girl down, pushing her gently away, pointing at two ambulances among the swelling crowds nearby. She moved hesitantly, then stopped, then moved again. I don't think she looked back, I don't really know. Looking up briefly, I saw the fire had really taken hold and was reaching high, floor after floor up the outside of building.

My instinct was to leave the scene quickly. I pulled the towel over my head and face, dropping my head down slightly, then put distance between me and those flats. No one challenged me. Why was I so indifferent to a life taken and perhaps a life saved? I really can't say because I don't know. A phycologist would have much to say about my behaviour, but I wasn't concerned.

Quickening my pace a little, walking as upright as I could, I cut across the play area, between the slide and the swings, my eyes were streaming badly still but the coughing had subsided a little. Before turning into Hamburg Street, it was like I had been touched on the shoulder. I turned to view a spectacle of absolute horror. By now the fire was totally out of control, reaching with ease up through the upper floors, lightening the night sky. Swelling, billowing palls of dense black smoke were building above the tower with falling debris and occasional burning molten panels falling to the earth. I could still see people on odd balconies on the northern side near the top. Their only option would be a fatal leap. This vile spectacle of destruction was ripping through a community that only a few hours ago had lay quietly at rest. Again, I started walking and turned the corner, leaving just the sound of sirens in the half light .My left shoulder was hurting as I moved my arm. How I had held on to that small child I don't know.

Gently, I prodded my face. The cheek felt sore, probably just a graze, and my nose was OK, which was surprising, but at least it didn't feel like I'd broken it. Using the stinking towel, I wiped carefully around my face hoping to tidy things up and was about to throw away the towel when I thought again, it was nearly dry, it was evidence of a sort.

That mile was a slow walk and I was hurting. Defrosting from somewhere deep, I could only hold one image now. It was the picture of Charlie and what I had done that grew. I knew there would be serious trouble. Fortunately, there were few people around on the streets at that hour of the morning. When I reached my building, there was only stillness and the echo of my own feet on the stairs as I made my way to my first floor room.

Stripping to my T-shirt and underpants, I climbed into bed and curled into the foetal position. Slowly, warmth returned to my body, but so did the searing images of the fire and the panic that had been all around me. Sleep was out of the question, but I did at least hover in a veil just above it.

In the morning, the fire was a secondary replay on full volume, right across the country's media. Pictures of the tower ablaze and shouting at a night sky; and then blackened, blitzed and smouldering like a gaunt skeleton against the dawn were everywhere. The fireball had rampaged free from any constraint or control, consuming everything in its path. It was said that, as an older building it had been upgraded with insulation products on the exterior which had fuelled the fire, but no sprinkler system had been installed. The death toll was estimated at 110, but because of the intensity of the fire, the true number of people might never be known. When I heard this I wondered about Charlie.

I left Melbourne about a year later and moved west to Adelaide, where I felt a new start might wipe away the scarred memories of my life. It had taken a long time for me to realise that I had spent most of my life pursuing the ultimately pointless. I had started to change, and begun to focus on the people around me more. Having only a few possessions, the decision to leave Melbourne, which had been fermenting for a while, was easy. I just collected my cards with my wages after clocking out of work for the final time and went home. I awoke around 5.30 the next day, washed and was gone, catching an early bus right into the city.

I chose on an impulse to get off the bus a few blocks before the station and crossed the St Kilda Road into Victoria Gardens and walked slowly among the trees. They were just turning the late autumn colours. It was a place I felt affection for and I had been there often. It calmed me, just breathing deeply and walking there. Through the trees on my left, I saw out takes of the modern Arts Centre building between the boughs. It had been originally designed to have a massive copper spire to top it out, I had laughed at the obvious cost of this and I suppose this was why it hadn't happened.

Taking the under-path beneath Alexander Avenue, I walked on down towards The Yarran and Princes Bridge. Stopping at the bottom of the steps, I stretched my fingers a few times and picked up my bag again. Dodging the downward flow, often swinging my bag at knee level to clear my path, I climbed the steps and crossed the bridge for Flinders St Station, the front of which was Victorian architecture at its best. Glancing up above the high entrance arch before passing through it, the clock was on 10.20. I thought how it didn't so much tell the time, as keep up with it.

The station was crowded with people trying to pick their way through so many bodies. Pressing into them, I passed the shops and bars and grazing outlets, weaving towards the platform areas and the overhead departure boards. I had just enough time to buy a single ticket, and get a paper. Slightly short of breath, I arrived at the barrier to the platform, where the inspector took my ticket before clipping it and passing it back in my direction without a second glance. It was only then that I actually opened the paper.

Block print leapt up at me.

Alan Bond bankrupt

This was April 1992. The news that Alan Bond had gone bankrupt for $1.8billion had been reported all over the world, and there was a big piece about him in The West Australian, the paper I had just bought. Some banking group, headed by the Hong Kong Bank of Australia, applied for a trustee to be appointed after 'Bondy', as he was known across Australia, failed to repay $194 million arising from a personal guarantee he gave on a loan to a former nickel mining project.

Alan Bond, who arrived in Australia at the age of 12 with his parents, had started out as a sign writer, and then gone into business. It all got a bit messy and he went to prison for corporate fraud. When he was out, he made another fortune. You may have heard people talking about him and his decision to back Australia to win the America's Cup back in the 80s. This prestigious cup attracts the world's top sailors and yacht designers as well

as wealthy sponsors – it's a rich man's sport – and Bondy sponsored the
Australian challenger. Well, he made history. In 1983, his sponsorship heralded a new age for the sport in Australia, and we won, taking the trophy from the New York Yacht Club for the first time since its inception in 1857. It made Alan Bond a hero back home. Now, here he was…. bankrupt.

Reading about his downfall and the futility of having everything – and then nothing - resonated with me. It made me reflect on my own life.

I walked part way down the platform before opening the door to a compartment. There were just two people inside, at the corridor end, so I was fortunate to get a window seat. Swinging my bag gently, I used my spare hand under it to lever it into the slung luggage rack above the seat, then sagged to the seat with the newspaper. Letting out a long breath, I looked about the carriage to see I was being examined by two elderly women. They could have been sisters.

Taking in my surroundings, I glanced above the padded tapestry headrests. Framed and fronted by glass was the long diagram of stops on the line to my destination, then an advert about the adventures of travelling by train. A hushed conversation among the two women started, but I didn't look at them. The minutes ticked on as I scanned the sport on the back page, then the door opened and more passengers came on. The sisters' chatter ceased abruptly.

The shrill of the whistle came, a sudden small jolt, and the train began to move. The sisters got off in the suburbs at some station, and my long journey was underway.

After a while, I gave up with the paper and stared out of the window. I was bored, and thought the best way to pass the time was to shut my eyes. I crossed my feet at the ankles, and drifted off to sleep. It was tedious, and took most of the day to reach Adelaide.

After living in two sets of rooms, I eventually settled in a flat above a bicycle shop. It was small, but comfortable and convenient. I missed nothing of Melbourne. For a couple of years after arriving here, I had worked in an abattoir, but funnily enough the violence towards the animals got through to me. They had spent a blameless life, harming nobody, but they were frightened and abused by both the abattoir workers and the system. I always found it difficult when I got the job of hosing down the killing floor. To wash away so much innocent blood was awful. I realised then how much time had changed me, because when I was younger, I had used the knife on a couple of occasions and had positively enjoyed hurting people. Physically twisting the blade had given me a greater sense of power.

Then, blood had never worried me, and I can tell you now that I have had blood on my hands both literally and metaphorically. I'm not proud of these things, but they are part of me nonetheless. I gave up all red meat shortly after leaving the abattoir, I called it my spiritual payback.

It was a small add on a postcard in a newsagent's window that had led me to Richard Barnfield, and to the flat above Barney's Bicycles. Barney, as he was known, had taken a long lease years ago on the shop and flat above, which he converted into two micro units at some stage. The flat I took was really two rooms, with a shower in the corner of the bedroom. The kitchen/living room was fitted out well enough, with a new vitreous enamelled sink, a fridge and a work top. There was a Belling electric cooker. It was all a bit on the small side, but fine for my purposes. Freshly papered with a magnolia colour throughout. Barney lived in the other flat across the hall with his companion Sly, a mid-sized, seven year old mongrel true to his name, an affectionate beast who followed him faithfully. The dog would wander around the shop, often lying in the warmth of the sunshine by the window or sitting near the inside staircase, watching the repairs. He would say hello to all the customers, but even with an open door, he wouldn't cross the threshold without instructions.

What started with a beer on a Saturday evening turned in time to a friendship that meant as much to me as any I've ever had. Barney was older than me by ten years or more, and was well known, but only appeared to keep his own company. An intelligent man, completely at ease with himself.

He had once been married, but he rarely mentioned it. He was raised up at Port Augusta and had drifted south with the swill of life to the city fringes. I started by helping out in the shop on the busy Saturdays while he worked on repairs. He was close enough to shout over to me if I couldn't find stuff for customers. He would be spread over the small section at the back with tools scattered around him. The smell of that shop I remember so well, it was distinct and singular.

We became a good team, and he taught me much about bicycle mechanics. I gradually came to like him and I became very fond of Sly. I even took to wandering the west side city streets on Sundays when the traffic was at its lowest, on a bike that I took for my own. First, I had borrowed it from the rack of second handers that came our way for resale in part exchange for new bikes. I was wobbly at first, but you never really forget how to ride a bike. They were slow speed days, drifting up back alleys and service roads exploring the mesh of byways that make up the arteries of my end of the city. Going slowly meant it was easy to stop to satisfy my curiosity about something I saw. It was easy to strike up small conversations, momentary relationships that glowed briefly then burnt out. These were small enrichments of what had become a simple life.

I'm not sure when I first noticed that Barney was forgetting words, or using them in an odd context, but I would brush over it. It took me a long time to recognise there really was a problem. I thought it might be stress-related in some way, and we would often just laugh it off. It was three years before I could persuade him to go and talk to a doctor about it, and when he did he either didn't believe him or he just took no notice.

By then, I was working full time in the shop for a low wage and a rent- free flat, happy to be a contributor to something useful that was of worth to both me and others in the neighbourhood. I knew things were worsening when Barney asked me to take over the ordering and accounts. He came across the landing to my door one morning, banged it, and then shouted out my name. Normally, he would have knocked just once and waited. When I opened the door, he stood there looking like a man who had got dressed in a charity shop in the dark. He was clutching an armful of files and papers. As he held them out to me, papers slipped to the floor, he didn't appear to notice.

'Here you are, see what you can make of them …'

And with a tired smile, he retreated to his own territory. I had never really been in his flat before. I had only got as far as the small hallway because that was as far as he wished me to go. It was dowdy, coloured from a forgotten decade, the ceiling paper was coming adrift at the seams. The low wattage light burnt brighter without its shade. Occasionally I would get a splash of a view through his doorway to reveal more of the same, but he kept the door held shut as much as possible when he spoke to me. This was soon to change.

I don't think he was embarrassed about the way he lived. It was more that he had no wish to share his private space with anyone. Occasionally, I would make a joke about 'the grandmother in the freezer' but he never rose to it, dismissing me as though he had never heard. His frustrations started to manifest themselves in darker ways, loss of temper and shouting at people, inappropriate conversations at inappropriate times. I tried to shield him from the strangers' stares, but it didn't really work. I didn't feel embarrassed by his behaviour, even when one day I came back from a delivery to find him somewhere between a child crying in frustration and a mad man's rage.

The terrified customer, a woman, had fled leaving her bike fallen among the new stock. I put my arm around his shoulders, talking quietly to him telling him the time had come to shut the shop, I don't think he even heard me, the froth of his anger was dying. But soon he was flat and peaceful again. I flipped the sign on the door to closed, and that's the way it stayed for several weeks. I took him to the doctor and he was finally diagnosed with Primary Progressive Dementia (PPD), the fast degenerative disease that is comparatively rare but still effects tens of thousands. Because of the change inside his head, he genuinely believed he was OK, perfectly normal. It was the world that was out of sync.

He started drinking heavily, on a daily basis. His routine, which he didn't like upset in any way, was simple. On the dot of five he would start drinking any alcohol that was around, until he could no longer focus on anything. When he was drunk, his memory loss of objects and what they were used for became more pronounced, and it showed where this illness was taking him.

Sly came to my open door eventually, fed up with the brutality that was being metered out to him when Barney was off his head. One day, I found Barney with a circular saw screaming away in his kitchen, trying to slice a joint of uncooked beef. His mind may have melted a little, but his body was as strong as ever. I was always careful, not knowing how he would respond to any situation. Neighbours complained and he barely recognised most of them anymore. I opened the shop mornings only, doing repairs in the early afternoons. Sometimes he would look in, but because of his increasing confusion, he was of little help.

The landlord of the shop had been to see me to ask whether I would take the lease over, but I told him I thought it was a bit mean to be thinking about that just yet. Eventually, Barney was sectioned by three doctors under the Mental Health Act. This was after he had two desperate attempts at suicide. I remember that day, because I returned to my flat, saddened that I had lost my best friend to a disease that had fogged his existence. I sat on the stairs, and I'm not ashamed to say it, I cried long, choking sobs for my loss. I'm not sure that I have ever cried like that before.

Sly sat in front of me for a long time. Sensing his master was missing, he didn't settle for days. At night he would sleep curled up by my front door, waiting for a master that would never return. That next day was the first time I went into his flat to really look around. I was hoping to find some contacts, maybe some relatives. But there was nothing. The living room was sparse with just two pieces of a three- piece suite. Books and newspapers covered the top of an old table in the corner. It was tidy, but blanketed in dog's hairs. I checked the small, modern bureau which had been left open. The over-flowing papers were not worth keeping. It was the kitchen that really surprised me. I say kitchen, more like a workshop with a food station in amongst it. Vices, spanners, boxes of tyres of odd sizes, oil, grease, cutting equipment and a fire extinguisher lay on the floor near the dirty cooker, which had a filthy frying pan on it.

How Barney didn't get food poisoning, I'll never know. I checked the bedroom carefully, especially the wardrobe and his clothes. I found only two things of any note. On top of the wardrobe, behind the small pelmet, I located a dust covered bank savings book with 420 dollars in it, which I passed to the Court of Protection. In the inside pocket of one of the coats was a thin wedge of ten dollar bills, held firm with a small green bulldog clip. I wet my thumb and forefinger with the edge of my tongue and flicked the notes quickly; amongst the tens was a single, badly-defaced five dollar bill. The total was 685 dollars, which went into my pocket to go towards the rent and the recent electricity bill. I left his flat without moving or touching anything else, my last look down the hallway before locking the door with the spare that I kept.

I did take over the shop and continued the business, having the lease transferred to my name. I bought what stock was not on sale or return from the Court of Protection. Being the only bidder, I paid very little for it, and I kept the name above the shop as a reminder of my friend. Over the last span of years here in Adelaide, I've thought about you Jamie, from time to time. When I see a dad lift a small girl to his arms, or a girl giving her dad a hug. It's the ache of it all. There have been so many times now since I have become older when I have thought about what families are all about, the real sustaining value they give to individuals and communities.

But nothing comes easy. It requires effort, patience and, of course, love. I have no excuses, the fault of failure lies squarely on my shoulders. I can live with that, with how it affects me relatively easily, but the guilt about how it affected you and your mother and whether it contributed directly to the mess you got into in your teens is more difficult. It's natural for both of us to miss what might have been, but I don't think now I had or have the strength to build or maintain any relationship.

I guess I could have tried to get in contact over the years, especially with all this social media stuff we have these days, but I'm not comfortable using it and I didn't know if you would still be using the same name, or living in the same town. It seemed easier somehow to back away. I have known many women over the years, some for company and some just for one night, but sustaining something lasting was beyond me. I never made any firm friends either, apart from Barney.

The shop gave me a sense of belonging in a way nothing else had done before. The pleasure of work using my hands repairing a bike, to have someone pleased to see me because I could help them – that felt good. Visiting Barney became harder as the disease enveloped him completely. As the months slid away, he rarely recognised me or anyone else around him at all. That stare, that unblinkingly emptiness haunted me. In the end, the very end, there was absolutely nothing left of the character I could recognise as the man I knew and called my friend.

He died in the middle of a Tuesday night, surrounded by only his own darkness. I arranged the cremation in a miserable, modern chapel at the crematorium over at Wallerville. It's a long, single storey building in dark red brick, L-shaped with a sweeping, curved driveway leading to the tidy car park. I got out of the back seat of the taxi and asked him to call back for me in an hour. I was dressed in my everyday clothes and had made myself presentable by shaving. I remember walking with my hands in my pockets across the car park just as mourners came out of the double doors at the other end by the chapel gardens.

Tight groups, heads still low, murmured conversations before departures. I was early, not too early, but the parson stood outside the door of number two chapel to welcome me. His attire was simple, all in black with the white band around his neck. His hand shake was well practised, and we walked past rows of empty benches to the plinth that held Barney's coffin. The very soft sound of organ music from a looped tape somewhere floated on the air. It irritated me in its lack of sincerity. There was just me and the parson standing beside the coffin. No family were there, but a clutch of people who had known Barney from the shop were thinly spaced among the front two pews.

There were two short prayers, no hymns, and even before the curtain had closed completely around the coffin, the sound of the electric motor could be heard winding up to take Barney away. I brought back the photo that I had framed, that had hung near his bed in the care home. I still have it on the wall of the shop. It's a photo of him, Sly and me outside the shop, with his name proudly displayed above the window.

Sly died peacefully about three months later, after falling into his last long sleep at my feet one evening.

I have kept my head down for nearly two decades now, staying well away from crime of any kind. Round here, I've been seen as helpful, but quiet and a bit reclusive. Then it just happened, I felt unwell outside our neighbourhood shops. It came first as a slight tightening in the chest. I remember raising my hand, vaguely thinking it was indigestion of some sort perhaps. It improved a bit, then it came back, I couldn't breathe so well.

Very quickly after that, there were pains in my left arm, dizziness, then it was pain like I have never experienced before, not the hot hurting stuff, this was so intense that steel would melt, an obliteration of everything. Reason and feeling left me completely and blackness overcame me. I passed out. I had landed face down on the pavement slabs apparently. The bloody nose was the least of my worries. A passer-by thought I had just fallen over, before realising it was worse than that.

I was unconscious, an ambulance was called and I was taken to hospital. They shoved a couple of stents into me straight away. I had been sedated all the time and when I awoke, I just lay there feeling weightless, moving only my eyes to take in my surroundings. There it is. One thing led to another, tested for this tested for that. Later I was found to have lung cancer. It was the cough and shortness of breath at first, but then I had been a life-long smoker. By the time I got checked out, the cancer had spread though the lymph nodes into the blood steam to several other parts of my body.

I am riddled with it. I'm told I've probably had it for years. Who knows? By the time you read this, I'll be done. I always felt that I should contact you. But in the end, I left it to my lawyers to pass on these notebooks to you after my death. Call it an explanation, or call it an apology, as you will. Jamie, you are my only mark in the sand, don't waste your life. Like I did.

You will also know by now, from my faithful old business lawyers, that I have left my estate, such as it is, in its entirety to you and you only.

The last page was signed with a scribble that Jamie took to be her father's signature. On the bottom edge of the page was a single, pale pink, bluish water stain. Jamie allowed the book to slip from her fingers to rest on her knees. Her emotions had again been turned over like a plough cuts through soil. She couldn't stop the tears. So many thoughts were crashing in her head.

Part Eight

Fareham, England. 2010

The investigation scene was kept on for four days before the aggregates depot opened again. Their search inquiries soon led to me at my yard. Two police detectives turned up while I was replacing the new top mounts on a small van, not a difficult job unless the nuts are corroded like these were.

I heard the yard gate open, it's an ill-fitting gate, it whines with a nasty screech on the top hinge. The van was up on a hand jack and I was working at the bench vice with part of the suspension unit, a spanner and wrench, trying with everything I'd got to get the rusted in nuts undone, when I heard it open. Wiping my hands on a rag, I turned to face them.

I knew they were police, you do, don't you? They must have parked further up the street, as I didn't hear them pull up. The woman was dressed in jeans and a heavy knit jumper and the man wore a bomber jacket. They showed me their IDs, then pictures of his face. It was him alright, it was Nat Gibson. I told them what I knew, about how he'd been with me for a couple of weeks and about his earlier life in Australia. It never occurred to me, as they suggested, that perhaps he might not have been telling me the truth.

The detectives wanted me to make a statement at the station later in the day which I did. Strange really, I never heard much more until later in the newspapers...

The noise of the car doors shutting had barely faded when Col turned in the driver's seat and said:

'Well, that's the lead we need.... and if the stories of travelling around Australia were true, that could fit in with his tattoo of a turtle. The experts said it was a Polynesian design, so perhaps we're onto something.'

'Yeah, if it goes anywhere ... having stripped out his room in Bellrose Gardens we're none the wiser really. With this, we may get a name confirmed. But no one we've linked in with knew of his movements or anything personal about him. His last hours are a bit of a mystery.'

DC Lloyd carried on: 'Hopefully, the DNA will link us to something, if we can find where he entered the water, we'll get a fix to start there too.'

'Yeah, if…'

Col reversed the car deftly into a short driveway and then, with the slightest wheel spin, pulled away. Over the next three weeks progress slowed considerably. The new leads were dead ends, tidal experts turned up nothing new and searches up and down the creek failed to reveal an entry point. They checked the dentists in the surrounding area in the hope of coming up with records, but drew another blank.

The first unconfirmed connection came in an e-mail from the immigration department at Australia House. It stated that a Philbus Nathaniel Gibson was recorded as entering Australia on 23 October, 1967 on a British passport; and recorded as leaving the country on 3 November, 1976. They knew already that a person of that name had left the UK on May 12, 1966 and had returned on 14 April, 1989. The dental plate, which was thought to be Australian, was, for some reason, not listed.

When the DNA report finally flicked in, it was immediately transferred to the case file, with flag alerts to both detectives. That evening, Lloyd was getting ready to go home, she was tired and feeling irritable. They were short-staffed and the extra workload was getting out of hand. Sagging back to a swivel chair at one of the hot desks, she clicked on the file, and started to go through it again. Her last task before she left was to request the long chance, to check the possibility of a DNA match within criminal records held in Australia.

Two days later a reply came back. She scanned through it.

'DNA match… robbery with violence conviction some years back. History of drug abuse. Female, recorded name Jamie O'Hagan. Last known address… Bulli. We can visit property and notify if required. We await your instructions.'

Part Nine

Arc of Doubt

Jamie, Sydney. 2010

Then with some solemnity, the lawyer placed everything back in the large envelope, pushing it gently in Jamie's direction before carrying on:

'To administer this estate has been straightforward and with your cashing of the enclosed cheque for 837 dollars and 30 cents, his personal estate will then be closed.'

Mr Williamson added: 'However, we also act for the trustees to what is commonly described as a blind trust. We have received instructions from the trustees of a third party to begin payment to you coinciding with Frank O'Hagan's death and the subsequent administration of his will. The payments will be on a quarterly basis and will begin on the 25th day of next month, as this is one of the official quarter days, either by cheque or bank transfer, as you wish. The full details relating to this trust will remain undisclosed.'

Drawing a breath he carried on: 'I can well imagine that you may have many questions, but unless they refer to Mr O'Hagan's will, I shall, unfortunately, not be in a position to answer them.'

'Well...how much money is there? Who owns this trust? What is it?'

The lawyer smiled patiently, saying:

'The payments and administration will be made by the trustees, all details of the trust are confidential. I can only say you are very fortunate to be a beneficiary.'

'Well, can you tell me how you got the books then?' asked Jamie.

'They were posted to our offices in Adelaide, as Frank O'Hagan was a client of ours. As you can see, they are handwritten, some are stapled together, some loose. They appear to be some sort of a diary. They came to us in what looked like a supermarket carrier bag.'

'Is there anything else? Possessions of any kind or sort? Papers from his past? Photographs?'

The words were rushing out. The lawyer allowed another short silence, then said: 'We, as a firm, are the executers of the will and the Trust. Those wishes have been carried out by the presentation of what you have before you. One thing I can tell you, Miss O'Hagan, is that the instructions we are following, in respect of the will and the Trust, are not the instructions of the same person. In regard to your affairs, we are following the wishes of two of our clients.'

Jamie looked shocked.

The lawyer slid his weight on the chair, placed his elbows on its arms and waited for Jamie's further response. There was none. Her face was blank, she couldn't take it all in. She took up the envelope and its contents, muttered about being totally confused, and put it in her bag.

The handshake signified the end of this meeting. Turning to shut the door, she took one last look at the man who - as of this meeting – had not closed an old wound, but opened it still further. With many more unanswered questions, she left the building. The return journey back to the bungalow and the life she knew was slow and tiring. As the key slipped through the escutcheon plate to the lock, and clicked as it turned in its worn chamber, she knew this was where she felt safe.

Over the next few days, she read and re-read the notebooks.

Then on the 25th of the following month, the first transfer of $15,000 fell into her account.

About the author

A H Pilcher has written several novels, but Arc of Doubt is the first one to be completed and published. He spent some time in Australia, but now lives by the sea in southern Hampshire.

Book and cover design: Macaulay Design
Published by Backleg Books, UK

Printed in Great Britain
by Amazon